12 HUNKS OF HERCU

LEIA

C. ROCHELLE

CONTENTS

TYPOS & LANGUAGES

While many people have gone over this book to find typos and other mistakes, we are only human. **If you spot an error, please do NOT report it to Amazon.**

Send me an email:
crochelle.author@gmail.com
or **use the form** (also found in my FB group, pinned under Featured/Announcements)

GLOSSARY NOTE: The men here are speaking Ancient Greek (plus a little Old Norse), which I've mostly written as English, since they "magically" understand each other. You will find a few unfamiliar words, italicized and written phonetically. Please reference the glossary in the back of this book for definitions.

SLANG NOTE: There is also a bit of American slang peppered in, but I didn't bother translating, as much of it is common lexicon at this point. When in doubt, use Google, or contact me using the methods above if you truly believe it's a typo.

WARNINGS & TRIGGERS

The 12 Hunks of Herculeia is a monstrously mythic, medium-dark rom-com loosely based on the 12 Labors of Heracles, with many ridiculous liberties taken. <u>This is book 1 in the Monstrously Mythic Herculeia duet.</u>

And before my fellow history nerds get their togas in a bunch, I am aware that Hercules/Herculeia is the Roman spelling (it gets addressed in the book, trust.)

For those wondering how weird this is gonna get in the sheets: Think monster shifters, who maintain fancy accessories (sometimes more than one!) in human form.

This book is meant for readers 18 and over.

This series includes:

- MM (Loads of it. With their own relationship arcs. Love is love.)
- Multiple POVs

- Slow build group of mates (slow-build, NOT slow-burn - I'm not that much of a monster)
- Cliffies

Possible triggers overall:

- Sweary dialogue
- Naughty irreverent humor including horse jokes
- An overly possessive, slightly unhinged group of mates
- Explicit sex, including kink (eg. primal play, praise/degradation, asphyxiation, and a breeding kink without traditional pregnancy) and edgeplay
- Light threat of violence with a knife and a brief but bloody graphic death (outside the main characters, barely a side character)
- Trauma/grief/anxiety related to past death in the family (father - car accident), a bad breakup (cheating), and a magical shipwreck (where our girl was thrown overboard)
- Ongoing familial betrayal involving lying and gaslighting (mother)
- Slut-shaming (from the Big Bad)
- Snakes (one of the men is a Hydra, so he has 9 snake heads and forked tongues, and various other creatures have snakes elements to their bodies)
- Signature weirdness and medium-dark elements
- Greek myths with many ridiculous liberties taken

In general, please do not read this if you own pearls to clutch, or if you regularly ask to speak to the manager, as you and I will probably not get along.

Please do not hesitate to email the author directly with any questions or suggestions for adding to the TWs.

STALK C. ROCHELLE

Stalk me in all the places!
(Including by joining my Clubhouse of Smut on Patreon,
my Little Sinners FB Group, and subscribing to my
newsletter)

"Ye are of the lineage of the invincible Heracles; Fear ye not a multitude of men, but let every man hold his [sword]... making Life his enemy and the black Spirits of Death dear as the rays of the sun." —*The War-Song Fragments, Tyrtaeus*

"Hit that pussy with an uppercut, call that Kraken Captain Hook." —*Megara Thee Centaur*

1

LEIA

My bare feet scrambled over the soaked deck of the cruise ship as it tilted alarmingly to the left. I desperately reached for anything to save me, miraculously grabbing hold of a pole painted like a palm tree. Wrapping my arms tightly around it, I was morbidly thankful for the howling wind devouring the screams of my fellow passengers. Roaring waves violently lashed over the railing, the soaked nightgown clinging to my skin offering little protection against the elements. Through it all, the storm continued to rage, showing no sign of letting up—showing no mercy.

A flash of lightning revealed a monstrous wave headed straight for the ship. I tightened my slippery grip on the pole, already knowing I was no match for this awesome force of nature. When it hit, I was thrown skyward before plummeting, barely taking a breath, before disappearing beneath the roiling sea.

The battered hull above me grew distant as I sunk deeper. As death closed in, I was overwhelmed with regret for everything I hadn't experienced and would never have the chance to.

"I can't die before I reach 1 million followers!"

. . .

Jerking awake, I was confused to find myself face down, still slightly damp. Another moment passed before I realized I was at my desk at work, lying in a puddle of my own drool. Closing my eyes again, I sent up a quick prayer to Our Lady Gaga that none of my coworkers had gone paparazzi for Instagram.

I usually only have wet dreams about Magnolia cupcakes...

Casually lifting my head, I glanced toward my manager Jasmine's glassed-in office, relieved to find no sign of the leggy nightmare. All my coworkers at Auracle PR were gone, which meant there was probably an art opening nearby with free wine and nosh. While I was tempted to try to catch up with everyone, I couldn't shake the uneasy feeling still lodged in my gut.

It was just a dream, Leia.

A really intense, stress-induced dream.

I'd been putting in longer hours lately—thanks to Jasmine loading me up with work—but I'd never passed out at my desk before. I was a New Yorker, born and raised. We survived like cockroaches on a diet of black coffee, dollar slices, and an intense hatred for anyone who walked slower than 20 miles per hour.

This is exactly why I'm going on vacation.

Tapping my phone awake, I frowned to discover my boyfriend, Dylan, was apparently unconcerned by my radio silence this week. Not that he contacted me much during our busy workdays, but it was almost the weekend. He usually at least texted to ask if I was 'bringing the booty' to his Lower Manhattan apartment, like the stockbroker bro he was.

I almost dropped my phone in surprise when it

suddenly *rang*. Nobody *called* me—nobody called each other—but when I saw it was my niece Iola, my blood ran cold.

Oh my god, she's been kidnapped! And she's trying to call me from the trunk of the black Mazda she's trapped in before it disappears into the Lincoln Tunnel...

...to New Jersey!

Frantically stabbing at the green button on my screen, I cursed when Iola abruptly hung up before I could answer. I was about to call her back when a text popped up in my notifications.

(Little Shit) *WhoOops [facepalm] so that's what that button does. Where you at, bish?*

You just gave me a minor heart attack, nbd. I'm about to leave Auracle and swing by Dylan's.

(Little Shit) *[barf] I was gonna see if you were down for shots at Clem's. But if you'd rather hang with Wall Street Dyldo, you do you, ho.*

I snorted and replied with the eggplant and money bag emojis before tossing my phone into my knockoff Kate Spade tote. Maybe Iola was finally wearing me down, but she'd made some fairly good points in her latest '10 Things I Hate About Dyldo' rant. My niece made no secret of her hatred for my boyfriend, even in his presence. Even if I didn't agree, that brand of straight talk was why she was my favorite relative and BFF.

And annoyingly nosey roommate.

You knew you came from an enormous family when your *niece* was closer to your age than your first cousins. But sharing a studio apartment with blood was far better than finding a Craigslist rando who would unalive you in your sleep. When things got too close for comfort, I always had Dylan's fancy high-rise to escape to when I needed space.

If I prove myself at work, maybe I can afford my own place someday...

I scoffed. Even being the account manager for one of the hottest up-and-coming natural beauty brands didn't mean I was headed for a promotion anytime soon. I knew I was nothing more than a warm body in an open floor plan-land. The turnover rate at Auracle wasn't bad compared to some of the other marketing firms in town. That number increased exponentially for those working beneath Jasmine Snowe.

Jasmine was a notorious hardass who didn't possess a shred of artistic talent or social media strategy. I'd always assumed it was her underhanded tactics and model-hot appearance that landed her a corner office, even if I couldn't prove it. While I usually sided with my fellow lady-bosses, she even said I was nothing more than an underling destined to slave for her glory. So the disdain was well-deserved.

I swear, I'd give up Magnolia cupcakes forever to knock that shady B down a notch.

Ok, maybe not forever...

My stomach rumbled, and I realized I hadn't eaten much today besides the Grey's Papaya special I snagged for lunch. Gathering my things, I headed out, stopping at the food cart in front of the building for a pepperoni slice. Folding it in half, I ate it on my way to the bus stop, debating my next move.

I rarely dropped by Dylan's without texting first, but I'd left my mother's amethyst ring in his bathroom last weekend, and figured I could pick it up on my way home. Not only did my hand feel naked without it, I was on-edge, the sudden anxiety left over from my dream making its absence even more noticeable.

I'll feel better once I get it back.

Climbing aboard the M55 bus, I looked down at my empty ring finger, trying to envision a diamond glittering beneath the flickering lights. Dylan and I met a year ago, at some lame loft party thrown by one of Auracle's clients, and it started as a one-night-stand more than anything. I went home with him because I drunkenly decided I'd rather take a quick cab ride to his place than smell the Q Train all the way to Brooklyn.

Ignoring the itch to mindlessly scroll through Instagram, I instead considered whether a future with Dylan was what I actually wanted. Our first few months together were fun, but we'd since settled into a fairly boring routine that wasn't doing anything for me. We didn't truly connect on anything other than being workaholics, and I'd honestly had better sex back when I was regularly partying with my niece. Why I'd settled down with a vanilla latte like him was something I'd been asking myself a lot lately, even without Iola's loud opinions.

I really need to get my shit together... especially with our trip coming up.

Getting off near City Hall, I walked to Dylan's apartment building and breezed past the doorman into the lifeless marble lobby. The uneasy feeling from earlier only intensified as I entered the elevator. I rubbed my stomach, vaguely wondering if it was the imagined shipwreck or the Grey's hotdog disagreeing with me.

Fiddling with my spare key outside Dylan's apartment door, I went over a few excuses I could use to avoid spending the night. The most obvious and truthful one being that I had a big client meeting tomorrow and wanted to wake up fresh.

Preferably with clean underwear.

Nu metal assaulted my eardrums the instant I entered the apartment. Blessedly, the guttural screaming and screeching guitar riffs were muffled by the bedroom door at the end of the hall. In no rush to increase the volume, I slipped inside the bathroom and flicked on the lights. I couldn't contain my gasp when the harsh fluorescents revealed my reflection in the mirror. While I'd gotten used to the green ombré dye job Iola insisted worked perfectly with my Mediterranean skin tone, there was no ignoring how ragged I appeared.

Setting my purse on the vanity, I quickly applied my favorite client's olive oil-based moisturizer before touching up my makeup. Once I looked alive again, I snagged my amethyst ring from the soap dish and slipped it onto my finger with a sigh of relief, immediately feeling my heart rate settle.

I debated sneaking out of the apartment to head home, but then my phone suddenly displayed another missed call —this time from my boyfriend down the hall, of all people.

What's with everyone calling me all of a sudden? Rude.

Sighing in resignation, I acknowledged it would probably be weird to leave without at least letting him know I was here. With my phone still in hand, I slung my purse over my shoulder and trudged toward Dylan's bedroom, my stomach twisting further as I approached.

I gaped at what awaited me inside. Front and center was Dylan's pasty ass, unattractively flexing with exertion as he unevenly pounded into whoever had their long legs thrown over his sweaty shoulders. His phone was bouncing on the bed next to them, and I realized with horror that he'd *butt-dialed* me while fucking another woman.

Dick-dialed, to be exact.

My breath caught. I recognized the custom Disney princess pumps dangling from the perfectly arched feet of the unlucky lady faux moaning beneath my now ex.

Jasmine fucking Snowe.

2

LEIA

"Girl, I don't know how you left that apartment without adding a double-homicide to your extensive rap sheet."

I barked a laugh, although there was very little humor in it. Throwing back my fourth shot of the evening, I gestured for the bartender before turning to face Iola on the stool beside me. After all, Clem's *was* the kind of bar you could talk about homicide in.

And what better alibi than my delinquent niece?

"Honestly, I barely remember anything aside from the glass I threw, Jasmine's unholy screech, and Dylan's flopping dick as he ran for cover."

A smirk curled my lips as I recalled how he'd locked himself in the en suite, leaving my half-naked manager to fend for herself against my wrath. Not that she'd seemed particularly scared. Jasmine actually had the nerve to *scold* me for not knocking first, her entitlement so shocking that I'd simply spun on my heel and walked out.

Those two deserve each other.

Somehow, my phone had recorded the entire thing,

which Iola found hilarious, and she'd made me play it for her no less than two million times. I hadn't decided what to do with this juicy ace up my sleeve, but right now, my adrenaline had faded, leaving me exhausted. I already knew I'd be in no shape to go into the office tomorrow—if ever again.

I should probably spend my PTO next week looking for a new job instead of...

"Ughhh," I groaned, laying my head down on the sticky bar in the same position I'd woken up in at my desk only hours earlier. "This means I won't get to go on that Greek cruise I booked for Dylan's birthday. Fuck my life, Io, seriously, just fuck it hard."

In signature unbothered fashion, Iola rolled her eyes. "Listen, hoebaggler, I say go on the cruise by your own damn self. You're the one holding the tickets, and some international dick would be just the thing to get you back on track." She paused her sage advice to kick back two consecutive shots, impressive, as always, that such a tiny girl could hold so much liquor. While we shared many physical characteristics of our Greek heritage, I was decidedly heavier in the lower regions, pear-shaped where she was slim and athletic.

An unfamiliar jolt of self-consciousness suddenly shot through me. My heavy thighs and big ass had never bothered me before—being at the receiving end of NYC catcalls was enough to boost my spirits most days. But now I was wondering if the reason Jasmine ended up in Dylan's bed was because her willowy figure epitomized western beauty standards.

Stop it, Leia. Thick thighs save lives!

"...and speaking of hard fucking," I brought my attention back to Iola's thrilling synopsis of 'How Leia Got Her

Groove Back Under the Grecian Sun.' "There's a party happening down the street that'll be full of those really slutty hipster guys who ride fixed gear bikes."

I gratefully smiled at my niece, even as I shook my head. "As tempting as ironic tattoos and Prince Albert piercings sound, I should probably just head home. One of my favorite clients wanted to meet up with me for lunch tomorrow. Even though I should probably just put in my notice with Auracle, I'd hate to leave without saying goodbye to them."

Iola thoughtfully observed me, but didn't reply, so I pulled out my phone to check on my wannabe influencer Instagram account. Nursing my latest shot, I sighed heavily over the low numbers in my insights, despairing over my apparent inability to find my niche or audience. Switching accounts, my eyes widened when I realized I was still logged in as Jasmine Snowe from all the times she'd lazily asked me to post for her.

"Ooh, let's change that bottom feeder's password to chokesondick420," Iola cackled in my ear, shamelessly peering over my shoulder. "Better yet, just give me your phone, bish. I want you to focus on having *fun* with me tonight, even if you insist on denying yourself the simple pleasure of rebound sex."

With another dramatic sigh, I handed over the offensive device to my niece and threw back another shot. I wasn't as upset about losing Dylan as I probably should have been, but the tired cliché of finding him in bed with my boss made my cheeks heat.

Time to drown my feelings in a bottle of Jack Daniels. Bottoms up!

———

I woke up hours later, fully clothed and face-down on my twin-sized futon, blessedly not drooling, but with a hangover that could take down a warhorse. Groaning in the language of dehydration, I peered through the blackout shade on my window, finding the sun setting beyond the water tower perched atop the roof next door.

Did I sleep through the entire day?!

I blindly pawed at my milk crate bedside table until I located my phone, praising Past Leia for plugging it in to charge last night. The lock screen confirmed it was already Friday evening, and there was a backlog of texts waiting for me.

(Little Shit) *Before you freak... I postponed your lunch with one of those sisters from Ancient Olive and called you out sick for work.*

(Little Shit) *P.S. I also posted that video you took to Jizzman Snowe's IG and packed you for your trip.*

(Little Shit) *P.P.S. I'm at fuckboy's tonight. Bon voyage, hooker!*

How Iola figured out who my client meeting was with today was beyond me. Gingerly lifting my head, I discovered she had indeed packed my small suitcase and carry-on, and neatly piled them near the door. A gift bag was temptingly balanced on top, but the idea of moving my body any more than necessary sounded worse than death, so I checked the next message instead.

(Wayward Mama) *HERCULEIA WHEN WERE YOU GOING TO TELL ME YOU WERE COMING TO GREECE? CALL ME.*

I groaned again, not only because of how much boomers loved ALL CAPS, but that this reeked of Iola's meddling. That chaotic bish knew full well there was no way I could back out of my trip if my *mother* caught wind of it.

Dr. Alcmene Hatzi-Loukanis was a world-famous archeologist specializing in Ancient Greece, with a slew of fancy degrees and accolades to prove it—not that she needed them. She was born a specialist in Greece. She lived and breathed it and made it her daily bitch, while running circles around the men in her field. Although my mother was rarely at home, I always admired her professional drive —even if her taste in Christmas and birthday presents was questionable. I'd been on the receiving end of countless hideous replica clay pots featuring naked Grecian wrestlers, no matter how many times I told her I had zero interest in history.

If being Greek was so important to her, she should have raised me there!

Despite my resistance, I'd still picked up a considerable amount about my Greek heritage, including the myths and legends, and a version of the language that hardly anyone still used. Absorbing this random trivia seemed to appease my mother enough to leave me alone, and even though *she* was disinterested in my actual interests, my childhood was full of love. My dad was parent enough for both of them. Even after Alcmene divorced him—her third divorce at the time—he never faltered at being invested and involved in my life.

Until he died five years ago...

Swallowing the lump in my throat, I scrolled to the next message, almost yeeting my phone across the room when I saw who it was from.

(Dyldo) *Have you seen my black socks? The Neiman Marcus ones?*

Not even the revelation that Iola had changed Dylan's name in my phone could quell my visceral reaction to his audacity. Before I could descend on my ex with the fire of a thousand dragons, my phone rang—*again*—and my mother's number flashed on the screen.

Choose the lesser of two evils, Leia.

"Hi, mama," I fumbled open a day-old Vitamin Water to ease the Sahara in my throat, attempting a cheery tone. "Soooo... guess what? I'm coming to Greece!"

She harrumphed. As in, I clearly heard the word 'harrumph,' before she replied, "So I've heard, Herculeia. And how were you planning on letting me know? By postcard, perhaps?"

I breathed evenly. Not only did she know I *hated* my full name, but my notoriously absent mother accusing *me* of being incommunicado made my head pound more than it already was.

"Yes," I hedged, deciding to save the news of my ruined romantic relationship for when we talked again in another year. "Dylan and I are going on a weeklong Nereid Cruise, but it leaves from Athens Sunday night, so I didn't think we'd have time to see..."

"Iola told me you were traveling tonight. Alone."

My gaze narrowed on the gift bag still taunting me from across the room, even as my mother continued to harangue in my ear. Stumbling over to the luggage pile, I snatched the envelope nestled in the bag's tissue paper, almost tearing it in half as I wrestled it open.

What kind of psychopath actually seals the envelope, Io?!

Sure enough, my shiny and new first class plane ticket

was neatly folded inside, showing a departure time of midnight tonight. Further investigation revealed a nonsensical handwritten poem and a P.S. about someone named 'Eury' meeting me in Athens to purchase Dylan's cruise ticket off of me.

I swear to all that is holy, Iola better not be setting me up on The Bachelor: Athenian Edition.

"Is everything all right, *kamari mou?*"

The anger instantly bled out of me at the nickname. My mother occasionally questioned why I chose to work in social media marketing instead of joining her in studying our rich heritage. It was futile to explain the rush I got from chasing the newest trend—of discovering something *new*—so I usually just changed the subject. Despite our inability to relate professionally, she still referred to me as her 'little pride'—especially when she wanted to pull on my heartstrings.

Well played, mother, well played.

"I think so," I sighed, although I honestly had no idea what my next steps in life would be after this trip was over. "And if you're able to meet me for dinner tomorrow, I would love to see you."

The connection grew muffled as she covered the phone to talk to one of her no doubt hot-bod crew members. My mother readily employed other women—made a point of equal opportunity. Regardless, I couldn't help noticing she was usually surrounded by tanned, shirtless dudes in group photos taken at the various dig sites she oversaw.

I wouldn't mind a harem of my own...

"Yes, Enrique will handle operations here in Delphi so I may dine with you," she hummed in approval as hottie Enrique chuckled sexily in the background. "There's a restaurant in the Plaka District called Hesperides that I used to frequent with your father..."

I swallowed hard, suddenly eager to cut the conversation short. "Sounds good, mama. I'll call you when I land." We said our goodbyes, and I warily eyed Iola's gift bag, feeling like Pandora staring down her box of woe.

It was a jar... not a box.

Annoyed by my random knowledge, I ripped the tissue from the bag and reached inside, frowning at the oddly shaped object wrapped in fabric. Shaking the object loose, I pulled the covering from the bag, rolling my eyes at the goddess-cut—and decidedly see-through—nightgown dangling from my fingers. Tossing it on top of my suitcase, I fished out the other item, laughing as my niece's note finally made sense.

Moving my mother's amethyst to my left hand, I slipped my new knuckle ring onto three fingers on my right. Admiring the sharp Manhattan skyline rising from the metal surface, I reread Iola's poetic message with a smile on my face:

"When in Greece, be a slut in the sheets. But don't let 'em forget, you came from the streets!"

3
LEIA

Aside from the baby howling from its posh first-class accommodations across the aisle, my red-eye to Athens was uneventful. After my fiery train wreck of a breakup, being able to lie flat after stuffing my face with canapés, quail eggs, and salmon was a welcome treat. I had no idea how Iola leveled up my seat, but I felt more relaxed than I had in months, and slept like...

Like the baby in seat 7B should have been.

Upon landing, I breezed through customs and snagged a public transit map, which I quickly scanned for the best route into the heart of the city. I'd last been to Athens in high school, but remembered Piraeus Port was on the opposite side of the Plaka District from the airport. That meant my bags would come along to dinner with my mother, but luckily, Iola had packed light for me. Peeking at her handiwork earlier, I'd discovered she'd rightfully assumed I'd be wearing mostly my bikini and beach wrap on deck and casual summer dresses with light layers in port.

The economy-sized box of condoms was a nice touch, too.

I headed for Arrivals, smirking down at the knuckle ring

my niece had given me. It was amusing that she thought I'd need to assert my street cred by punching someone while on vacation. After scanning the transit map, I lifted my gaze to look for Bus X95. Instead, I was surprised to find an attractive older man holding a cardboard sign with the name H. Baggler scrawled in Sharpie, waving as if he recognized me.

This has Iola's fingerprints all over it.

"Are you Hannah?" he asked in a thick Greek accent, stepping closer. His perfectly straight white teeth gleamed against tanned skin as he smiled invitingly, drawing me in. This man was *devastatingly* handsome, but in a way that felt like a facade, like a Bond villain. He was wearing what was clearly a Very Expensive Suit, and I probably could have paid for this vacation many times over with the Cartier watch glittering on his wrist.

"Depends who's asking," I curtly replied, immediately recognizing 'Hannah' as the fake name I gave to annoying men when out drinking with Iola. My neglected vajay was greatly considering jumping this man's bones. However, the rest of me wasn't interested in spending my first night in Athens hacked up and stored in a body freezer. Until I understood how he knew me, I would continue to stonewall like a pro.

Mama didn't raise no fool.

He chuckled, the smooth sound invoking an oddly thrilling full-body shudder. "I was told to look for a young lady with green hair and piercings. One who would answer with deep suspicion when asked her name. I'll admit, I wasn't properly prepared for your incredible beauty, but I believe you otherwise fit the description to perfection, don't you?"

I sniffed, dedicated to appearing unimpressed. "I'll need

your name first, stranger—*with* I.D." This earned me a joyous laugh, but he immediately dug out his leather wallet and flipped it open so I could check credentials. "Eurystheus, hmm?" I murmured, examining the I.D.'s hologram under the lights. It was a very good fake, or he was telling me the truth, but I still leveled him with a hard stare, worthy of my Tri-State upbringing. "That's quite a mouthful."

Again, his sexy chuckle threatened to derail my resolve. "So I've been told. That's why I go by Eury."

Ohhhh...

"Why didn't you just *say* you were the guy buying my cruise ticket?" I smiled pleasantly, even as I discreetly snapped a photo of his I.D. before handing it back. "I thought you were a random creep trying to lure me into his windowless van."

He smiled, flashing those too-perfect teeth again. "Ah, forgive the confusion, little *planetes.* I live near the airport. It was easy enough to meet you here rather than attempt to find you in the busy Nereid cruise terminal. May I offer you a ride?" My awareness snagged on how he'd used the Greek word for 'wanderer'—how he'd been mixing Greek with English this entire time—yet I'd understood him perfectly.

It's probably the jet lag...

Chewing the inside of my mouth, I weighed my options. Driving *would* be faster than taking the bus or metro, but I didn't know this man, and was traveling light enough where I could easily manage my bags myself. A quick glance over Eury's shoulder revealed a restroom, and an excuse to buy some time.

"Hold that thought. I have to piss like a racehorse, so excuse me while I go break the seal." I replied, before breezing past him and into the safety of the ladies' room.

Being 'unladylike' always throws them off their game.

Once inside, I immediately called Iola, smiling in petty as she fumbled to answer, sounding like death warmed over. "If this is Leia's kidnapper looking for ransom money, you're barking up the wrong tree, my dude."

"Well, I haven't been kidnapped *yet,*" I hissed into the phone. Admittedly, I hadn't bothered to calculate the time difference between us, but at the moment, I gave zero fucks. "No thanks to you and your dark web ticket trading, Io."

She cackled, and I heard her on-again, off-again fuckboy murmur something in the background, reminding me she'd spent the night at his place. "Oh, so the mysterious Eury tracked you down, hmm? Listen, *Hannah,* the only reason you had to meet in person was because Nereid requires all transfers to involve paper tickets, to avoid fraud or some shit. He's already paid—way more than *you* did originally—along with covering the penalty fee for you to now have a double-occupancy room, all to your slutty self. So stop giving Mr. Moneybags the stink-eye, hand over Dyldo's ticket, and go meet Auntie Meanie for what will surely be an unpleasant dinner."

If only this were FaceTime... I'd show you stink-eye...

"Yeah, thanks for sending Alcmene my ETA immediately after the biggest breakup of my life—real classy," I snapped. The last thing I wanted was to endure an afternoon with my mother, but Iola had left me little choice. For some stupid reason, tears pricked my eyelids at her uncharacteristic insensitivity.

Since she was my ride or die, Iola knew better than to continue poking the bear. "Yeah, I probably should have asked first," she sighed, sounding annoyingly genuine. "But something told me I needed to get you two together. We both know if I'd asked, you would have just said hell no." A pause. "Listen, Leia... I think it's time for you to stop blaming your mom for..."

Oh, not today, Satan.

"What was that? You're breaking up... Ok, well, I'm gonna hand off this ticket and catch the bus. Love you, byeeeee!" I muffled my voice and turned on the sink full blast to mimic a faulty connection. It wasn't my proudest moment, but dinner was going to exhaust me as it was. I didn't need some love and light forgiveness crap on top of my recent shit sandwich.

Especially from the devil on my shoulder herself.

Leaving the restroom, I found Eury casually leaning against a pillar checking *Instagram,* of all things, looking like some sort of distinguished gentleman plotting an evil influencer scheme.

"Ah, there you are," he looked up from his phone before shoving it in his pocket. "I was wondering if I'd have to send a search party, or perhaps dredge the Acheron to bring you back from the underworld."

Rolling my eyes good-naturedly, I dug into my purse and handed him Dylan's unwanted ticket. "Can you blame a girl for checking her sources before blindly trusting a handsome stranger? Besides, you're keeping busy, researching stock market trends or whatever it is you suits do all day."

He was observing me thoughtfully, a smile twitching his lips, and it took me a moment to realize I'd just admitted he was handsome. I boldly maintained eye contact, refusing to be embarrassed by the fact I had eyes and recognized a hot piece of dick when I saw it.

"The only trends I follow are those directly related to the reputations of my clients. On that note, have you considered my offer?"

I blinked, remembering he'd offered me a ride. "Yes, I did, and I'm fine with taking the bus," I stiffly replied, suddenly itching to be on my way and away from *him*. "Here's the ticket. I've been told you already paid soooo... I guess that's it then."

Eury's hand brushed mine as he accepted the ticket, and I flinched. "Yes, our trade is complete and you are obviously a woman accustomed to taking care of herself. However, please allow me to give you a small token, to welcome you to my homeland."

He placed a thin bronze coin in my palm, and I gasped at the dizzying sense of déjà vu that suddenly washed over me. It was warm from being in Eury's pocket and surprisingly heavy for such a small object. I took a closer look, but its surface was so worn it was impossible to recognize the imprint. Even though I didn't have the knowledge of artifacts my mother did, I knew this coin was old, and probably extremely valuable.

Why would he give me this?

Furrowing my brow, I attempted to hand it back, but he shook his head and added, "A good luck charm for your travels. I highly suggest keeping it on you at all times. Although I wouldn't recommend using it as fare, at least not for *that* mode of transportation." He canted his chin, and I followed his gaze to see the X95 arriving outside the lobby doors.

The next bus wouldn't be arriving for another hour, so I brusquely saluted and rushed outside for my chariot. It wasn't until we were pulling away from the terminal that the strangeness of our interaction fully hit me. I wanted to brush it off as a classic culture clash, but I felt deeply unsettled—and not only because of his inappropriate gift.

Needing more time to process, I opened the photo of

Eury's I.D. and committed his deceptively handsome face to memory. If I saw him on the cruise, I'd just head in the opposite direction, preferably toward a buffet of food or dudes.

I refuse to let anything ruin this vacation.

4
LEIA

"*You've lost weight. Are you eating enough? How is Iola? Here's another helping of Moussaka. Or try the octopus—it's quite tender. Remind me, what was your boyfriend's name again?*"

Dropping my head back against the padded sun lounger, I contentedly sighed, soaking in the warm rays heating my skin, and the fact I'd left my mother far behind on the mainland.

Dinner two nights ago had played out pretty much as expected. My mother dominated the conversation with news on her latest dig and speaking engagements, while tossing out just enough surface-level questions to feign interest in my life. Only when I'd offhandedly mentioned my recent breakup with Dylan did she perk up and genuinely listen.

Tea is always the hottest item on the menu.

Not much was offered in the way of condolences, besides an empty platitude on how there would always be more men in my future. It was a good thing this woman had insisted I attend therapy growing up, or else I might have mistakenly assumed she cared.

The more you know!

On a positive note, the food was delicious. While I didn't love my mother's scrutiny, being told to eat *more* was a welcome change from the calorie counting commentary I was surrounded with at Auracle.

My mother suggested we visit the Acropolis together after our meal, probably to bore me with as much history as possible before I made my escape. Soon afterward, I aimlessly dragged my luggage through the aptly named Archaic Gallery, politely enduring the continuation of our one-sided conversation instead of sneaking in a scroll on Instagram.

Although, a selfie in the museum would probably get some likes...

Before I could whip out my phone, a flash of something silver caught my attention. Abruptly veering around the glassed-in case, I saw a small coin tucked in among other artifacts. I wasn't sure why this relic had caught my eye, but now that I was looking at it, I couldn't seem to tear my gaze away.

"Ah, an Athenian *obol*," my mother hummed, pulling a nerdy magnifying loupe out of her pocket for a closer look. "See the owl design, signifying Athena, the goddess of wisdom? Sadly, this isn't a *rare* find. What I wouldn't give to discover a true *'Charon's obol'*—typically bronze or copper and often placed over the mouth of the dead to pay the toll to the underworld."

I shivered, wondering if the bronze coin from Eury was also an *obol*. The last thing I wanted to do was bring it to my mother's attention, but this could be one of the creepiest gifts I'd ever received.

Although, men have done weirder things before to get into my pants.

Not that Eury would be getting anywhere near my pants. I'd glimpsed him at the Nereid Cruise Line terminal during boarding, but the mass of fellow passengers had blessedly herded me in the opposite direction. I'd eaten enough with my mom to sustain me through the entire week at sea, so I grabbed some nosh and disappeared into my cabin the first night. Since then I'd slept late and spent my days by the pool, usually wedged in among noisy families—the ultimate man deterrent. While I couldn't deny Eury was easy on the eyes, I'd officially decided I didn't like him, and I trusted my instincts about people implicitly.

Well, except with my longtime ex-boyfriend...

Determined to eat my feelings, I blindly reached for another olive on the empty chaise-turned-buffet-table next to me. I'd already filled my plate at least a few times today. It was currently holding a mountain of spanakopita and grilled pita complimented by dipping oils and some of the best tzatziki I'd ever tasted. I was never one to shy away from delicious food, plus I was surely *schvitzing* away a few pounds while tanning under the Grecian sun.

Now all I need is some toxic dick to consider this vacation a roaring success.

A shadow passed over me. While the sudden shade was a welcome respite from the Mediterranean heat, I couldn't ignore how my guts twisted, already knowing who'd tracked me down.

"Is this seat taken?" A familiar voice rudely snapped me out of my dreams of vitamin D, and I squinted up at the backlit figure blocking my sun.

"Yes, Eury," I adopted a bored tone. "As you can see, my

personal buffet is occupying the seat next to me, and I'm afraid snacks trump all else, including social interaction."

He chuckled, the sound causing my neglected pussy to traitorously suggest we throw the nosh overboard and make room. "Fair enough. I was merely stopping by to ask if you're enjoying your solo adventure so far?"

Thanks for bringing up the solo part, dude.

"I am," I coolly replied. "Considering I'm usually wedged between an ass and an armpit on the subway, some alone time is a delightful change." To punctuate my point, I then pulled out my phone and start scrolling in the universal language of fuck off.

To his credit, Eury picked up what I was putting down. "I'll leave you to it, then." He nodded and turned on his heel, calling back over his shoulder, "See you at dinner, *Hannah.*"

I frowned down at my phone, annoyed by the interruption and discouraged by the sad engagement on my latest Instagram post. Long before the Jasmine-Dylan debacle, I was scheming to eventually leave Auracle and set out on my own. Even after devouring every blog post and podcast episode on influencer success stories, I couldn't seem to hit the mark. I knew better than most that mastering social media was a combination of authenticity, consistency, sticky content, and plain ol' viral luck, but I hadn't moved the needle in months.

Maybe I'll find some new inspiration during this trip.

Tossing my phone into my purse, I settled back on the lounger and closed my eyes, ready for a catnap. As I drifted off, a vision of the Acropolis' obol surfaced... the silver shifting to bronze as the owl on its surface morphed into a lion... then into a man wearing a skinned lion's pelt as a cloak and helmet.

Jesus, maybe the tzatziki went bad in the sun...

Fully awake—and thoroughly unsettled—I gathered my things and headed for the pool to cool off with a dip before returning to my cabin. The clubs on board looked promising, so I'd decided on the later dinner seating followed by dancing.

I'll see where the night takes me from there!

———

Wiping steam from the bathroom mirror, I paused a moment to take in my reflection. I wasn't as haggard as I'd appeared in Dylan's apartment, but something still seemed off.

Popping open my travel-sized Ancient Olive moisturizer, I smoothed the buttery heaven over my face, feeling a pang of regret for bailing on Friday's business lunch with my favorite client. The company was founded by three Greek sisters who were the epitome of boss bitches. Even though they had a small army working for them, one of the three always made the time to meet with me whenever they were in town.

I'd planned on pitching the concept of curated lifestyle shots while on vacation, but realized now how stupid that would have been. The models their ad agency historically used were waif thin and Swedish blonde, so the idea of *me* repping their beauty empire was laughable, in hindsight.

Thank fuck, Iola cancelled that lunch before I could make a fool out of myself.

At the thought of my niece, I sent her a selfie mid-prep. I immediately followed up with the words 'cruisin' for a dicking' and a combo of cruise ship, eyeballs, and water droplets emojis.

(Little Shit) *Girrrrl... make sure to find yo'self a butt pirate [peach].*

Jolly Roger! Just call me Land Ho.

(Little Shit) *Sample the seamen but watch out for scurvy.*

Don't worry, I'll eat my daily dozen of veggies [eggplant x12].

My stomach rumbled, reminding me I needed to finish up and get to the dining room for the 8:30 seating. Much to my horror, when I arrived at the dining room, I discovered the night was pirate-themed. Dodging the overly enthusiastic hostess who was handing out accessories, I snuck inside before she could slap an eye patch on me.

I'd hoped Eury would go for the early bird special followed by an old man's bedtime, but I spotted him at a back corner table with plenty of open seats. Pretending to wave at someone on the opposite side of the room, I joined a table of Spring Breakers closer to Iola's age than my 29 years. Coincidentally, they were interested in hitting up the clubs, and one guy mentioned his older brother and friends would join us.

Oh yeah, it's all coming together.

I paired my surf and turf with a couple of glasses of Pinot Noir, so by the time we all stood to leave, the deck was a'tilting. Promising my new friends I'd catch up on the dance floor, I stopped in the bathroom to splash some water on my face and freshen up. Stumbling back into the hallway, I audibly groaned when a familiar face was waiting for me.

"Look, *Eurystheus,*" I snapped, before he could speak,

content to let the wine do the talking. "I don't know how else to say this, but I'm not interested in fucking you. So go breathe on someone else. K, thanks, byeeee."

He cocked his head, observing my belligerence with amusement edging suspiciously close to condescension. "Oh, I have no interest in sleeping with you."

My eyes rolled so hard I saw my brain. "Why is it that guys always go for the 'you're ugly anyway' line when they get rejected? So predictable." I slung my purse over my shoulder and attempted to leave when he grabbed my arm to stop me.

Oh, you did NOT just put your hands on me!

"I said nothing about you being *ugly*, little wanderer," his tone had turned dangerously low, making me instinctively freeze. "In fact, your beauty is more convenient than you know. I was merely checking that you had your coin on you. The forecast calls for rough seas tonight, and I would hate for you to be unprepared for your journey."

He abruptly released me and stalked away, leaving me rooted to the spot as I processed this latest level of creepiness. It was bad enough that Eury had given me a dead person coin as a welcome present. Now his unnecessary weather report and insistence that I *needed* the coin for my 'journey' seemed one step away from luring me into a pit to make a skin suit out of me. Unpleasant encounters with pushy men came with the territory back in the City, but this interaction had shaken me to my, albeit drunken, core.

Leia, you are a luscious goddess who eats fools like him for breakfast.

Brushing the proverbial dirt off my shoulder, I continued on my original path to the club, noticing a thick fog had rolled in outside the porthole windows. I frowned as I remembered Eury's prediction for rough seas, knowing I *didn't* actually have his coin on me. It had seemed safer to leave it in my room, so I wouldn't accidentally use it to pay for something before I had the chance to pawn it.

Maybe I should just throw it overboard...

What *was* in my purse was the knuckle ring from Iola. I slipped on my fingers, grimly deciding our boy was going to catch hands if he came for me again.

Hours later, I was pleasantly wasted and peeling off my sweaty clothes back in my cabin, unfortunately alone. I'd danced my ass off, but wasn't interested in any of the guys in the club, despite my alcohol-infused plan to finally fuck my ex out of my system. Pulling Iola's scandalously sheer nightgown out of my suitcase, I snorted in amusement at her nod to Greek culture with the goddess-cut style.

If I'm the goddess of anything, it's blue ovaries and annoyingly high standards.

Rebound sex used to be my no-fail breakup cure, but something was holding me back this time—and I wondered if I even *wanted* to return to my pre-relationship ways of carelessly fucking whoever crossed my path. This was an extremely uncomfortable realization, as I'd always been a staunch supporter of women doing whatever the hell they wanted to with their bodies.

Don't tell me Dyldo and Jizzman have ruined this for me!

Saving psychoanalyzing my hang-ups for another, more coherent day, I completed my nighttime routine and crawled into bed—keeping one foot firmly planted on the floor to lessen the spins. I'd grabbed Eury's creepy coin from the room safe and was now absently running my fingers over the worn imprint on its surface.

Why would he give this to me?

I usually removed my jewelry to sleep, but I'd left my

amethyst and knuckle rings on, feeling oddly comforted simply by wearing them. With the coin clutched in my hand, I allowed the gentle rocking of the ship to lull me to sleep, confident that tomorrow would bring me more clarity.

And dick. I would love some clarity with a side of di...

4 1/2
LEIA

I awoke when my face hit the floor.

This can't be good...

My disorientation was magnified by the emergency lights illuminating my cabin and the echo of frantic voices and pounding feet outside my door. I scrambled to stand, desperately fumbling for my phone to check the time—as if it mattered—and the familiar glow centered me enough to finally think straight.

Grab only what you need to survive, Leia.

I grabbed my raincoat and sealed my phone, credit card, and I.D. inside a waterproof pocket. My precious rings were already on my fingers, so I shoved my bare feet into sneakers and quickly threw my raincoat over my night-gown, deciding that was enough. The flashing lights reflected on something half-buried in the sheets as I took a last look around my room, reminding me I'd fallen asleep while drunkenly admiring Eury's coin. Sighing, I recalled my ominous benefactor's earlier comment about rough seas and being 'prepared' for my journey.

I'll take all the luck I can get.

Before I could change my mind, I grabbed the coin and flung open the door, joining the frantic wave of passengers running down the hallway toward the exit. The scene above deck wasn't much better. A blanket of thick fog made it difficult to know which way to go, and I couldn't hear anything above the cacophony of shouting and fearful wails. Luckily, someone grabbed my elbow—presumably a crew member wanting to point me to safety.

"Did you follow my instructions?" Eury's familiar voice in my ear was both comforting and chilling. I mutely nodded, too overwhelmed by the chaos to resist as he led me *away* from the crush of bodies muscling their way to the lifeboats. The ship was leaning at an alarming angle and my gaze snagged on a pole garishly painted like a palm tree.

Was my dream at Auracle a... premonition?

"Show me the *obol!*" he hissed, simultaneously yanking me from my thoughts and confirming the coin's provenance. Again, I obeyed—unclenching my hand to reveal the coin in my palm, shaking with cold and terror as my body went into shock.

Eury snatched it away and spun me to face the sea, tightening his arm around my waist to hold me in place. Realizing I was about to die, I gaped in horror at the enormous wave curling overhead just as he forcefully shoved the coin into my open mouth. I was torn from his grasp as the wave hit—the last thing I heard being the screams of my fellow passengers and the echo of Eury's voice.

"Safe travels, little wanderer..."

5

AMBROSE

I absently swirled the wine in my *kylix,* noticing how the deep red liquid coating the bottom resembled freshly spilled blood.

It's been too long since I indulged in the thrill of the hunt...

Nowadays, I mostly hunted for sustenance—which I hardly required. That restraint was more because of the disappearance of my abilities rather than any desire to reform. I couldn't help wistfully thinking of the old days, when I was one of the most feared creatures in this godsforsaken land. Exactly how long ago that was remained unclear, but I'd grown used to my drink-dulled memories.

Taking another sip, my gaze swept over the cliffs to the white-capped waves beyond. Their movements were monotonous—crashing upon the rocks far below only to be swallowed up by the sea once again. As usual, no ships dotted the horizon, long since obscured by a thick fog stopping anyone from coming or going. Unfortunately, no ships also meant no sirens would appear to lure men to their doom for my amusement.

How utterly boring.

I reached for the *amphora* to refill my cup. My fingers brushed the indigo envelope, taunting me like a bruise against the light ash of my desk, but I ignored it. I had no intention of opening the letter, no desire to humor Julius' latest strategies and schemes.

We'd tried countless times to escape this cursed island —especially in the early days. A punishing storm would always blow in, tossing our ship to the waves and spitting us back onto the shore. Some of us successfully made it to the edge of the fog, only to discover it was as impenetrable as my armor. That was the moment we discovered we were truly trapped here by forces greater than ourselves.

I'd reached this level of resignation more quickly than the others. Our destiny was woven by the Fates themselves. Unless the gods were suddenly interested in granting us an audience, we had no hope of reclaiming what was rightfully ours. The restlessness brought on by my bewitched condition was maddening. However, planning a rebellion against an unreachable foe was a fool's errand, and I refused to be tortured by misplaced hope.

Far better to just drink myself into oblivion.

I added water to my *kylix* before topping it off with more wine, frowning to realize the jar was almost empty. Rising from my chair, I stalked to the opposite window, looking beyond my courtyard to the countryside beyond, where I was still free to roam. The late afternoon sunlight glittering off the lake of Lerna in the distance reminded me it was high time I paid Timyn a visit. My oldest friend never forced me to talk about the past unless I wanted to. Although, he also conveniently never stopped me from getting so drunk that I lost control over my speech.

Painful memories arose of the vineyard beyond the forest, and the night too much wine—and misspoken words—changed everything.

Immortality certainly encourages one to dredge up the past.

The ground suddenly lurched beneath my feet. I was thrown to my knees so quickly, I barely stopped my face from connecting with the stones. My collection of battle-worn shields rattled against the walls and I watched in annoyance as the amphora rolled off my desk to unceremoniously shatter on the floor.

I could have finished that!

Grasping the arm of a nearby couch, I climbed into the seat to wait out the seismic disturbance. The sky had turned a sickly green, the fluttering leaves of my olive trees showing their undersides, implying a storm was on its way. Earthquakes weren't uncommon in Greece, but this felt *different,* like a foretelling of events too inevitable to ignore.

What more could the gods take from us?

Just as abruptly, the vibration ceased, leaving an eerie silence in its wake. I stood and slowly approached the sea-facing window again, amazed by what I saw. An enormous tidal wave was roaring across the glassy surface of the water, hungrily devouring everything in its path as it raced towards land.

The remains of an unusually large *ship* crested into view before splintering against the stark white cliffs, like a toy discarded by a careless child. This was most unexpected, as the fog had historically not only trapped us here, but restricted the outside world from getting in. Morbidly fascinated, I tracked the tidal wave as it continued its path of destruction, vaguely wondering if the sirens were to blame for this strange occurrence. Before it reached my cliff, the wave collapsed inward, smoothing itself out once again to gently foam over the beach, like a caress.

Well, that was anticlimactic.

When the surf receded, something was left fluttering between the large rock formations dotting the pebbly beach —like a sail wrapped around some wreckage. I leaned out of the window to improve my awkward vantage point. Unfortunately, the harsh sun had reappeared, forcing me to squint and shade my infuriatingly weak eyes.

Things would be so much easier if I wasn't stuck in this form...

I sharply inhaled as I realized a human *foot* was sticking out of the rags. The instant I saw it move, I turned and raced down the stairwell, eager for a fight. The beach path was littered with debris, although interestingly, none of it looked like more bodies or body parts. I nimbly sidestepped the obstacles, the adrenaline in my veins bringing predatory focus, and I prayed my beast would be set free if a battle awaited.

As I drew closer, the survivor groaned, and I stopped in my tracks at the realization it was a *woman*. The first outsider to reach our shores in gods knew how long was not a hero coming to vanquish me while I was at my weakest, but a *helpless female.* My thirst for battle dissipated, and I crouched to gather her in my arms, careful not to damage her naturally fragile form.

The instant my skin connected with hers, a jolt of... *something* traveled through me, like a wave of pure power. It almost reminded me of the last time I was my truest self— the last time I'd felt whole.

Who are you, little Siren?

The woman abruptly coughed, spraying seawater in my

face and revealing a glimmer of bronze under her tongue. Arranging her on a nearby patch of grass, I gingerly opened her mouth and removed an *obol*. This only added another layer of intrigue to her arrival. Coins like this paid passage to Charon for those needing to cross the River Acheron— and were often placed over the mouth to protect the deceased's soul during the journey.

But this isn't the underworld...

I quickly checked her for injuries, only then registering she was dressed in nothing but a thin shift, soaked through to the point of being transparent. While vaguely aware there was etiquette stating I *shouldn't* gaze upon a half-naked woman in a semi-conscious state, I couldn't help assessing her. Yes, her soft skin and deliciously thick curves were causing my fangs to lustfully ache beneath my gums, but there were other, more unusual details that captured my attention.

Bits of metal were purposefully *embedded* in her face. Besides the delicate hoop in one nostril, there were studs beneath her bottom lip and pierced through the skin of her left cheek. Her earlobes were stretched over hollow wooden rings, and I spied a few tattoos, implying she was a slave, a criminal, or deeply religious. Most curious was that her hair was a vibrant shade of *green,* although when I warily poked at it with a stick, no hissing came from the tangled pile.

Definitely not a Gorgon, then.

"*Holee fuckin' shitballsss...*" she slurred, and I was so caught off guard by her delirious curse that I almost fell backward onto my ass.

Realizing I should contain her inside before she fully awoke, I tossed the woman over my shoulder and headed back up the path toward my villa. After stopping in the wine cellar, I decided my guest would be more comfortable in my room instead of the dusty women's quarters.

The better for me to control the situation.

While her arrival was fascinating from a logistical standpoint, I didn't believe in coincidences. No one had ever made it through the fog—in either direction—so why now, and why *her,* was an intriguing mystery I planned to discuss with the others.

I set the jar on the bedside table, next to the waiting pitcher of water and empty *kylix,* before tossing the *obol* in a drawer. My quarters were spare, but clean, with abundant natural light—vastly different from my previous home. Since I'd discovered the villa fully furnished, with odd accoutrements like cookware and clothing, I'd simply grown accustomed to living in this cultured way ages ago.

What other choice do I have, after all?

My visitor began to stir as I laid her on top of the linen bedspread, and I tensed, suddenly concerned she'd feel exposed in her transparent garment. Shucking off my robe, I hastily threw it over her body just as her eyelids fluttered open. Her warm brown eyes immediately focused on me, not with surprise or relief—as I'd expected—but with deep suspicion.

"Why the hell are you standing over me with your cock out?"

I glanced down, not quite understanding what the problem was. Yes, I was larger than what Greek warriors found 'civilized,' but that was to be expected of my kind.

I've certainly had no complaints.

It wasn't entirely clear if her question was rhetorical or not, and the wine was calling to me, so I made myself another drink while deciding how to reply. She sharply inhaled as I brandished a knife to break open the clay stopper—which was interesting, considering the harrowing experience at sea she'd already endured.

My guest seemed like the type to speak plainly, so I assumed answering in kind would set her at ease. "If I was going to kill you, it wouldn't be with a blade," I scoffed good-naturedly before frowning at her wary reaction.

Why doesn't she look reassured?

"As to why I'm naked," I carefully continued, mixing water with my wine before taking a sip. "It's because I gave you the robe I was wearing. I didn't want you to be uncomfortable in my presence when you awoke. While nudity matters little to me, I'm not sure of the customs... wherever you're from."

Her expression was calm as she nodded, although her gaze darted around the room. "Where are we now?" she asked evenly, those pretty eyes of hers meeting mine again, although they first lingered on my cock.

Perhaps the gods were feeling generous after all.

"That's a difficult question to answer," I laughed, offering her the *kylix*, which she promptly refused. "It could be Aeaea, but I've seen no pigs. Or perhaps it's Thule, as Pytheas wasn't particularly clear about where the island was located after he discovered it—"

"What the fuck kind of answer is that?" she swore again, to my surprise and delight. I'd encountered few women in my time—and even less since arriving here—but I didn't recall their vocabulary being so colorful. "How can you not know where you live?" Her anxiety was clearly getting the better of her, as she twisted the amethyst ring on her finger in what was probably a nervous habit.

I grimaced, gulping down the contents of my cup and wondering if I should start drinking it straight again. "Amnesia..." I offered, at a loss for how to handle this unprecedented situation. As I was still unsure whether this woman had been sent to ruin me, and not wanting to frighten her regardless, I didn't dare give her the truth...

That we were banished to this island eons ago, and it appears the Fates have similar plans for her.

6

LEIA

Something wasn't adding up here. Last thing I remembered was being tossed off a boat during a shipwreck, and yet somehow I'd woken up in a naked dude's bed. My heart was pounding as I frantically tried to make sense of the situation, but if there was one thing I excelled at, it was playing it cool. I had very few people in my life to rely on—especially now—and I refused to let anyone see me sweat.

Especially my rescuer.

Who may actually be my kidnapper—unclear.

It might have been my PTSD looking for a distraction, but it was a struggle to keep my gaze above the waist while this hunk of man-meat spoke to me. Some deeply buried voice of reason suggested I keep it in my pants until I figured out where the hell I'd washed ashore—or what this man's intentions were—and I agreed. Begrudgingly.

Just call me Saint Stranger Danger.

I diligently focused on his face, although that only made it worse, since he looked like the cover model from a bodice-ripping romance novel. His naturally highlighted strawberry blond hair fell in perfect waves over his broad shoulders, his aquiline nose resembled a Greek god's, and his cheekbones were sharp enough to cut glass. Desperate to find a neutral zone, I dropped my gaze again, only to then zero in on the chiseled planes of his sun-kissed chest and abs. This resulted in my focus inadvertently traveling lower as my lizard brain took over, unhelpfully reminding me the original goal of this trip was finding international dick.

Fuck it, I'm no saint.

"What's your name, Siren?" he cocked his head, his amber eyes fixed on me with unwavering focus. I suddenly realized he was speaking in a dialect of Ancient Greek, yet I somehow understood him perfectly.

All those useless lessons from my mother were useful, after all.

"Leia," I replied, surprising myself with my honesty. "Let me guess, your name's *Fabio* or something?"

"Leia..." he gazed off, rolling my name around his tongue as if he were tasting it. "No, I go by Ambrose nowadays," he replied, refocusing on me while he took a slow sip from his weird bowl-cup, languidly licking the rim in a way that made me clench.

I now identify as a weird bowl-cup.

Determined not to let my pussy run the show just yet, I smiled sweetly. "All right, *Ambrose*—can I use your phone? There are a couple of people I need to call so they don't think I'm, you know, *dead.*"

His amused expression faltered, and he lowered his gaze, as if suddenly finding the contents of his bowl-cup fascinating. "You won't be able to contact anyone, I'm afraid, and the sooner you accept your fate—"

"Excuse me?" I sat up, the stress of the situation finally

making me snap. "Listen, Fabio, being someone's captive wasn't on my agenda today, or ever, so this is what's gonna happen. You're going to put on some pants and drive me to the nearest town so I can—"

"Why would I put on pants?" he interrupted, either not caring that he was flapping in the breeze or an absolute master of the deadpan. In reply, I pointed at his—very impressive—dick, but he simply shrugged. "If it bothers you, I can find another robe, or simply tie it back."

"Tie it back?!" I squawked, my anger now taking a back-seat to pure confusion.

Ambrose was eyeing me as if *I* were the crazy one. "Yes, I have a *kynodesme* lying around here somewhere. It's used... *was* used during athletic events. It ties around the foreskin before being connected to a belt around the waist." He thoughtfully took another sip from his bowl-cup, as I tried —and failed—to absorb the nonsense he was spouting. "Although I've also seen humans simply connect it to a loop around the scrotum, although that always looked a bit odd to me."

I was starting to wonder if I'd actually drowned in the shipwreck and was now existing in some sort of absurdist afterlife. Either way, I had absolutely zero interest in seeing this man's cock wrapped up like a foreskin dumpling and tied with a bow.

"Let's just pretend that *isn't* an option," I muttered, handing him back his robe before realizing I was wearing nothing but my rings and the ridiculously sheer nightgown from Iola. While this man was clearly comfortable being on display—and I admittedly didn't hate it—his dick was distracting me from organizing my thoughts. "But... um, maybe you could put *something* on?"

A smile played on his lips as he dutifully tied a thin

cloth around his hips like a mini sarong, which did little more than accentuate his muscular thighs and ass—among other things. Channeling my inner Hugh Hefner, or an off-duty drag queen, I gathered the purple silk robe around myself and left the bed to better poke around the joint.

I followed enough travel bloggers to know the architecture of this place screamed Italian villa, which either meant I'd been blown *way* off course, or it was Ambrose's decorating style. Not that there was much to the decor. It actually looked like some old-timey historically accurate museum, and I almost expected to find an olive press and a lute stashed in a cupboard. My hottie host quietly followed me from room to room, intently watching me snoop through his belongings, but his scrutiny didn't set me on edge. In fact, I was so weirdly comfortable in his presence that I worried I was full-on disassociating from my trauma.

It wouldn't be the first time.

"Nice place you have here," I casually remarked, trying to get him talking about whatever the hell was going on.

He dismissively shrugged, as if it were common practice for one to live in an exotic seaside villa, routinely naked aside from silken robes. "Mmm, the cave I previously inhabited was more to my liking. However, when that was no longer an option, I came upon this unoccupied house and decided it was sufficient, if small."

I'd started to suspect Ambrose didn't actually know our location, and if he'd lived in an actual *cave,* it was probably safe to assume he'd washed up here too. Greece had thousands of islands, with only a couple hundred inhabited by people. My heart dropped as I realized a fully furnished villa just sitting here for the taking implied something terrible had happened to the previous occupants.

Something like a crazed castaway caveman murdering everyone...

While my natural paranoia immediately reached this conclusion, I couldn't bring myself to believe Ambrose was dangerous, or meant me any harm. If anything, Hottie McNoPants seemed just as lost and confused as I was. The oddly automatic trust I was feeling towards him made no sense, especially when compared to how Eury—*Eurystheus* —had creeped me out almost immediately, even as he'd pretended to be helpful.

Before throwing me into the fucking ocean.

I took a steadying breath to calm my racing thoughts, reminding myself I was alive and in no immediate danger. "Are you the only one here... on the island?" I quietly asked, unsure what I *wanted* the answer to be.

Ambrose hesitated, just long enough for me to realize *he* was playing his cards closely, too. "No," he carefully replied. "There are quite a few of us here, mostly... *men*, and we've been here a very long time."

This does not bode well.

My stomach sank, but I refused to give up hope, if for no other reason than stubborn determination. I was made of stronger stuff and hadn't survived a humiliating breakup, and shipwreck, only to give up now. "Well then," I said, straightening my spine to address him. "It looks like we're in this together, until we find a way off this island, so consider me your unwanted guest!"

"Oh, I don't see you as unwanted, Siren," he murmured, his voice vibrating so deeply I felt it in my core. "More like, incredibly *unexpected*. This entire situation is simply..." He gestured vaguely. "Unexpected."

Preach.

Since my suspicions about Ambrose's motives had died

down, I allowed myself the pleasure of discreetly admiring his hotness once again. Despite being hornier than a rhinoceros, I'd been hesitant to go after anyone post-Dylan, second-guessing whether I had it in me anymore to bed-hop like I used to. I also had to admit that being off the market for so long, and then discarded as harshly as I was, had knocked my self-esteem down a few pegs.

All that uncertainty went out the window in this man's presence, however, as I was currently experiencing an irresistible *pull* in his delicious direction, despite the circumstances. Plus, learning this island was inhabited by a bunch of—possibly hot, probably naked—*men* made me salivate, from top to tail.

And by tail, I mean pussy.

I desperately wanted to contact Iola and find a way home, but it was tempting to make the most of my current situation—like a karmic reward for all I'd recently been through. This almost felt like *permission* to unpack my baggage, a lot of which came from my ex, in my own way, without the usual judgments. There would be no swiping left, no next-day walks of shame, and no unanswered texts to dampen my rebound rodeo.

Here, I could do whatever I wanted, and maybe I'd even rediscover the old Leia along the way.

As they say, what happens in Greece...

7

AMBROSE

Intriguing wasn't a strong enough word to describe this woman. Captivating would be more appropriate —tantalizing, even.

What I wouldn't give to sink my fangs into her skin.

Besides looking like a delicious afternoon snack, Leia was proving to be witty and intelligent, and impressively self-sufficient. We'd tramped around my territory for hours, and she'd not only matched me physically, but with stimulating conversation. The tension between us had lessened considerably since yesterday, when she thought herself sly, attempting to pry information from me so she could escape.

As if I would let her get away.

Little did she know, I'd tracked prey for centuries. The idea of her running off whetted my appetite so fiercely, I allowed her to sleep in a separate bedroom last night, just to see if she'd try. Although I would have enjoyed the chase, I was equally pleased it no longer felt like Leia wanted to take flight. She was such good company, even with the nonsensical jargon—and amusing curses—endlessly streaming from her tempting mouth.

"Pumpkin spice basic bitch!" Leia yelped after injuring her delicate feet on some tiny pebbles yet again. I'd found her a linen *peplos* to wear, instead of her ruined dress, but she'd insisted on imitating me by going barefoot, despite my warnings of the rocky terrain. "Ambrose, are you *purposefully* trying to put me out of commission with the route you've chosen here?"

I chuckled low, scooping her into a bridal hold, despite her unladylike protests, noticing yet again that her skin against mine simultaneously awakened and settled my beast. "Yes, you've discovered my sinister plan. I want you so incapacitated, you have no choice but to let me carry you back to bed."

She immediately stopped struggling and gazed up at me through long eyelashes, her fascinating piercing extruding as she nibbled her lower lip. "I guess I'm not totally opposed to a big, strong man being useful."

Oh, it's endearing that you think I'm just a man.

Despite the possessiveness already flooding my veins, I couldn't wait for Timyn to meet this little Siren. Thanks to the loose boundaries of his habitat, he'd remained connected to the outside world the longest, but Leia was clearly from a modern era farther along than what any of us had experienced first-hand. I already knew my friend would eagerly drink down any knowledge she offered.

Among other offerings...

As if reading my thoughts, Leia asked, "Hey, when can I meet the other castaways on this island? Do they live far?"

I gazed across the rolling hills, considering how well she'd kept up with me today. "It's about a day's walk to get to the lake of Lerna, where my friend Timyn resides. He may have some insight into how you infiltrated the mists surrounding the island, and would surely enjoy meeting you, regardless. We can pay him a visit tomorrow, if you'd like?"

"Yeah, it was really foggy the night of the shipwreck..." she murmured, before immediately becoming distracted again. "Hey, are those actual *olive trees?*" she gasped, wiggling out of my grasp as we arrived at my humble grove. "I think I recognize them from this skincare line I work... *used* to work on."

I brightened, more than happy to share *this* part of my life with her. "Indeed, they are. I cultivate olives as a hobby. It's given me a purpose since hunting lost its *flavor.*"

When I first found the olive grove, left wild by the previous owners, I cared nothing for the trees. As the years passed, I realized I needed to distract my mind from all I'd lost—all that had been taken from me. So with encouragement and mild teasing from Timyn, I stopped licking my mortal wounds and got to work. Others weren't as supportive of me changing my focus from revenge to horticulture, but the Fates worked in mysterious ways.

"Do you make olive oil from your harvest?" Leia asked, poking at a hanging olive.

"Sometimes," I absently replied, distracted by the ripe fullness of her ass before she turned to face me again. "But there's only so much oil a man needs on hand."

"Oh, but it's so good for your skin and hair!" she exclaimed, tentatively nibbling an olive before spitting it out with a sour expression. "Olive oil has more uses than just cooking, you know."

Why would I use it for cooking?

Knowing full well what I used it for, I conjured up a vision of Leia spread open before me, coated in oil for me to take her. It was inevitable at this point; me ending up inside her, but I was *trying* to be cognizant of any trauma still lingering from her unceremonious arrival. The last thing I wanted was to inflict harm on my new obsession. At least, not in a way that wasn't pleasurable.

"If you don't mind me asking," I carefully spoke, gauging her reaction. "Do you remember what caused your ship to capsize? Anything... out of the ordinary?"

Like a Titan-sized Kraken, perhaps?

She chewed on her plump lower lip again, which only made my trapped fangs ache all the more. "Things were chaotic above deck, and I was still a little drunk from the night before," she mumbled, picking another olive to inspect. "Although the enormous tidal wave that took us out was hard to miss." She opened her mouth again, before snapping it closed with a shake of her head. "That's all the news that's fit to print, anyway."

Leia wasn't telling me everything, but I couldn't fault her for being cautious. We were still mostly strangers, and the gods knew I was behaving similarly, for possibly the same reason of self-preservation. I wanted to trust this woman—and strangely, felt I could. However, I knew it was wise to keep certain things to myself, at least for now.

All of a sudden, I wished Julius was here. He may have been stubborn and incorrigible, but no one could extract valuable intel out of someone as skillfully as he could.

Although that talent is exactly why I'm living in this blasted house.

Alone.

Refusing to allow my thoughts to linger on *other* missing acquaintances, I turned my attention back to the tantalizing woman before me. Leia had an otherworldly aura to her. If I wasn't almost entirely certain she was human, I might have mistaken her for a creature I hadn't seen in a very long time. This impression was only enhanced by her strange hair color and bizarre body modifications, but I suspected there were other reasons for those.

"Who is your master?" I bluntly asked, needing to know who might come looking for their property. Registering her confusion, I pointed to where a colorful underwater scene adorned her left bicep. "Your tattoos. Who branded you?"

"I... no one," she stuttered, before a smile twitched her lips. "We get tattoos for fun where I come from, Ambrose. Only *cattle* get branded."

"Ah, I see," I murmured, pretending to thoughtfully consider her answer, even as my beast purred with possessive satisfaction. "So you don't belong to anyone, then?"

Her smile instantly faded, and I realized I'd struck a nerve. "Not anymore," she sighed, but before I could amend my oversight, she snorted. "It's cool though—he was a douche."

"I don't know what that is," I cocked an eyebrow, endlessly amused by her strange choice of words. "But I assume it's something unpleasant."

She barked a laugh before looping her arm through mine and pulling me toward a small hill. "Yeah, you could say that. Dylan was a most unpleasant and highly frowned upon practice that disturbed the natural balance of my vagina. But hey, you live and learn!"

I couldn't help but be drawn to her humor, even with the language barrier. Leia's casual mannerisms were like a breath of fresh air after being suffocated by hopelessness for far too long.

Tearing my gaze from her appealing face, I realized she'd led me to a strategic vantage point for watching the sunset. We stood in comfortable silence a while—her watching the sun creep toward the horizon and me sneaking glances at her, enjoying the view. I'd existed here for more sunsets than I could count, and I suddenly realized I'd rarely appreciated any of them. I believed there would always be another one the next day, for all eternity.

But what is the point of immortality if you're not truly living?

"I lied," she barely whispered, and I turned my body to give her my full attention. "Not all tattoos are for fun." She was rubbing a thumb over her wrist where a series of numbers were inked, plain and nondescript. Something told me not to pry, so I simply nodded in acknowledgment, grateful for the piece of herself she offered.

Part of me was desperate to learn *how* Leia arrived here, and how the rest of us might escape, but I also relished the idea of having an endless amount of time to discover *her*. Mystery surrounded this woman, and for the first time in forever, I was actually looking forward to what tomorrow might bring.

8

LEIA

Despite the possibility Ambrose's good looks were disguising an axe-murderer, my first full day on the island was legitimately enjoyable.

There wasn't a neighbor or getaway car in sight as we explored scantily clad Fabio's vast estate, but I stopped caring as the day went on. Whenever my anxiety flared up, I focused it on the materialistic loss of my phone instead of the panic-inducing memory of the shipwreck I'd survived. The concern wasn't a stretch—not being able to reach my family to let them know I was alive was killing me.

Yeah, yeah, I also miss checking Instagram.

...but mostly the family thing.

It didn't take long for my stupidly attractive tour guide to make me forget any FOMO I was experiencing. Ambrose wore his confidence like a second skin, yet he became adorably shy when explaining the cultivation process of his olives. Something about seeing this long-haired lumber-snack talk about his trees like they were precious babies made my formerly uninterested ovaries rally to attention.

That's new.

Back in the City, I'd never taken the time to truly enjoy the sunset. It was always more of an annoyance, blinding me between tall buildings as I speed-walked to my next destination, but here it was spectacular. I wasn't sure if my appreciation was because of my brush with death, or that I was essentially *forced* to be in the moment without my phone. Either way, it was like nothing I'd ever seen before. Jewel-toned purple faded into mauve and tangerine, with the sea reflecting the colors back to the sky like an endless mirror. The only interruption was the thin strip of fog on the horizon, and I frowned, recalling how Ambrose seemed to think *that* was what kept everyone trapped here.

It didn't take long for me to get distracted by a different vision—my hottie host. He heard my stomach growling and suggested we get back to the house to cook dinner together. I eagerly agreed, even if by 'together,' we meant *Ambrose,* since I didn't do 'kitchen.'

From where I'm supervising, he's doing a bang-up job!

The kitchen itself was roomy—with a table big enough to seat an enormous family or small army—but it was missing some key modern elements. There was no fridge or dishwasher, no appliances except for a brick oven and an odd, freestanding grill that needed an actual fire built beneath it. This was what Ambrose was currently using, while I admired the way the fire and oil lamplight high-lighted his ridiculous muscles.

Much to my amusement, he'd shed his sarong as soon as we returned, only to then don an apron—wisely protecting his sensitive parts from grease spatter, I assumed. His ass was still fully on display beneath the apron ties, however, and I wasn't complaining one bit.

A girl could get used to the nudist castaway life.

Ambrose also finally convinced me to try his diluted

wine in my very own weird bowl-cup, which he referred to as a *kylix,* although I had no intention of ever calling it that. Draining the delicious contents, I snorted in amusement as an image of two naked men 'wrestling' was revealed at the bottom.

How historically accurate.

"I wish I had my phone with me," I murmured, mesmerized by the homey glow on his flexing forearms as he flipped a pair of juicy steaks on the grill. "So I could document this adventure."

His brows furrowed. "How would you document something on a phone? I thought telephones were for talking to each other through a series of wires."

Either this guy is an Oscar-worthy actor or he's suffering from extreme amnesia.

"Ambrose..." I carefully began, setting aside the cup and hopping down from my counter perch. "How long do you *think* you've been here?"

I observed his profile, searching for any sign of deception. Ambrose claimed he'd found this abandoned villa as-is, but he'd never specified how long ago that was. He didn't look to be any older than his late-30s, but if he'd never even heard of *cordless* phones...

My gawd, that means he doesn't remember the internet!

Tamping down my horror at his nonexistent social media presence, I stepped closer, inexplicably compelled to touch him. His shoulders dropped as I brushed my fingertips down his arm, and I could have sworn I felt a shiver run down my spine in response.

"I truly don't know, Leia," he grimaced, his frustration palpable and seemingly genuine. "I remember who I was before this, but how and when I ended up on this island—as I am now—is maddeningly unclear."

Realizing I should probably drop the subject, I removed my hand, but he snatched it back with a growl. "None of that matters when you touch me, however. I think I'd be willing to forget everything about my past if I could just bury myself inside you."

Well, tell me how you really feel!

I threw my head back with a laugh. "Shit, you don't beat around the bush, do you? I usually at least *try* to play coy, so I don't scare anyone away."

Ambrose chuckled. "Please understand, even before I ended up here, I didn't encounter many women. So you'll have to forgive me if I don't behave as *civilized* as I should." Then he smirked, clearly *not* seeking forgiveness, his blatant invitation practically blasted on a Times Square billboard above his handsome head.

And I am buying whatever he's selling!

He released my hand with a sly smile, revealing noticeably sharp canines, before transferring both steaks to a single plate. I helpfully topped off our bowl-cups and followed my host to the enormous farmhouse table, where a single place setting awaited. He sat at the head and I aimed for the next seat down, but was forcefully pulled into his lap instead. I yelped as my ass landed heavily on his already hardening dick, my thin layers and his ridiculous apron doing nothing to disguise how much he wanted me.

"As I said," he growled against my ear. "I want your skin on mine... unless hearing that scares *you* away?"

"Not at all," I chuckled, wiggling a little to get him to growl like that again. "I think I'm just jealous you get to be so blunt."

Ambrose circled his tree trunk arms around me to cut the steak, apparently intent on feeding me as well. "Why wouldn't you speak as plainly as me? Do you not agree that directness is best?"

The simplicity of his questions stunned me into silence, and I gladly accepted a bite of steak while I contemplated. Being a PR firm, Auracle employed mostly women, but the owners and c-suite execs were all men. During meetings, the likelihood of being talked over by these higher ups—or having your idea parroted back to you as if they'd thought of it—was extremely high. Even though I could hold my own in real life, and never filtered who I was around Iola and my other friends, I was used to playing small at work.

"I suppose it's how I've always been *expected* to behave," I haltingly replied, feeling my own hackles rise as I heard myself articulate it. "Where I come from, if a woman speaks her mind, she's considered aggressive, and if she protests, she's shrill. Unless you're in a position of power, it's just easier to smile sweetly and nod agreeably than risk rocking the boat."

Ambrose stilled, with the fork poised at my mouth. I took the bite, then twisted in his lap to better look at him, finding pure confusion clouding his handsome face. "I see nothing wrong with a woman who knows what she wants and does whatever it takes to attain it," he muttered before zeroing in on me with predatory focus. "What do *you* want, Leia?"

The proximity of his lips to mine almost made me forget the question, but I quickly recovered. "Well, at this exact moment, I'd like you to eat some of *your* steak before I devour both pieces."

"Both steaks *are* for you," he smiled indulgently. "So devour away."

It was my turn to look confused. "But why wouldn't you cook one for yourself? You must be hungry."

"Mmm, these are much too well-done for my taste." Again, that secretive smile, his amber gaze trailing down my body. "Besides, what I hunger for is decidedly... *juicier.*"

CLENCH!

My lady bits gave such an enthusiastic pulse of approval, I barely registered that the steaks in question were so rare they were practically still mooing. My desire must have been written all over my face, as Ambrose chuckled knowingly before nuzzling against my neck for a deep inhale.

He growled again, low and rumbling, and the pure animal sound of it flipped a switch in my brain. "Show me," I rasped, physically unable to form coherent thoughts in the presence of such primal hotness.

In one motion, he swept the table clear, the plate and bowl-cups clattering to the floor, before flipping me onto the surface. I gasped in surprise as my back hit the worn wood, but Ambrose was already moving my dress out of the way and parting my thighs, sliding his chair closer until I could feel his warm breath on my wetness.

Then, nothing happened.

I lifted my head to peek at him, finding him simply staring at my pussy, his brow furrowed, jaw clenching as he breathed raggedly.

Does he not like what he sees?

I cleared my throat. "Uh... are you all right down there?"

He snapped his attention to my face, a wide grin brightening his face, his too-sharp canines somehow looking even sharper. "Oh, I am more than all right. I simply wasn't expecting such..." His gaze dropped to my pussy again as he licked his lips. "Mouthwatering perfection."

Marry me.

My self-confidence soared through the fucking roof,

prompting me to give a saucy little wiggle in reply. "Well then, it's your turn to eat up. I'm already full."

Again, that low rumble of his vibrated through my core. "Not yet, you're not," he murmured before lowering his head and running his hot tongue up my center.

I squeaked as a shockwave of pleasure rocketed down my back. My hands involuntarily flew to Ambrose's flowing locks, and I yanked him closer, wrapping my legs around his neck before he could even think about backing off. He chuckled against me, sliding his large hands under my ass and lifting my hips, burrowing his face deeper as he went to town.

My legs were already trembling, my nails raking down his arms as he sucked my clit into his mouth. Maybe it was how hard up I was—or that no one had ever licked my pussy like a Magnolia cupcake—but the sounds I was making were rivaling those primal growls of his. The instant Ambrose lightly bit down on my clit, I exploded, gasping my way over the edge as I soaked his face.

Holy shit, I hope he's still alive.

I tried to sit up—immediately self-conscious about *everything* that had just come out of me—but he held me down with a firm hand on my chest. "Oh no, Siren," he raised his head, licking my release from his lips with a grunt of approval. "That was just an appetizer."

9
LEIA

There was no way in hell I was going to stop Ambrose from delivering main course orgasms, especially since he was enjoying the meal just as much as I was.

Go little rockstar!

Of course, there was nothing *little* about this man. Besides the massive, rippling muscles of his overall physique, that enormous cock of his was now fully erect, centimeters away from impaling me as he rose to stand at the end of the table. Wrapping his hand around my thigh—fingers still dripping from massaging my g-spot until the floodgates opened—he spread me wider still.

"Should I be gentle with you?" Ambrose asked, his gaze riveted on where he was rubbing the head of his cock through my wetness. "Or should I fuck you like I want to?"

My brain officially broke at the clearly rhetorical question, but after a beat, I noticed he was watching my face, patiently waiting for my answer. Of course, my hussy vagina was begging for instant ruin, but the small part of me that wanted to survive this physically intact won out.

"Maybe start out gentle? I mean, I do like it rough, but I haven't been with many... *any* as big as..." I awkwardly replied, finding it difficult to maintain eye contact as my gaze drifted south. Dylan was on the larger side—probably one of the few reasons I stayed as long as I did—but this was some next-level aubergine. "So, um, how about you work up to the part where you destroy my pussy?"

Ambrose's hand was suddenly gripping my chin, forcing me to look at him again. "Of course I will, Leia," he whispered, kissing me softly as he curled his body over me. "This cunt is mine now and I protect what belongs to me."

Daddy? Sorry, Daddy?

That skillful tongue of his forced its way into my mouth, tangling with mine as he quickly slathered some oil on his cock and eased his way into me. I whimpered at the stretch, but quickly locked my heels behind his muscular thighs to urge him on. He gently pumped his way in—deeper each time—nipping and licking my lips to distract me from the pain turning into pleasure.

His gorgeous mane of hair was draped over me, lightly tickling my neck, and I noticed he smelled like a summer's day at the beach—fresh and salty. Just being in his arms was like sunlight on my skin, and I was getting all warm and fuzzy, even as he filled me up with his monster cock.

Careful, girl. Don't go catching feelings.

He shuddered as he finally bottomed out, lifting himself off of me so he could stare down at where we were joined. His jaw muscles were working again, his chest heaving as he breathed through his nose, as if calming himself before continuing.

"Are you okay?" I teased, assuming he was trying not to prematurely blow his load.

Which of course just means my pussy is magic!

He smiled again, although it was softer this time. "Yes. I feel better than I have in a while. It's simply... unexpected."

There was that word again—*unexpected.* There could be a deeper meaning here, but I chalked it up to Ambrose being mostly pussy-deprived for an indeterminate amount of time.

Wait... does this mean he's been fucking the other men on this island?

I'd spent my fair share of evenings watching smut online, and was not ashamed to admit a lot of it was gay porn. Never in a million years would I have disrespected my gay or bi friends by asking them to *perform* for me, but Ambrose didn't seem like the type to keep it behind closed doors.

So maybe...

"Siren," he rasped, his amber eyes seeming to flash gold, even in the low lamplight. "If you continue... *tightening* around me like that, I may no longer be as gentle as you'd prefer."

Smirking, I sat up enough to shimmy out of my borrowed *peplos,* tossing it to the side in what I hoped was a sultry move. Ambrose's gaze hungrily roamed over my naked body—clearly liking what he saw—and my confidence gave a smug little curtsy.

"I think gentle time is over," I licked my lips, purposefully clenching around him again as I laid back down. "My safe word is Lincoln Tunnel. If you hear that, stop everything. Now, my big, strong man—show me how you *want* to fuck me."

He growled so intensely, his dick turned into a vibrator. "As you wish. But in return, I want you to scream for me."

"Yes, Ambrose," I whimpered, as he dragged his cock

almost all the way out of me. "I promise I'll scream your name when I come."

"Not only when you come," he grinned, his sharp teeth catching the lamplight just as a breeze blew it out, plunging the room into darkness. "And that's not my real name."

Before I could fully register his latest bizarre statement, Ambrose slammed back into me, yanking a ragged scream from my throat as I arched off the table. He immediately captured my mouth with his—greedily swallowing my cries, as if consuming my pleasure. Licking his way along my jaw, down to my neck, he nuzzled closer, practically folded me in half as he began fucking me, slow and very, *very* deep.

His skin on mine was like a drug. Dizzy with need, I feverishly ran my hands down his broad back, holding him tightly against me so as not to lose the sensation. He was trailing tentative little bites along my neck and shoulder, each one making me shudder, as if testing how I'd react to the idea of more.

"Go ahead. Bite me," I panted, suddenly wanting nothing more than for him to sink those canines in. Ambrose growled again, the full-body vibration sending me barreling toward another orgasm just as his teeth pierced my skin.

Holy! Those fuckers really are sharp!

I came hard, and he immediately began rutting into me like an animal—his huge cock seeming to grow larger as he carried me through this climax and into the next. My hands continued to dance over every inch of him in the dark, registering a hell of a lot more fur than I'd previously noticed, which only enhanced the Daddy vibes.

I'll allow it.

Ambrose somehow hadn't stopped growling—like a

deep rumbling purr. It only intensified as his hips stuttered, his bite bordering on painful as he emptied inside me with an inhuman sound. To my surprise, he then immediately tensed, hurriedly releasing my neck and untangling himself from my arms, as if he couldn't get away fast enough.

Weird. I would've pegged him for a cuddler...

"A-Ambrose?" I faltered, confused by the sudden change in intimacy, especially since the man was still buried inside me. More concerning was how much I *cared* about his aloofness, since he was only supposed to be the first stop on my rebound sex island tour.

"Don't move," he gruffly answered, but his voice sounded strange—more growly, were that possible. After a beat of awkward silence, he added, "This may hurt for a moment, Leia. But I'll... get you something to clean up with."

Why would it hurt...?

A sliver of moonlight was the only illumination left, so I couldn't gauge how serious his statement was. My answer came soon enough. He slowly began pulling out and I seized up, yowling like a goddamn cat as what felt like actual *barbs* scratched my tender inner walls.

"Holy crapola!" I yelped, cupping my throbbing pussy protectively after he'd withdrawn, as if that would help. "How did I not notice you had Hellraiser dick piercings? What the *fuck,* dude?"

Ambrose murmured an apology as he backed away from me and headed for the sink. I strained my eyes, but all I could see was the faint outline of his form, looking monstrously larger in the low light.

I quickly sat up, but froze when a deluge of cum leaked out of me—way more than seemed humanly possible. Oddly, this didn't disgust me. Instead, it triggered the strangest sense of *loss*. Despite having firmly existed in the no-kids camp for my entire life, I found myself weirdly disappointed that I'd recently renewed my birth control shot.

Jesus, I must be high on dick right now.

I sighed in relief as Ambrose stealthily appeared at my side again and pressed a warm cloth against my battered vajay. He quietly cleaned up his mess, and I relaxed into his gentle touch, wishing the lamp hadn't blown out so I could get a better look at his expression.

And his hardware, full disclosure.

Still unsure why my overly affectionate man was acting like such a weirdo, I reached for him, stupidly satisfied when he immediately gathered me into his arms. Caressing his back, I frowned at how the 'fur' I'd felt while under the influence of too many orgasms had seemingly vanished.

"You may have my bed tonight, Leia," Ambrose rumbled, easily navigating the darkened house as he carried me upstairs. "I'll take one of the guest rooms so you can rest."

Maybe I was still riding high on endorphins, but the idea of us sleeping apart made my gut twist uncomfortably. "Please, don't leave me alone," I blurted out, tightening my grip on him. "I want to sleep next to you."

Ambrose immediately stopped walking, and I inwardly scolded myself for being so needy. Before I could rescind my statement, he haltingly replied, "You... wish to sleep next to me? After what just happened?"

"Yes, Ambrose," I huffed a laugh, my insecurity evaporating with how unsure *he* sounded. "Even though you ravaged me like a wild beast on your kitchen table and scratched my paint with your piercings, I wish to sleep next to you." I paused for a moment before feeling compelled to add, "And I wanna do it again."

"I also want to do it again," he whispered against my skin, continuing up the stairs, sounding more like himself again. "As long as you'll let me."

10

LEIA

I awoke with a groan. My joints were painfully sore, reminding me that—as much as I liked to pretend otherwise—I was no spring chicken, and my body had been through some *shit* in the past 24 hours.

Including surviving King Dong.

Rolling over on the lumpy, but comfortable mattress, I found Ambrose fast asleep, adorably snoring in a way that only made me want to climb aboard for another ride.

Don't mind if I do...

This man made me wetter than a fire hydrant, but I knew my pussy would hate me later if I didn't prep the runway a little first. As quietly as possible, I opened the bedside table drawer, hoping to find more of Ambrose's artisan olive oil to use as lube. Next to the knife he'd used to open his wine jar, I found a small bottle, which I generously applied to myself, relishing the way it felt on my skin.

Slipping the thin sheet off of Ambrose's body, I took a moment to admire my personal Adonis. He truly looked as if he'd been sculpted by the gods themselves, and I briefly wondered if his friends were as hot as him. My gaze landed on his dick—of course—and I frowned when I saw no evidence of piercings or body mods to explain the pain I'd felt the night before.

Maybe we didn't use enough oil...

Unbothered, I went to return the bottle when the glint of something metallic in the drawer caught my eye. I froze, realizing it was a coin that looked a heck of a lot like the one Eurystheus had given me in Athens.

Panic flooded my system, my heart pounding and vision blurring as I fought to breathe. With no recollection of how I got there, I was suddenly straddling Ambrose, my shaking hands holding the knife against his throat.

"What a thrilling way to wake up," he purred, peering up at me through one eye with an infuriatingly sexy smile playing on his lips.

"Start talking, asshole," I growled, my voice thick with an overwhelming cocktail of rage and betrayal as my mind replayed everything that had gotten me to this point. Eurystheus had *stalked* me, demanding I carry the *obol* at all times, even though I owed him nothing. As if that wasn't enough of a violation, he'd then *shoved the coin in my mouth before throwing me overboard.*

Ambrose claimed he'd found me on the beach, but I only remembered waking up in his bed. His story still didn't add up, but I was so eager to get laid, I hadn't even considered my rescuer might be working with the very man who sent me here.

He's playing me—just like Dylan did.

I'm so fucking stupid.

"Where did you get that coin in your drawer?" I hissed through gritted teeth, tightening my grip on the knife.

He hummed in understanding. "Ah... the *obol*. It was under your tongue when I found you. I didn't wish for you to choke, so I put it aside for safekeeping." Ambrose turned thoughtful, as if this were a normal conversation, not a come to Jesus at knifepoint. "Although, I've been meaning to ask where *you* acquired such an object—"

"I'm the one asking questions here!" I barked, noticing his cock stirring to life beneath me as I increased the pressure on his neck. This caused my oiled-up pussy to flood with wetness, but I refused to let another traitor run the show. "Are you working with... with *HIM?!*"

His serene expression instantly faded, replaced by confusion and concern. "Who are you talking about?" When I didn't answer, he slowly blew out a breath. "Leia, I am finding it exceedingly difficult to give this conversation the focus it deserves while your deliciously wet cunt is rubbing on my cock."

Oh, are you having trouble concentrating?

Wiggling in Ambrose's lap, I shifted so his swollen head was teasing my opening. "How about we play a game?" I smirked down at him, deciding to get some pleasure out of this exchange. "For every truth you tell me, you get an inch." He groaned, and I grinned, relishing the control I had over him.

I am awesome at being a hot man interrogator.

"This isn't wise," he rasped, his desperate gaze shifting between me and the bright morning sun pouring through the window. "I don't want to... we can *see* each other now..."

"Excuse me?" I choked out, tears pricking my eyelids as my emotions spiraled yet again. Dylan had made similar comments about seeing my less-than-perfect body in the light of day. I was in no mood for Ambrose to do the same, especially considering the circumstances. "Are you seriously telling a woman with a *knife* you don't want to *see* her when you fuck?"

Pure horror washed over his face. "By Olympus, no! How could you even *think* that? I... *look at you!*" Ambrose ran his gaze over my naked—and harshly lit—body, raw hunger his only expression. "You are absolutely breathtaking, with every curve created by Aphrodite herself. From now on, I will wake you each morning with my face between your luscious thighs, so you know exactly how much I desire you."

Okay, he gets at least a few inches for that.

I lowered myself down, sighing in satisfaction as his thickness stretched me, despite the hint of soreness from the night before. Ambrose hissed through his teeth and tentatively reached for me, but not to guide me further down. Instead, his large hands wrapped around my thighs, his nails digging into my flesh as he firmly *stopped* me from taking any more of him.

Holy mixed signals, Batman.

"Leia," he gritted out. "I don't want *you* to see *me*. Please, I can't..." His jaw was clenching, as if he were warring with himself. "I can't control what I become with you. Please..."

Realizing I'd crossed a line, I hurriedly pulled myself off of him and tossed the knife aside, my hands flying to his throat to massage away any hurt I'd caused. I attempted to slide off his body completely, but Ambrose wrapped his arms around me and pulled me flush against him in a crushing hug.

"I'm sorry. That I called you an asshole," I mumbled into his chest, too embarrassed to meet his gaze. "And for the knife. And that I didn't stop when you asked me to..." I trailed off, feeling like a complete trash human. If Ambrose was struggling with whatever happened between us last night, the last thing he needed was for me to be alternating between knife-wielding psychopath and sex-starved creeper.

The only asshole here is me.

Ambrose quietly chuckled, caressing my back with his large hands, the feel of his addictive skin calming my frayed nerves. "You have nothing to apologize for. You recently suffered a traumatic event, and now find yourself in a world you don't fully understand. I should have brought up the *obol* before now but I didn't want to frighten you with my theories." He paused, as if debating whether to continue. "For me to have found it under your tongue, Leia... there are certain implications—"

"You think I'm dead," I flatly stated, lifting my head as tears began blurring my vision again. The idea that this could be purgatory... that I could be trapped here forever, never seeing Iola or my mom again. No longer able to visit my dad's grave...

Jesus, get it together, Leia.

"No, Siren, I *don't.* That's why I've been mulling over how to address it," he soothed, before observing me curiously. "How do *you* know an *obol* placed under the tongue buys passage to the underworld? That's a tradition not practiced much... nowadays, correct?"

I sniffled, sloppily attempting to dry my tears with the heel of my palm. "My mother is a Greek historian and archeologist—a pretty famous one, actually—so I've picked up a few things."

"Interesting..." he murmured, gently batting my hand away so he could wipe my face with a cloth, like the Daddy he was. "Perhaps this world won't be so strange to you, after all."

While it was incredibly tempting to just let Ambrose take care of everything—no questions asked—the self-sufficient New Yorker put her foot down. "If there's something I need to know, you need to *tell* me. I'm not fucking around, Ambrose."

The indulgence in his smile came across as sweet rather than condescending. "Leia, it's simply that *I'm* not ready to share certain things about myself. *Yet.* However, I promise, I will always try to be honest with you, to the best of my ability."

Don't catch feelings. Don't catch feelings.

"Ok, deal," I replied, before remembering something odd he'd said while I was delirious on dick the night before. "How about you start by telling me what you meant by *Ambrose* not being your real name?"

He took a steadying breath before replying. "Ambrose is the name a... very dear friend gave to me, soon after we all mysteriously arrived here together." The sorrow on his face affected me more than it should have, considering we'd only just met, but I had little control over my emotions with this man.

"What was your name before?" I dared to whisper, hoping I wasn't making things worse, but desperate to make it better.

"I don't think I had one," he sadly replied, tucking a strand of hair behind my ear. "So, Ambrose it is."

I'm totally catching feelings.

As enjoyable as it sounded to laze in bed with Ambrose like a couple of giant house cats, we clearly needed help with solving all the mysteries on our hands. "We should probably get going to see your friend, hmm?" I reminded him.

His eyes widened in alarm before he puffed out a laugh. "Oh, you mean *Timyn*. Yes, of course. I assume you'll want to freshen up and that you'd prefer a bath over using a *strig-*

il?" When I simply stared in reply, he laughed. "That's what I thought. Allow me to heat some water so you can wash and relax. While you bathe, I'll prepare for our journey."

A little while later, I was lowering myself into the perfectly heated waters of an alabaster basin with a groan of pleasure. The lavender and bay leaves my host had left floating on the surface were an extra touch that made me feel guilty all over again for suspecting him of foul play.

Unless he's seasoning me to eat later...

I snorted in amusement at my train of thought, as Ambrose had been nothing but a gentleman since I'd arrived. A mostly naked, dirty-talking piece of man-candy who turned into an absolute animal in the sheets. Making a mental note to encourage more of his primal growling and biting—assuming *that* wasn't what had freaked him out—I sank deeper into the glorious depths.

Stretching out my legs, I jumped as my foot brushed against something solid in the depths. Blindly groping beneath the surface, my hand closed around what felt like a thin metal disc. Lifting the object out of the water, I stifled a scream, almost throwing it across the room in terror. Although its markings were different from the one Eurystheus had given me, I instantly recognized the coin for what it was.

Another *obol.*

The fare for the dead. A message heard loud and clear.

If only I can figure out what it means.

11

LEIA

"It's finally dark out, Ambrose," I teased, scooting closer in our army-style canvas tent. "The perfect time to get busy, under the cover of night."

Some might call it The Dicking Hour.

He chuckled, low and throaty, pulling me against his wall of muscles. "Very well, my insatiable little Siren. Although I'll be gentle this time—for both our sakes."

I grumbled, but quickly got over it, as Ambrose's version of 'gentle' translated to slow and deliciously deep. There was no pain this time as he pulled out, and I chalked up our first encounter to nerves and girthy thickness.

And I am down with the thickness.

As promised, Ambrose had packed and clothed me for our outing while I bathed like a queen. The Kelly green *peplos* he'd found perfectly matched my hair and hugged my curves like a dream. However, paired with the gladiator sandals and blood red Spartan tunic he wore, we looked like a couple of eerily accurate historical re-enactors.

At least now we're both wearing clothes, like civilized humans!

We'd walked all day to reach the rocky shore of an enormous lake stretching to the horizon. As the sun set, Ambrose announced we'd camp for the night and knock on his friend's door first thing in the morning. Then, he disappeared, only to return with a dead rabbit that looked like it had been mauled by a bear. A full bowl-cup and the sweet smell of bunny roasting on an open fire soon erased any guilt I had about eating Thumper. I couldn't help noticing my brave hunter didn't join me, and realized I hadn't seen him eat anything since I arrived.

Can Ambrose actually survive on a pussy diet?

Hours later, I was awakened by a large splash from the lake, and I held my breath, listening for monsters. All I heard was the wind gently buffeting the canvas flaps and a faint chorus of peeping sounds that were weird but non-threatening. Nature was also calling, and my bladder decided the coast was clear, so I slipped out of the tent to visit the facilities.

Luckily, the moon was full, so it was easy to navigate the enormous boulders dotting the shoreline. I quickly crouched and took care of business before gathering the long skirt of my *peplos* and wading into the moonlit lake to freshen up before returning to the tent. The water was pleasant, and I serenely gazed out over the nighttime landscape, feeling like a goddamn yogi with how one-with-nature I was.

My hippie phase was short-lived, as something slimy brushed against my ankle underwater. I yelped and stumbled backward, only to have *two somethings* wrap around the other ankle and give it a gentle tug. Frantically kicking myself free, I tore out of the shallows like Nessie was after me, only to stumble over nothing and face-plant on the rocky beach like some kind of helpless damsel.

Please don't let me be eaten by lake snakes!

Before I could get my bearings, the *something* that had touched me in the water firmly coiled around both calves. I was so frozen in terror, all I could do was whimper as a bigger version wrapped around my waist and immediately constricted. The texture was smooth yet cool on my skin, with shockingly powerful muscles undulating beneath the surface as whatever it was began flipping me over.

My brain was screaming at me to shut my eyes, but the New Yorker in me knew I needed to identify the perpetrator in a lineup. Street smarts and city grit aside, I was *not* prepared to face what awaited me.

A multi-headed *dragon* was leering down at me, its forked tongues snaking out from between ridiculously jagged fangs. The appendages holding me in place tightened as what appeared to be the main head moved closer. I opened my mouth to yell for Ambrose when an overwhelming sense of calm washed over me, erasing my panic and lulling me into complacency.

What a cute wittle lake monster...

"You smell good enough to eat," a male voice smoothly chuckled in my head and I tensed, my instincts scrambling to regain control. A second wave of relaxation hit before the dragon used his tail—tails, plural—to spread my legs apart. *"What I meant, Water Lily, is that your scent roused me from my slumber. Now that I'm awake, shall I show you what my tongues can do?"*

Despite whatever reptilian mind spell he had me under, the dragon didn't make a move. Instead, he stared down at me intently with multiple sets of eyes, as if waiting for my consent. The tongue from his first head flickered out to test the air above my parted thighs, mesmerizing me with how fluidly it moved.

I mean... since you're offering.

"Yes," I whispered, resting my head back as another tail slithered under my neck like a pillow, adding to my comfort. "Show me what those tongues do."

The dragon seemed to grin as three heads descended on me together. The tails wrapped around my legs spiraled upward, pushing my skirt higher and caressing my thighs before the tips gently spread me open like an offering.

"Look at that pretty little cunt," he murmured in my head, his dulcet tone enveloping me like warm caramel. *"The perfect snack."*

Sweeping his ridiculously long tongue up my center, he teased my folds before dipping inside, curling upward in a way a cock never could. I writhed as he hit my g-spot, massaging it with an expert's precision while I moaned garbled words of appreciation—seeing stars from how good this freaky shit felt.

He chuckled low at my reaction. *"So responsive. I wonder how much of me you could take."*

"More," I gasped, not entirely sure what I was agreeing to, but game all the same. I'd never understood what 'tongue fucking' meant until this moment, but this skillful muscle was officially my new favorite toy. I rode his tongue as much as I could with how he'd restrained me, already barreling toward an orgasm, when the two heads on call joined the party.

Fuck yes, I'm being eaten by lake snakes!

One newcomer hovered above my clit, his seemingly endless tongue unfurling to circle around the sensitive bud before stroking it. The thick tail surrounding my waist constricted, lifting my bottom half off the ground, and I could only groan as a third tongue tickled my back door before sliding in like silk. I violently shook, screaming through my release, not caring in the least that a goddamn talking dragon and its many heads were my cunnilingus MVPs.

"You came so beautifully for me," the voice cooed, and I smiled dreamily, pleased that I'd pleased him. All I could think about was sleep—my eyes fluttering closed as I was gently set on the ground. *"Now to fill you with my seed..."*

What the what now?

My eyes shot open, and I gasped to find a very attractive *human* man gazing down at me. His jet black hair somehow reflected the moonlight, and his green eyes seemed to glow like luminescent algae against his olive skin. When he smiled, a decidedly boring tongue appeared to wet his full lips, immediately bringing me back to reality.

The realization that I'd hallucinated the entire encounter hit just as I felt him rubbing his cock through my wetness. All at once, I understood that this stranger—this naked man who was *not* a sexy dragon—mistakenly thought he was going to fuck me. Without a moment's hesitation, I clenched the fist wearing Iola's knuckle ring and punched him straight in his handsome face.

12

LEIA

"Ow, that fucking *hurt!*" Hottie Not Dragon laughed, clutching his nose, his eyes glittering in perverse excitement. "Is this how you normally reward men for feasting on your perfect cunt?"

When they think dinner means dessert, yes.

"Timyn!" Ambrose's stern voice had me scrambling to my knees, guilt clawing at my insides. "Why is it impossible for you to behave? I was waiting until morning to introduce you to Leia."

The other man snorted, drawing my attention back to him. "Oh, we've met. She was too tempting a treat to resist, and before you interrupted, I was about to devour her whole."

"You're a *pescatarian*," Ambrose grumbled, his tone conveying he thought *that* was a questionable choice. "So stop pretending to be frightening and leave my poor Siren alone."

Timyn cackled, rising to stand with freakishly smooth grace. "I don't think she's *yours* anymore, Ambrose. You'll simply have to share." He extended a hand, but I ignored the gesture, not wanting to make things worse by appearing to be choosing him.

What have I done?

I dropped my gaze, unsure about what had actually happened and what it meant for everyone involved. On the surface, Ambrose didn't *look* pissed about what he'd walked in on, but he was so naturally chill, I didn't know how to interpret how he felt. To add insult to injury, clocking faux dragon in the face had somehow shattered my knuckle ring, severing my last connection to my niece.

I wish Iola was here with me.

Before I could get myself too worked up over *all the things,* Ambrose's familiar arms were wrapping around me, gently helping me to my feet. "Let's get you back to bed," he rumbled. "Since *I* just awoke from *an unnaturally deep sleep myself.*" This last part seemed aimed at Timyn, but I couldn't blame Ambrose for being angry with his friend.

Or me.

Guiding me back into the tent, he arranged the blankets around me like a nest before tucking me in, which I found extremely comforting. "Try to get some sleep, Siren. I need to leave you for a bit, as there are some matters I must discuss with Timyn."

"Get your ass out here and make me a fire, you furry bastard!" the other man called from beyond the tent. "You know how I get cold."

Ambrose sighed a sigh I recognized on a soul level. It held long-suffering annoyance combined with unconditional love—a sound I often made in the presence of Iola. "Allow me to apologize on my friend's behalf. He shouldn't have cornered you like... helpless prey."

"Oh, but she was a very willing participant and enjoyed herself immensely!" Timyn sang out again.

Traitor!

My stomach dropped with the truth of his words, and I awkwardly cleared my throat. "I'm the one who should apologize, Ambrose. I was definitely more than okay with what happened, even when I believed..." I trailed off, unsure how to explain what I *thought* I saw, but knowing I needed to come clean. "Even when I believed he was a multi-headed lake dragon licking me like cake batter from a spoon."

Ambrose went eerily still, and I knew I'd fucked up. Big time. It wasn't like we'd discussed our relationship status, but I should have brought it up before getting down with his *friend*.

I really am an asshole.

We'd traveled here so Timyn could help us figure out how I ended up on the island—and possibly how I could get home. But I'd skipped the friendly handshake and gone straight to his face between my legs. I was so focused on getting back at my ex and reclaiming the old Leia that I wasn't thinking about anyone else except myself. Now that this situation had come up, I realized the last thing I wanted to do was hurt the man in front of me.

I've definitely caught feelings.

Those dragon tongues, though...

"You saw him as a *dragon?*" Ambrose faltered, oddly fixated on my weird hallucination instead of how I hooked up with another man. "And you *allowed* him to pleasure you in that form?"

My cheeks burned. I was incredibly thankful in that moment for the darkness of the tent hiding my shame. "Yeah... It was kind of hot and felt like three guys at once, which is something I've always wanted to try anyway and...

oh gawd, can you just leave before I keep talking and embarrass myself even more?"

To my surprise, Ambrose chuckled and leaned down to give me a passionate kiss. "You are a gift from the gods, Leia. Again, you have nothing to apologize for, and now *I'm* only sorry I missed the show." Before I could confirm he was essentially agreeing to make a sandwich out of me, he loudly added, "Now it's time for you to sleep."

Just like on the beach, I was suddenly hit with a wave of peace—this time so strong I could feel myself immediately drifting off. Part of me struggled, realizing something weird was happening, but I was so tired and the blanket nest felt so comfy...

———

When I woke up again, pre-dawn light was already filtering between the flaps of the tent. I groped around for Ambrose, but all I found was another *obol* tucked into the cold blankets next to me. This implied he'd never returned to bed, and that *someone* had left me an unwanted gift. Death coins randomly appearing was slightly disturbing, but since I didn't know who was behind the deliveries, it was probably best to keep it to myself.

For all I know, they're trying to help me.

I heard the guys talking quietly outside the tent, and since no one knew I was awake yet, it seemed logical—and completely valid—to eavesdrop.

"...It's fascinating that she made it through the fog," Timyn was musing. "While I know for a fact this is not the underworld, I would wager the *obol* you found on her somehow provided safe passage." He paused, and I crept closer to hear better. "I wonder... if we got our claws on more—enough for all of us—could we use them to escape? Perhaps this tasty morsel of yours is fated to be our savior... as well as our plaything?"

Ambrose scoffed. "Yes, about that. I cannot fathom how you thought it was appropriate to present yourself to her in that way." He barely spoke above a whisper, but his stern tone made me rub my thighs together. "She thinks you're a... *dragon.*"

Timyn snickered, clearly unbothered by Dad scolding him. "That's fine by me. Apparently, women nowadays read books where *dragons* are the love interests."

I feel seen!

A beat of silence followed before Ambrose murmured, "How could you possibly know that?"

"I have my sources," Timyn sniffed. "Regardless, the more important takeaway is that she liked it, so there's hope for you yet. Now we just need to get you feeling like yourself again."

"I started to change," Ambrose interrupted, a note of unease in his normally confident voice. *"Parts* of me changed while I was inside her."

Timyn hissed through his teeth. "Ouch. Yet, she's still here. As you said—a gift from the gods."

Ambrose hummed. "Perhaps. But I also suspect Eurystheus sent her, and if that's the case, she's less of a gift and more of a Trojan Horse."

Wait a goddamn minute!

Something must have given me away, as Timyn suddenly raised his voice. "Come out and join us, Leia! I hunger for breakfast."

Wetness immediately flooded my pussy at his not-so-subtle invitation. Tucking the *obol* into my travel bag, I wrestled my way out of the tent and stomped toward them, scowling all the way. I'd intended to scold, but was immediately distracted by the incredible hotness of both men—casually seated on driftwood around a dying campfire, like Ancient Greece L.L.Bean models. Ambrose was still wearing his red tunic, but Timyn was dressed in a classic toga, which did nothing to hide the noticeable bulge between his legs.

"Sit on my lap, Water Lily," he patted himself invitingly. "And tell me a fairytale."

Ambrose rolled his eyes, but a smile twitched his lips as he subtly nodded at me in approval. There was nowhere else to sit—and I didn't totally hate the idea—but I huffed dramatically while approaching the other man. Timyn was solid, with a swimmer's definition to his muscles, so he barely budged, even when I plopped my full weight down onto him.

"Oh, all this delicious *flesh*," he groaned, pawing at my thick thighs, apparently unfamiliar with boundaries. "It makes me want to sink my fangs in. That is... *if* I had fangs." He ended with a low chuckle against my neck—his oddly pleasant scent of wet earth making my breath quicken. My gaze warily flickered to Ambrose, but he was simply watching us, running his tongue over his teeth, which only reminded me of him taking a bite while pounding me into his kitchen table.

Stop getting dickmatized!

"All right, time-out!" I gasped, pleased when Timyn immediately stopped feeling me up. "First things first. How the *fuck* do you know Eurystheus? That dickhead is numero uno on my shit list."

Ambrose cocked his head, observing me closely. "That's good to hear, Leia. I was concerned you were an accomplice of our greatest enemy."

"And then we would have been forced to kill you. Which would've been a shame," Timyn casually added, making me stiffen. I twisted in his lap to look at him, finding nothing but unblinking eye-contact waiting for me.

Another master of the deadpan... I hope.

"Oookay..." I murmured, slightly unnerved, yet oddly turned on at the same time. "I'll go first. Eurystheus bought my extra cruise ship ticket, acted like a creeper, gave me an *obol* I didn't ask for, then threw me overboard in the middle of a storm after shoving the coin in my mouth. That about sums up the extent of our relationship." Both men silently absorbed my thrilling tale, but neither offered their own history with Eurystheus in return.

Frustrated, I refocused on what I knew. Timyn's interest in the obol at least confirmed they weren't the ones leaving creepy coins for me everywhere. They also genuinely seemed to want off the island, so going along for the ride could be my only way home.

It would still be nice if they told me what they knew.

I exhaled, deciding to take Ambrose's advice that directness was best. "You both have said this isn't the underworld. How do you know that?" I knew there were larger issues to focus on, but some superstitious part of me hadn't ruled out being dead as a possibility. Both men had made our existence sound like an irrefutable fact, and I figured getting them to talk about this first would lead to juicer subjects.

To my annoyance, Ambrose simply pressed his lips together, continuing to offer me nothing. He'd mentioned not being comfortable telling me everything about himself yet, but I would have thought realizing Eurystheus was our shared Big Bad would bring us closer together.

I want to know you.

"It's the stars," Timyn broke the silence, startling me with his willingness to answer. "We're still seeing stars, and I've... *heard* the underworld doesn't have any of those." I followed his gaze to where a few constellations still twinkled in the brightening sky. Surprised to recognize several, I smiled, remembering how this weirdo had asked for a fairytale.

"That's Cancer," I pointed to a faint cluster, ignoring how self-conscious I was to be sharing my long-buried knowledge. "In Greek mythology, Hera sent a giant crab to distract Heracles while he fought the Hydra during his second Labor. He almost lost, because every time he chopped off one of the Hydra's nine heads, two more grew in its place."

I trailed off as my gaze drifted to the neighboring constellation resembling a long water snake. Something was tapping at the edges of my awareness, but I couldn't put my finger on it—like a half-forgotten dream.

Maybe I should have paid more attention when my mother was lecturing me...

Timyn chuckled again, grinding me down onto his lap, breaking my concentration. "Mmm, this Hydra sounds impressive. But what does a sweet human like you know about that idiot Heracles?"

I choked on a laugh. "Well," I replied, deciding I may as well own my heritage for once. "My mom is a Greek historian named Alcmene, so of course she named me Herculeia."

13
TIMYN

Thankfully, Leia wasn't facing me when she revealed her given name. I'm sure I turned as pale as a bloated corpse that had been underwater too long, tangled in the reeds. Not that I would know anything about that.

I'm kidding.

I know everything about that.

Ambrose had better self-control than I did, as he simply blinked once and calmly asked, *"Herculeia, you say?"*

There was no way for Leia to know who she was sitting with, despite her knowledge of the legends related to her namesake, and brush with our true forms. Humans were so eager to believe in logical explanations, even when it would be in their best interest to be wary. While I oddly believed she saw Eurystheus as the enemy, it didn't mean the bastard wasn't using her for his own agenda—regardless of whether she was aware of it.

Oblivious to the tension radiating from the two dangerous creatures in her midst, our tasty prey continued to reveal her provenance. "Yup, Herculeia, and holy shit, was mom pissed when the delivery room nurses spelled it the *Roman* way on the paperwork. If she hadn't left to return to her dig site a few days after I was born, she probably would have sued Mount Sinai hospital for all they were worth."

Per usual, Ambrose immediately let down his guard for a pretty face. "Your mother *left* you when you were a newborn?" he asked, adorably horrified, despite neither of *us* having a mother who was particularly maternal. Leia casually shrugged in reply, but I noticed her twisting the ring on her finger while Ambrose busied himself with preparing a disgustingly overcooked meal for her consumption.

I sighed, disappointed to realize I probably couldn't bring myself to kill the woman either, even if she had been sent here to defeat us. The instant my prehensile tails wrapped around her ankle, her panicked pulse music to my ears, all I could think about was pursuing and protecting her at all costs. She was mine. Mine to possess in every way —my mate.

I'll have to look elsewhere for bloodshed, I suppose.

"You realize none of this is a coincidence, right, Ambrose?" I called out to the man ruining eggs over the fire. "And if Eurystheus is behind it, we need to get Julius involved." My friend sighed heavily, but nodded in agreement, and it was all I could do not to clap my hands like an excited child.

We're going on an adventure!

Ambrose was notoriously averse to Julius' schemes, but I was always up for a little violence, especially if it involved our enemies. We may have been banished here, but the twelve of us had each been created as a worthy foe. Our small army had collectively fought back at first, but over time, we'd scattered across the island—some to regroup, others to accept their fate, and some simply unwilling to lose more than they already had.

Like Ambrose.

If I had a heart, it would go out to him. The tragic loss of his cave meant he'd lost his connection to his true self—cursing him to forever remain in human form.

Although, it's interesting that breeding Leia made parts of him temporarily change back...

My gaze wandered to where our curvy water nymph was bent over, cleaning up the remains of breakfast. Ambrose and I had discussed her unusual appearance, but I'd scared off enough cult members in my day to not be intimidated by body modifications, despite the priestesses' supposed connection to the gods. I was exponentially more interested in what lay between Leia's thighs, and how long it would be until I could sink into that glorious cunt of hers.

"Hey, buddy—ever heard of personal space?" Snapping out of my daydream, I discovered I was rubbing myself against her as she washed dishes in my lake.

How'd that happen?

"No." I stared down at her, unmoving. "I haven't." Unable to resist, I gave her thick ass a pinch, just to see what she'd do.

She straightened and spun to face me, the squeak she emitted making my predator writhe beneath the surface. "Do you *want* another punch in the face?"

I considered her question. The blow had caught me off guard in my easily injured human form, but I *liked* the sting of pain. "Yes, I do," I smiled, before cocking my head for a question of my own. "Do *you* truly want me to leave you alone?"

Her warm brown eyes glowed in the morning light as she appraised me. "Nah, I'll keep you around," she finally replied, unable to hide her smirk. "But that's only because you're a fucking wizard with that tongue of yours."

I clamped my mouth shut as the tongue in question suddenly threatened to tumble from my mouth and find its way under her dress. My control over my true form was usually immaculate, but then again, I'd never come face-to-face with my mate before.

And by the gods, do I want to lick every inch of her.

After the campsite was properly disassembled, Ambrose and I split up the ridiculous amount of items he'd packed for Leia's comfort before we all headed toward Julius' lair on Mount Erymanthos.

Leia kept up with our brisk pace all morning, apparently well accustomed to walking many miles per day back in the modern world, despite there being other modes of transportation. When we stopped for lunch, she muttered about craving 'a slice,' and I vowed to track down someone I could carve up for her pleasure.

We are nearing the centaurs' valley...

My mate's mood noticeably improved after she was fed, and she quickly resumed chattering like a bird once again. "All right, boys," she gaily chirped, picking her way over exposed roots as we entered the scrubby forest. "It's time to spill. How do you know Eurystheus?"

I shot a wary glance at Ambrose, but he surprised me by readily answering. "Eurystheus is the reason we're all on this island... as we are..." Leia only nodded, which meant Ambrose must have already shared parts of this historically sore subject. "He did it while we slept—

rounding us up, one by one, and trapping us here for all eternity."

My mate furrowed her brow, understandably unsatisfied with his vague reply. "Wouldn't people have reported you missing, though? I listen to true crime podcasts, so I know you can't just kidnap a bunch of people and expect no one to notice. And how did Eurystheus even pull this off on his own? He's just a shady fucker who liked to stalk me outside cruise ship bathrooms—"

Ambrose vehemently growled, showing that fearsome side I dearly missed. "He was *stalking* you? By Ares, if that man thinks he will impregnate you with his seed, I will—"

"Listen," she boldly interrupted. "Never say the word 'seed' again, because I just threw up in my mouth. That goes for both of you." Leia threw a mouthwatering glare at me over her shoulder. "Second, no one is *impregnating* me—"

"But what if I was a dragon?" I teased, a smirk twitching my lips. "Would you let me then?"

"Yeah, sure, dude," my mate huffed a laugh, properly disarmed. "If you were a sexy lake dragon, I would be more than happy to have your little snek babies. Can we move on now?"

"What about Ambrose?" I continued, not at all interested in moving on. "What if he were a big cat?"

"Timyn," my friend's tone held a clear warning, but I was enjoying myself too much to care. Something about this girl made me want to play, especially if it brought Ambrose back to himself again.

"You know what?" Leia murmured, cocking her head at him appraisingly. "He *does* remind me of a big kitty cat! That long mane of hair, the way he moves, how he purrs in bed."

To my delight, Ambrose *blushed*. "I can't help the purring," he mumbled, attempting to hide his reddening face behind that lustrous hair of his. "It just happens."

Big kitty indeed.

A flicker of gold through the cypress trees caught my eye, but when I tried to focus my weak human vision on the source, I found nothing.

Although I have my suspicions about who it is.

Squinting up at the sun, I gauged the time before addressing Ambrose. "We should probably call on Pholus and see about spending the night at the vineyard. Otherwise, we'll be stuck out in the open on the way to Mount Erymanthos."

"Ooh! A vineyard sounds fun," Leia skipped closer to me, amusingly excited over what was essentially a compound full of farm animals. "But wait. Let's rewind. *How* did Eurystheus pull off this mass kidnapping? And why would he do you dirty like that, anyway?"

I glanced at Ambrose, eager to watch him squirm, but instead of signature discomfort, I found something much worse. He'd gone perfectly still, his gaze locked on something far afield that had his full attention. Although I already knew what awaited, I turned to find a golden stag standing among the fertile grass, shining like a beacon in the sunlight. Its enormous rack towered overhead, its head cocked and large eyes riveted on the man hunting it.

My predator instinctively responded as Ambrose's beast flickered over his human features for the first time in centuries. I still suspected my Water Lily had somehow unlocked its cage, and while this alone was good news, at the moment it did not bode well for her. Up until now, Leia had been blissfully unaware of *what* she was sharing a bed with, but as we'd just stumbled upon Ambrose's favorite prey, she was about to find out.

The stag tensed.

Ambrose licked his lips.

Let the wild hunt begin.

14

LEIA

The scene before us looked like a magazine spread from Napa Valley. Golden sunlight sparkled on the plump, dew-kissed grapes decorating the vines, birds sang in the forest at our backs, and my mouth was watering just thinking about the wine this vineyard would offer.

Good thing we packed the bowl-cups!

My gaze swept across the nearby field, again wishing for my phone and Wi-Fi, if only to share the splendor before me with the world. Just as I questioned *how* there was a working vineyard in the middle of a remote island, I spotted the most majestic fucking animal I'd ever seen.

"Guys, guys," I hiss-whispered, giddy with excitement. "Look at the deer! Ohhh, it's so beautiful."

Ambrose responded with one of those clit-vibrating growls of his, making the birdsong immediately cease. I turned to face him, irrationally annoyed at him for harshing my vibe.

"Leia, don't look—" Timyn warned me, but it was too late.

What I found wasn't Ambrose. Instead, I came face to face with something out of a bad horror movie as the man I'd started to care for convulsed and contorted—his body morphing into something else entirely.

Something *inhuman.*

His already enormous muscles rippled violently, expanding outward to tear through his red tunic like it was paper. Ambrose—or whatever he was—fell forward onto all fours, hands and feet exploding into gigantic paws as tawny fur appeared over every inch of his skin. His gorgeous hair became an actual mane, his handsome features distorting into a feline appearance, and the same fangs he'd buried in my neck distended well past his lower jaw.

Holy shit. I fucked a lion.

That was too tame a word for what stood before me. This creature was about four times the size of any lion I'd ever seen in the Bronx Zoo, and not at all cuddly looking. In fact, instead of looking soft, his coat of fur was molded over his deadly physique like a suit of armor.

Apparently uninterested in actual survival, my imploding brain fixated on the many red flags I'd ignored since meeting this man—from his purring and biting, to his obvious aversion to wearing pants. As more damning evidence rose to the surface, I began backing away from the monster, desperate to put as much distance between us as possible.

"Stop. Moving," Timyn hissed, and I froze. The Saber-Toothed Lion tore his gaze from the deer to stare at *me* like I was next on the dinner menu.

"These steaks are much too well-done for my taste..."

"He's going to eat me," I hissed in reply, my instincts finally kicking in and telling me in no uncertain terms to get the fuck out of there. Ambrose growled low, and I tensed, readying for flight.

"*Leia!*" Timyn barked, somehow speaking to me *inside* my head.

Just like during our midnight adventures at the lake...

Shivering uncontrollably, I shifted my gaze to the other man, only to find decidedly reptilian eyes staring back at me as Timyn struggled to keep whatever *he* was buried beneath the surface.

Fuck.

This.

Noise.

I took off running, no longer interested in listening to a goddamn lake snake. My sudden movement caused a chain reaction as Ambrose roared and the deer I'd been admiring bolted toward a sprawling compound in the distance.

I followed its lead, clumsily weaving between rows of grapes to lose the much larger creature barreling after me. The deer quickly left me in the dust, reminding me of the old saying that you didn't have to outrun a lion, just the guy behind you. Hot breath blasted against my neck and I screamed, hiking my skirt up higher and pounding the grass until my thighs burned.

I REGRET EVERY CUPCAKE I'VE EVER EATEN!

Desperate, I attempted to jump over a half-toppled grapevine like it was a subway turnstile and the house on the horizon was the last rush-hour train. Unfortunately, I misjudged the height, and one of my sandals caught on the protective netting strung over the trellises, pitching me forward. I hit the ground hard and immediately began rolling down a steep hill, loudly cursing as I hit every rock during my descent.

My momentum was so great that I actually caught up

with the deer, taking it out at the knees to tumble along with me. We ended up in a tangled pile of netting and limbs at the base of the slope, with a wide river cutting off our escape from behind. Frantically wiping my hair out of my eyes, I gasped to find the lion slowly padding our way, as if it had been casually keeping pace the entire time.

My terror instantly evaporated in the presence of my growing rage. Not only had Ambrose *lied,* but now he was toying with me—and a helpless deer—in the same way a house cat would bat around a mouse before eating it.

Not today, furry Satan.

As he reached us, I threw myself over the dazed animal next to me. "Fuck off, Ambrose," I choked out, determined not to go down quietly, and suddenly feeling a psycho-level protectiveness for the deer. "You want venison? You'll have to go through me first."

The lion froze, its confused expression oddly human. Then it started huffing—almost as if it were *laughing*—and I watched, half-horrified, half-fascinated, as it seamlessly morphed back into the naked man I knew.

"Well, well, Krysos," he chuckled, looking infuriatingly delicious, all sweaty and self-satisfied. "It appears Artemis isn't your only fierce protector."

"The chase always was your favorite part," a bitter voice sounded beneath me, and I scrambled backward in alarm as the majestic stag suddenly shifted into a breathtaking—naked—man. He was leaner than Ambrose and Timyn, with paler skin, a mop of blond hair, and pretty gray eyes. Everything about him was pretty—almost to the point of being androgynous. Almost, if you ignored the prominent golden antlers... and the enormous golden cock.

Because why not?

Still smiling, Ambrose stood and offered me a hand,

which I angrily batted away before standing on my own two feet. He then did the same for Krysos, who accepted, although he sniffed haughtily while doing so.

"I could have been miles away already if this graceless *fawn* hadn't tripped over herself." Long Dong Deer shot me a withering look before focusing his venom on Ambrose. "But bad luck seems determined to follow me—in the form of *you.*"

Ambrose's face fell, and I instantly realized there was a history here that went beyond the present situation. "You know I don't believe in bad luck," Ambrose softly murmured, his gaze holding so much longing for the other man, I momentarily forgot how pissed I was at him. "Only bad timing."

"Ho there!" an unfamiliar voice called out, and I bristled, wondering who the fuck thought they knew my life. Following the sound, I saw a shirtless, gray-haired man observing us from over a trellis. "Was that the long lost Nemean Lion I spied tearing through my vineyard?"

Nemean Lion?

"Ho there, Pholus!" Ambrose cheerfully answered, and I noted how expertly he'd buried his emotions behind a charming grin. "We were just about to come by and see about a room for the night."

"Were you planning to do that before or after you *ate* me?" I hissed under my breath.

"He wasn't going to eat you," Krysos scoffed, eyeing me with a mixture of annoyance and amusement. "That was foreplay."

"Anything for an old friend," Pholus replied before running an assessing gaze over me, either oblivious to our group's tension, or choosing to ignore it. "Especially if this *rare* guest will join us."

"Fuck, these legs are slow," Timyn suddenly appeared, slightly breathless and back to his deceptively human-looking hotness as well. "Although, I suppose now that the big cat's out of the bag, I didn't need to stay in this useless form anymore than necessary."

"The Hydra's not invited, however," Pholus sourly interrupted, his arms crossed and resting bitch face firmly in place as he gave Timyn a judgmental once over.

Hydra?

"Too bad, centaur," Timyn widely grinned, his mouth suddenly crowded with monstrous teeth. "We're a package deal."

Centaur...

I need to sit down.

"The human is looking green," Krysos vaguely gestured at me, although he didn't seem at all concerned. "Should we dunk her in the river Ladon, to wake her up? It might make her less clumsy as well."

My gaze drifted to the golden antlers sprouting from beneath Krysos' messy blond hair—every repressed memory of being bored to tears by my mother's 'history' lessons suddenly flaring to life in my foggy brain. If Ambrose was the Nemean Lion, and Timyn was the Hydra, then this glittery David Bowie lookalike was most likely...

"The Golden Hind," I croaked, before everything went dark.

15
AMBROSE

I knew well that leaving Timyn and Pholus together was a recipe for disaster, but I refused to abandon my post at Leia's bedside to play peacemaker. After all, it was *my* fault she was lying here, drifting in and out of consciousness. If only I'd told her the truth of what I was. Then she could've had time to grow accustomed to the idea, instead of me terrifying her the way I did. While Krysos was correct—I had no intention of eating her—she was a fragile human unfamiliar with creatures like me, so she had no way of knowing she wasn't in danger.

I only wanted to play...

"Whaaa dafuq is a hind, anyway?" Leia groggily mumbled, and I was reminded of when I'd discovered her on the beach in a similar state. Per my usual modus operandi, I'd been half-drunk, so hadn't fully appreciated the significance of our meeting. Now that I'd had time to ponder—and witness how the others responded to her, it was clear what the jolt of power I felt between us meant.

She's my mate.

Timyn had also declared her *his* mate back at the lake—which wasn't unheard of in some cultures—except legends like us rarely had a mate at all, much less a shared one. Our sole purpose was to provide an obstacle for heroes to overcome, and to repeat this cycle of challenge and defeat for all eternity. Being deprived of a worthy adversary had negatively affected us all, but Leia's appearance seemed like a blessing after centuries of despair.

Yet I may have just scared her away.

"So that's what I smelled burning," Leia's voice snapped me out of my thoughts. She was awake, cautiously observing me even as her signature humor surfaced. "Ambrose, deep in thought."

"Leia... I..." I awkwardly began, clenching my fists to temper the overwhelming urge to gather her into my arms. "I want to acknowledge how unfortunate it was that you had to discover my true form this way. I hadn't changed in so long... I didn't think I would need to address it yet, if ever."

"So you *lied* instead?" she snarled, her chin lifting defiantly, making me instantly harden for her. "So you *lured* me into your bed under false pretenses with your magic tongue and that spiky dick of yours that's probably scarred my vagina for life?"

"Oh calm down, monster-fucker," Timyn chuckled from the doorway. I glared at him over my shoulder, but he ignored me, brushing past my chair to stretch out on the bed next to Leia. "First, *I'm* the one with the magical tongue —tongues, to be exact—which you enthusiastically discovered. Second, the barbs on Ambrose's cock serve a purpose and are quite enjoyable once you get used to them... even when they're *stuffed in your ass."*

He delivered the last part of the sentence in an exaggerated stage-whisper, which made Leia intoxicatingly blush. Her honey-brown eyes darted between the two of us, her blush deepening, as if she were picturing me inside Timyn, and liking the idea immensely.

Interesting...

I banished the image of her watching us together, knowing now wasn't the time. "Leia," I tried again. "I am truly sorry I withheld information from you. It was selfish and entirely done because I didn't want to risk losing you. For reasons I'm struggling to explain, you have become so incredibly precious to me in such a short time. I feared you wouldn't want anything to do with me if you knew I was a—"

"Monster?" Timyn offered, unhelpfully.

Leia swatted him playfully, a smile twisting her perfect lips. "I don't think you're *monsters!* At least, not in a bad way. It's just... this is a lot to process, okay? To find out that the legends my mother drilled into my head are *real*—that there's an actual Nemean Lion, and a Hydra, and a... what the hell *is* a Golden Hind? I thought all of Artemis' deer were female... Oh! Does this mean the *gods* are real, too?!"

Wanting to atone for my previous mistakes, I immediately attempted to address some of her questions. "A hind is a sort of deer. Of the original five Artemis found, she only yoked four of them to her chariot—leaving the last one here in Ceryneia, as a future Labor for Heracles."

My gaze briefly met Timyn's, as I again considered the implications of a woman named *Herculeia* being sent to this island by our greatest enemy. However, I was the one being questioned at the moment, so I refocused on the topic at hand.

"Krysos is special," I continued, feeling my cheeks heat as I spoke of my tragic love. "His golden coloring is breathtaking, but he also has solid bronze hooves, is notoriously difficult to catch, and breathes fire when angered."

Not that I'm intimately familiar with that last feature or anything.

"And he's most *definitely* male, as I'm sure you noticed," Timyn again chimed in, winking mischievously at Leia. "Unfortunately for me, Ambrose doesn't like to share his hind, although, I have a feeling he'll make an exception for you. Would you like that, Water Lily? To share and be shared?"

Leia's pupils dilated, her breaths becoming labored, and I realized we needed to get out of this room before I shifted into my true form and frightened her again. Timyn had a theory that breeding Leia had somehow uncaged my beast, and the way it was currently pacing just beneath my skin was both exhilarating and concerning. My mate and I appeared to have found a truce, and I was determined to earn my way back into her bed—not simply take her like a wild animal unleashed.

Although, she seemed to enjoy that...

"Where is Krysos?" I swallowed hard, tearing my gaze from Leia's heaving breasts, painful as it was. "He didn't... leave, did he?"

Timyn smiled at me as sympathetically as a cold-blooded creature could. "No, he didn't leave," he softly replied before brightening. "He's helping Pholus and the others prepare for a party tonight. Apparently, we arrived just in time for their semi-annual centaur Symposium, and you know what *that* means!"

I groaned, not only because the last Symposium we'd attended did not end well, but that the wine served came from Dionysius himself.

And I'm really trying to cut back.

"Is this Symposium a big deal?" Leia cautiously asked, her gaze dropping to her torn and filthy *peplos*. "What's the dress code?"

"Naked, usually," came a voice from behind me that made my soul ache.

Krysos glided into the room, his antlers catching the light from the flickering sconces, giving the impression of an angelic halo over his head. Despite his insinuation, he was dressed in a violet toga, carrying a bundle I assumed was for Leia, as Pholus had already found new clothing for me. Arriving at the bed, he shook out the fabric to reveal a swath of fine silk in a suspiciously similar violet shade.

Well played, old friend.

Before I could remark on the clothing, Krysos turned and began herding Timyn and me from the room. "Shoo, both of you! I have been tasked with helping Leia prepare for tonight, so she may enjoy the festivities in comfort, without being further traumatized by you two. Out!"

Knowing it was always best to defer to Krysos when he was in this sort of mood, we obediently retreated to the hallway before heading toward the great hall. As expected, Timyn quickly broke the silence with a cacophony of commentary. "Did you *see* how he matched the color of Leia's dress to his toga? That sly fox, publicly claiming her like that. Either he did it to piss you off or..."

I stopped in my tracks. "Or he feels the mate bond too!" If Krysos was drawn to Leia—and she stayed, even after my unforgivable deception—then I might have the chance to win him back.

Perhaps I can have them both?

Timyn was observing me shrewdly. "The Fates work in

mysterious ways, hmm? Oh, and don't forget to let Leia know those meddling sisters are real as well."

I nodded, the wide grin stretching across my face as natural as breathing. "Yes, along with the gods. It appears even they have a sense of humor, after all."

16

LEIA

I made Krysos take the scenic route on our way through Pholus' vineyard mansion so I could properly snoop around.

Since I don't remember being carried inside.

The Doric architecture and marble busts reminded me of the classical wing of every museum I'd visited, but that's where the resemblance ended. Instead of the usual bleached white appearance, everything was painted in brilliant hues of rich greens and purples, mirroring the scenery outside, now bathed in orange from the setting sun.

Imagine waking up to this view every day...

Annoyed with myself, I banished the ridiculous fantasy from my mind. My focus needed to be on getting off this island and back to my old life—with a pit stop to find Eurystheus, so I could beat his ass. There was absolutely no reason for me to be worrying about breathtaking vistas, or *who* I could theoretically enjoy them with.

Especially since they both lied to me.

The last thing I needed was to add another man to my roster, but I couldn't help stealing glances at Krysos as we walked, captivated by his unique beauty. His bone structure alone would have immediately landed him a modeling contract with Elite, but there was something ethereal about him that drew me in. We stopped to admire a fresco, but my gaze drifted to the man beside me once again. The violet shade he wore perfectly accented his gray eyes, and the sharp line of his jaw brought me to full lips, forming a perfect Cupid's bow.

"Do you like what you see, Fawn?" He glanced sideways at me as he knowingly smirked.

"Sorry," I stammered, feeling like a total creep. "I know I shouldn't stare, but you're just so—"

"Pretty?" he offered, his smirk growing larger as he turned to face me. "Yes, I know. And I don't mind you looking. You can look *and* touch, if you want."

I actually had to take a step back, as the full force of Krysos' androgynous hotness washed over me. He pursued my retreat, backing me into a random alcove and looming over me despite his lithe build. Lowering his head, he brushed his pillowy lips against mine, trailing long fingers down my bare arms and sighing as if the contact brought *him* pleasure.

Following his lead, I raised my shaking hands to his mop of blond hair, running my fingers through the fine strands until I hit the base of his golden antlers. I traced the velvety curves and branches, fascinated when a particular stroke made him moan against my mouth.

So much for not adding to my harem.

"*There* you are," Timyn's amused voice made me snatch my hands away, like a guilty teenager. "Ambrose was concerned when we couldn't find you two at dinner, but I assumed you were simply making out in a corner somewhere."

I laughed, physically unable to stay mad at the Hydra. To his credit, he'd originally come to me in his true form, and probably would have outright told me what he was just to see my reaction. With Ambrose, the deception had been calculated, but I begrudgingly understood why he did it. And I'd be damned if that man didn't know how to deliver a sincere apology.

He still owes me a wake-up call, come to think of it...

Krysos responded to Timyn's words with a sly smile, taking my hand as we followed the Hydra along the terrace. The warm summer breeze caressed my ankles beneath the silk dress I was wearing and I shivered, but mostly in antici-pation of the evening ahead. I'd never been to a Symposium —hosted by centaurs, no less—and had a feeling it was about to put any loft party or art opening I'd attended to shame. The muffled sounds of music and laughter grew louder as we approached an enormous set of carved wooden doors built into the side of a mountain.

As Timyn reached for the handles, I grabbed his arm, suddenly feeling nervous about this new experience. "Is there anything I need to know before we go in there?" I blurted out. "Like, any etiquette? I don't want to embarrass myself... or you."

Both men looked confused by my questions. "Just try not to kill anyone unless they strike first," Krysos shrugged.

Reassurance fail.

Without waiting for my reply, Timyn flung open the doors and strutted into the great hall with the big dick energy I expected from him. This got me thinking about how big his dick *was,* and whether he also had barbs or another fancy accessory.

My deep thoughts were quickly forgotten as I entered the hall and took in the chaotic scene before me. Hundreds of centaurs filled the cavernous space—some were dancing and loudly singing, while others were seated at tables in what I assumed were specially made centaur chairs. All were pounding wine from tall bowl-cups inlaid with silver and gold. Raucous music was playing from somewhere deeper in the cave hall, and every table was overflowing with a king's feast.

Ain't no party like a centaur party.

I was led to a table off to the side where Ambrose was seated, engaged in conversation with Pholus, who was standing above him. Our host had been partially obscured by the grapevines when we'd first met, so I hadn't been able to fully appreciate he was an *actual centaur.* Now there was nothing stopping me from taking in the fantastical view.

The other centaurs all had bare chests seamlessly connecting to the bodies of horses. Pholus was a man from head to toe, with the hindquarters of a horse awkwardly attached to his ass. I wasn't sure why he was special, but either way, he was still *hung* like a horse with an impressive dick on full display. In fact, the only men wearing clothes were the ones I'd arrived with, which made me realize I was the one female in attendance. Ambrose said there weren't many women around, but being so outnumbered in an enclosed space with a single exit made me a little nervous.

As if sensing my anxiety, Krysos pulled me close to whisper in my ear. "As an addendum to my previous statement, *we* will kill anyone who strikes first. So all *you* need to do is enjoy yourself." He booped my nose as punctuation before releasing me and taking a seat.

It was slightly unsettling how comforted I felt by such a psychotic declaration. If my romance novels had taught me anything, however, the 'touch her and you die trope' was popular for a reason.

Sexy psychopaths for the win!

I noticed Ambrose intently watching my interaction with Krysos, but his expression didn't hold any jealousy. If anything, he looked adorably hopeful, which made me instantly soften. In sharp contrast, Pholus glared at Timyn, who was blatantly ignoring him in return, before the centaur turned to address me.

"Welcome to my humble Symposium, *Herculeia!*" I stiffened at the use of my full name, but he seemed so thrilled by my presence, I let it slide. "Please, sit and dine at my table, but I should warn you, the wine tonight is strong." With that, our host threw one more scowl at the Hydra before trotting off to rejoin his party.

Ambrose shyly pushed a plate my way, overflowing with goodies, to fatten me up. Again, he simply smiled at me expectantly, and I sighed before sliding into his lap, no longer interested in staying mad. He immediately exhaled, wrapping his tree trunk arms around me before cutting up my food in that Daddy way I secretly loved. Timyn was already digging into his meal, but Krysos took his time filling a plate, watching Ambrose and me with interest.

"Don't drink that," Ambrose gently batted my hand away as I reached for my wine, instead guiding me to a boring cup of water. "At least, take it slow, Siren. This wine comes from Dionysus himself, so it *is* quite potent."

While helping me dress earlier, Krysos had confirmed the gods were real—although none had been seen on the island—so I understood Ambrose was being literal with this statement.

I still eyed his bowl-cup judgmentally. "Yet, you seem to have already drank enough to reveal the *potent* ass-fucking scene at the bottom of *your* cup, my thirsty lion."

Timyn snorted. "That's because he's a professional drunk who enjoys ass-fucking immensely."

Ambrose sighed heavily while Krysos threw him a look of alarm, which I assumed was more in response to the revelation of drinking, and less the ass-fucking.

These men are so dramatic.

"Attention, attention!" Pholus' voice suddenly rang out, somehow bringing the din to an immediate halt. "Welcome, honored guests and... others," his gaze landed on Timyn, who popped an olive in his mouth and enthusiastically waved to the crowd. "I am overjoyed to be hosting another Symposium in your company. Gatherings like these remind me of what we still have, despite all we've lost."

The silence in the room took on a somber tone, and I instinctively straightened as our host continued. "I needn't remind you how, many moons ago, we awoke to find ourselves here. Since then, we've remained on this isolated replica of our once much larger world, suspiciously lacking the *humans* we once had direct contact with."

At these words, the tension in the room suddenly skyrocketed to level 11. Hundreds of centaurs focused on me, causing Ambrose to growl and possessively pull me against his chest. Timyn and Krysos also shifted closer, their true forms flickering over their skin, clearly ready to make good on the promise to unalive anyone who looked at me funny.

Well, this is awkward.

17
LEIA

While I didn't think Pholus was trying to record scratch his own party, the silence was thick as he once again angrily focused on Timyn. "Of course, there is one centaur noticeably absent today..."

"Here we go," Timyn rolled his eyes, his shoulders shaking in silent laughter.

"...our beloved Chiron—who now lives among the gods in the heavens—met his untimely demise during a past Symposium, when he was fatally poisoned, in cold blood."

Timyn snorted in amusement, apparently unbothered by the murder accusation. "First, I *am* cold-blooded, so that's not an insult. More importantly, it's no secret my blood is poisonous, so *beloved Chiron* got what was coming to him." He then pointedly turned his attention back to his meal as Pholus' speech turned into what sounded like a shareholder report on the vineyard's annual wine production.

I gaped at the Hydra before frantically waving my hands in his face. "Wait, wait, wait—time out! Did you kill his friend or not?" I hissed, suddenly unsure if the psychopath vibe was sexy or not.

"Ehhh," Timyn bobbled his head back and forth, as if considering. "Accidentally?"

Was that a question mark?!

"Chiron *should* have been more careful," Krysos agreed, equally blasé about the whole thing. "One shouldn't drunkenly wave a knife around the Hydra. Everybody knows that."

My stomach dropped. "What if they try to kill *us* in retaliation, guys? They could've... poisoned our *food!*" I violently shoved my plate away, eliciting another sigh from Ambrose, who was in the middle of gathering another bite for me to eat.

"Leia," he calmly spoke. "Centaurs wouldn't bother poisoning our food. If they wished to kill us, they would simply slit our throats while we slept."

"What?!" I squeaked, twisting in his lap so I could see if he was fucking with me or not. When I found nothing but a serene expression on his handsome face, I slowly asked, "Aren't you worried about us sleeping here, then?"

Ambrose shrugged. "I'm merely theorizing."

"Well, stop theorizing," I scolded. "No more theorizing, all around." None of the men looked concerned, but I was sweating bullets. Needing some liquid courage, I took an enormous swig from my bowl-cup before anyone could stop me, which earned me raised eyebrows, but no commentary.

They're smarter than they look.

I immediately regretted my rash decision as I swayed precariously in Ambrose's lap as soon as the wine went down. Flinging out a hand to steady myself, I knocked over my cup, spilling the remaining contents onto the table.

"Oh, you are such a clumsy little Fawn," Krysos cooed, the heated look in his eyes making it crystal clear he found my flailing hot as hell. How a prey animal could have such a *predatory* expression was beyond me, but I felt my cheeks flush and thighs dampen at his singular attention.

Timyn hummed in agreement, catching the runoff wine into his cup before downing the contents as if it were nothing more than water. "She is decidedly delicious, although a bit high-strung. I know! In the spirit of Symposium, I propose we *all* take her up to the bedroom and fuck this silly anxiety out of her system."

ALL of them?

As if it were an actual vote, Krysos and Ambrose murmured "aye," and I was suddenly lifted and thrown over Timyn's shoulder like a rag doll—not that I was complaining. I'd already decided staying mad at Ambrose and Timyn wasn't worth it, and if Golden Hind David Bowie wanted to hop on board the rebound express, my doors were wide open.

Just like my legs... heyoooooo!

I giggled at my self-deprecating humor as the Hydra carried me through the cave hall to the exit. My vision was alarmingly blurry, but it looked like the gathering had turned into Symposium After Dark, as every centaur in attendance was now busy fucking their neighbor.

Neighhhhbor!

"What's so funny?" Timyn chuckled, shifting me in his arms until he was carrying me bridal style. "Have you finally realized Pholus is the living embodiment of a horse's ass?"

I howled in approval of his joke, earning me a smile full of razor-sharp teeth, which quickly shut me up. Timyn must have noticed my startled reaction, as he murmured an apology and slipped on his mask of pearly whites yet again.

"Noooo..." I slurred, pawing at his mouth. "I like your smexy dragon fangs."

He laughed again, flashing some fang while easing my hand out of harm's way. "Careful—they're sharp enough to tear through human flesh."

By now, I realized Timyn's style of flirting was like the boys in grade school who would painfully pull your pigtails to get your attention. Except, I wanted this man to pull my hair and make it hurt.

Circle 'yes' if you like me, danger dragon.

"Aren't you a *pescatarian?*" I scoffed, doing my best imitation of Ambrose's disgust. "What's the point of such big *skerry* teeth if you're only using them to eat sushi?"

"All our features have a purpose, Leia, we just haven't been able to fully access them in a very long time." His gaze flickered to where Ambrose walked ahead of us, before he stage-whispered. "And that includes spiky cocks."

Krysos snorted, throwing a pointed glance at the Hydra. "Don't frighten her, Timyn. We want our little Fawn completely relaxed, so she can take *all* of us."

"I can take it," I blurted out, assuming he meant the foursome that hopefully awaited me. "I want all of you."

Timyn shuddered, and I felt something *other* ripple under the surface of his skin, reminding me the meat suit was only a facade. This should have scared me. It should have sent me running for the hills to even think about letting a trio of actual *monsters* into my bed. Judging by the smoke signals my pussy was sending up, however, my body was calling in the troops.

We finally reached the bedroom—far enough away from the festivities, and revengeful centaurs that I stopped worrying about casual murder. Ambrose was already inside, lighting candles and smoothing the enormous bed, like some sort of sexy mother hen. Timyn dropped me down on the blankets, then moved aside so Ambrose could approach. My lion lifted his finger, and I watched, fascinated, as his human fingernail turned into a razor-sharp claw, which he used to slice my dress in two.

"Meow," I snickered, wiggling out of the scraps of fabric and scooting over to make room—almost falling off the bed in the process.

Ambrose furrowed his brow, sitting me up and forcing a cup of water into my hand. "Siren, are you certain you want this? We can wait until you're sober."

"She's certain, you idiot," Timyn snatched the water out of my hand and shoved past him to kneel over me, pushing me onto my back. "She's starved for dragon dick."

He's not wrong.

"I want to see it first," I rasped, my hungry gaze riveted as he began unwrapping his toga from around his muscular body. Krysos crawled onto the bed to recline beside me, claiming his front-row seat to the strip show.

Timyn flung off the toga with a dramatic flourish, and I gasped at the big—very big—reveal. While the general shape of his cock was similar to a human's, Timyn's was bent like a cresting wave and featured thick ridges spiraling around the shaft to meet at the tip. My gaze traveled lower, and I tensed, noticing a set of spiky rosettes at the base, but I was quickly distracted again by the beautiful ombré of his skin—iridescent green fading into a deep maroon.

Not skin.

Scales.

Timyn closed his eyes as this coloring spread over the rest of his body. "Oh, it feels divine to let the beast out a bit, and so much *easier* than usual," he purred, his gaze snapping open to reveal reptilian slits within his green irises. "It doesn't bother you to see me like this, does it, Leia? I would hate to have to fuck you like a... *human."*

I was speechless. Even though part of me was dying to give his dragon dick a test drive, I hesitated, feeling incredibly out of my element.

He nodded at Krysos, who shifted closer, nuzzling against my neck with a series of kisses that instantly calmed me. "Allow me to show you how harmless he is," he chuckled, depositing one last kiss on my lips before leaving my side to crawl toward the Hydra. Before my brain could catch up with what was happening, he grabbed Timyn's cock and licked his way along one of the twisting ridges as the other man dropped his head back with a groan.

Oh. My. Gawd.

It's OnlyFans monster edition!

Ambrose did not respond as enthusiastically, roughly grabbing Timyn's hair to hiss in his ear. "Focus on Leia, and stop baiting me."

Timyn chuckled wickedly, cracking an eye open to wink down at Krysos. "I can't help myself, Ambrose. He's just so fuckable."

My Nemean Lion growled so intensely the walls shook, shoving Timyn forward so he landed on all fours, with his face inches away from my pussy. "You want to play games, Hydra? Because you're looking quite fuckable as well."

18

TIMYN

It was so *easy* to wind Ambrose up, but if anyone should be annoyed, it was me. I was the one being forced to watch him and Krysos alternate between angrily glaring or sadly mooning in the other's direction.

Just fuck and make up already.

I assumed Leia would eventually mend *that* broken fence, but if someone needed to get in the middle at the moment, I supposed I could play the hero. To my delight, Ambrose was already pouring some of his homemade olive oil over both of us before notching himself against my asshole. His cock was lovely, but it wasn't self-lubricating, like mine.

It's a good thing he has those barbs to make up for it.

"I don't want to hear another word out of you until you've made her come," he snarled. Then he shoved my face between Leia's scrumptious thighs, as if that was supposed to be a punishment.

Leia was propped up on her elbows, hungrily watching our heated exchange, and I appreciatively eyed her in return. Everything about this woman was absolute perfection. Her pert breasts were heaving in anticipation, and a thin layer of sweat had created a lovely sheen on her tanned skin. I wanted to unleash all nine of my tongues—lick every inch of her while filling her again and again with my seed. My cock was aching to do just that, but I agreed with Krysos that relaxing our mate first would help her better take us.

"Would you like to watch Ambrose fuck me while I lick this pretty little cunt?" I whispered in her head, so our grumpy lion wouldn't hear. She eagerly nodded, so I turned to Krysos and loudly added, "Pull your cock out. I want to gaze upon its beauty while I taste her."

As I'd hoped, Ambrose responded by slamming into me so violently I momentarily blacked out. Krysos lightly laughed and removed his clothing as Ambrose found a torturously slow pace—angling himself so his spurs deliciously dragged along my insides.

I do so love a little pain.

Ready for my snack, I gently parted Leia with my thumbs, admiring the slick wetness already decorating her folds. She looked like a flower—a water lily, of course—open and begging to be pollinated. Closing my lips around her clit, I sucked it into my mouth, wrapping my forked tongue around the needy little bud before beginning to thrum.

Leia arched off the bed with a strangled cry. "Holy fucking, fuckfuck*fuck!*" she gasped, those deliciously thick thighs crushing my head as she writhed beneath me.

"So responsive," Krysos praised. "Let's have you taste me while Timyn continues to feast on your cunt."

Leia made a muffled sound, and I glanced up to see Krysos' golden cock disappearing down her throat. The man in me was impressed by how much she took, considering his length, but my beast possessively reacted to his claim.

Being this far from the lake of Lerna usually meant my Hydra lay dormant unless threatened in battle. However, just as Leia had somehow reconnected Ambrose with his lion, she also seemed to be a conduit to my true form. It was all I could do to not fully shift and drag her off to keep for myself.

Mine.

The others were drawn to her as well, and Leia obviously enjoyed being shared, so I calmed my beast and refocused on her pleasure. Sliding my fingers into her wetness, I allowed Ambrose's thrusts to set my rhythm, relishing the feel of her needy cunt fluttering around me.

"Come for us, Leia," Krysos urged, and she whimpered as her legs shook, so close to the edge. "Be a good little Fawn and soak Timyn's face. Then we can all watch you ride him until you come again." Leia cried out as best she could around Krysos' cock—his answering moan inspiring Ambrose to pummel me harder.

I gently bit down on her clit with my human teeth, causing her to explode in a torrent of wet heat that obscenely dripped down my chin. I groaned at her flavor, the sweet nectar inviting me to collect every drop. The need to fill her up—to breed her—was almost blinding. As I felt Ambrose emptying inside me, I shuddered at the thought of doing the same to her.

Ambrose pulled out, the drag of his barbs making my dick twitch as I reached for my mate. Before I could snatch Leia away, Krysos withdrew from her throat and came on her perfect breasts, shooting me a bratty wink as he marked her as his.

Cheeky bastard.

Undeterred, I hauled Leia into my arms and sat back against the headboard, arranging her so she straddled me. She started to lower herself, but I grabbed her waist to stop her descent, making her whine indignantly. My beast deeply related to her dismay, but a moment of clarity had me realizing this *human* probably wasn't fully comprehending what was coming.

Besides me, that is.

"Leia," I haltingly spoke, choosing my words carefully. "You're in control here, so you can choose how much of me you want to take. Just don't... don't sheath yourself fully unless you want to... ah..."

"Unless you want his dick to lock into place until he's finished," Krysos smirked. He then positioned himself behind her juicy ass, expectantly holding out a hand for Ambrose to give him the oil.

Oh, no you don't.

"Just the tip, hmm?" Krysos smiled sweetly at me over Leia's shoulder until he registered my glare. "Ok, *fine*—just my fingers. You're no fun anymore, Timyn."

Mine.

Leia warily glanced down at the rosettes of spikes at the base of my cock. "Why would he need to lock into place?"

Ambrose chuckled as he climbed onto the bed, gently tilting her chin to deposit a kiss on her lips. "It's evolutionary. My barbs stimulate ovulation while Timyn's spurs fit inside you like a lock and key, holding you steady and ensuring his see... his *cum* makes it to your womb."

Her eyes widened as she processed Ambrose's words, and I braced myself for rejection. It wasn't as if creatures like us didn't fuck for pleasure—that's all we'd been doing on this island for centuries—but this instinctual *need* to impregnate a female mate was almost impossible to ignore.

I desperately wanted her to understand, but Leia was a human from the modern world. This revelation could very well be the thing to make her run.

Please don't leave.

A sly smile crept over her lips as she made eye contact with me again. "Ohhh... you want to come deep inside me, Timyn?" She slid herself down a few inches on my throbbing cock, making me groan. "You want to make little dragon babies together?" Another inch.

"Fuck," I rasped, my many appendages uncontrollably rippling under my skin, my body fighting against my crumbling restraint.

"You like to talk dirty, Fawn?" Krysos laughed mischievously. Leia gasped and glanced over her shoulder, no doubt in response to him sliding a finger, or four, into her ass. "Tell him how badly you want his cum dripping down your thighs—how you'll let him collect it to shove back inside you."

"Krysos, *enough!*" I choked out, my hips involuntarily snapping upwards, imagining this exact scenario and desperate for her to take my lock. More than anything, I was terrified of fully shifting and tearing Leia in half, although my beast seemed oddly aware that he needed to stay at a comparable size. "I can't control myself... she's my *mate.*"

Leia's attention shot back to me. "Your mate, hmm?" She caressed the scales along my cheekbones with her fingers, making me shiver. "Well, in that case..." With a moan I was determined to commit to memory, she dropped her full weight into my lap, locking my spurs into place.

I released a snarl that would have scared a lesser woman away, but Leia just wrapped her arms around me and began to ride. Krysos' cum was sticky on her chest, slickly rubbing between us, and I couldn't resist distending my tongue so I could lick it off her nipples.

Ambrose was kissing Leia like her lips were his last meal, and Krysos was doing gods knew what to her ass, but I was singularly focused on my cock lodged inside my mate. Despite our differences in anatomy, my lock fit perfectly and I was soon mindlessly thrusting, like the hind during his rut.

Mine mine mine.

"Shit, Timyn!" Leia gasped, her hooded gaze trained on my face like I was a *man* fucking her, not a monster. "Your ridges feel so good. I'm gonna... ahh..."

That glorious cunt of hers started clenching around me, stimulating every curved ridge along my shaft and ripping an orgasm out of me that made it hard to breathe. Fucking the others was never like this—could never *be* like this. This was too much, beyond anything I'd ever experienced.

I growled through my release, my cock pulsing as I filled her with everything I had—every drop, every long-buried primal urge trapped in this human body, everything I'd never *felt* before.

Mine.

19
LEIA

I woke up sore and sticky, with so many snarls in my hair, I wondered if it would just be easier to shave it off.

There was also a tongue between my legs.

"Good morning," Ambrose paused his Best Wake-up Call Ever to smile up at me. "It occurred to me I hadn't yet delivered on my promise to honor your beauty in this way. Plus, you smelled so delectable, I couldn't resist."

He resumed gently lapping at my pussy with his pleasantly rough tongue. For a moment, I worried exactly how I smelled and tasted, especially after what we got up to last night. I could still feel cum dripping out of me from Timyn, but that didn't seem to deter my big kitty cat one bit.

And who am I to rain on his pussy parade?

I almost laughed at how my inhibitions were trying to resurface *now*. I'd fucked an oversized armored lion and a lake snake—complete with prickly pricks. Then I'd let an androgynous deer-man play with my ass after stuffing his firehose of a cock down my throat. If Ambrose wanted a creampie for breakfast, that was downright chaste in comparison.

Closing my eyes, I settled back with a contented sigh, deciding I was perfectly fine with receiving this well-deserved honor. Of course, some cockblocker chose that moment to loudly bang on the bedroom door.

"GO AWAY OR I WILL FUCKING EAT YOU!" Timyn roared from underneath his pile of blankets—obviously not a morning monster.

The Hydra is my spirit animal.

The lurker outside the door must have gotten the hint, as there were no more knocks. Timyn eventually emerged from his nest as Ambrose brought me to the edge, happily assisting by lazily running his forked tongue over my nipples until I added *more* wetness to the other man's face. Krysos walked in while I was still shaking through my release, his gray eyes darkening as he took in the scene. I returned the heated look tenfold when I noticed the tray of food in his hands.

Eating after being eaten? Yes, please!

As tempting as the pretty hind was, I needed my strength if I was going to keep up with these monsters. Not to mention, it was probably wise to give my lady parts a rest before tackling his impressively long dick.

One doesn't simply take on Cervid the Impaler.

I snickered at my own joke before sitting up and taking the bowl of honey-drenched *loukoumades* Krysos was handing to me. My laughter turned into a moan as the first perfectly prepared ball of caloric goodness hit my tastebuds —the sound vicariously echoed by my men.

"Don't I deserve a honey token for my Olympian efforts this morning?" Timyn eyed the bowl and my lips with equal amounts of hunger.

Ambrose scoffed, the evidence of his more legit efforts still dampening his face. True to form, he seemed downright unbothered by the mess, but personally, I was dying for a power wash. Between the sticky breakfast and the layers of love juice coating me, I felt in danger of becoming glued to the sheets.

"Soooo... have we worn out our welcome with Pholus yet?" I popped another *loukoumades* in my mouth and rose from the bed to stretch. "Because I want to take advantage of that luxurious bathtub in the next room to scrub last night off of me before we leave."

All three men stared at me in uncomfortable silence. "You wish to wash us off of you?" Ambrose finally asked. His voice was deadly calm, even as his gaze warily flickered to Timyn, who looked like he was about to burst a blood vessel.

I may have made a monstrous faux pas.

Obviously, none of these men gave a shit about bodily fluids—judging by Ambrose's face and Timyn's willingness to lick Krysos' cum off my tits the night before. I'd assumed they were just game for anything, but there was more going on here. Ambrose had explained they were physically designed to impregnate females, and Timyn actually called me his 'mate.' This biological drive was probably why they all seemed determined to cover me with manjam—inside and out—which I oddly didn't mind. While I still intended to clean up, I didn't like the idea of them thinking I wanted to wipe my hands of the entire experience.

I just don't want to be the living embodiment of a cum dumpster!

"It's not that I don't want to *smell* like you," I soothed, cupping Timyn's face in my hand, gasping when his skin instantly turned to scales under my fingertips. "I just need to wash these tangles out of my hair and freshen up. I promise, you can rub yourselves all over me again later." This seemed to appease my monsters, and Timyn and Ambrose refocused on eating, while Krysos grabbed me a change of clothes and followed me into the bathroom.

"It's because they've claimed you," he absently murmured, heating water for the bathtub like a pro. "When I take you, I'll behave in the same way." Krysos spoke so matter-of-factly, it took my overtired brain a moment to catch up with the audacity of his statements.

"Listen," I snapped, wanting nothing more than a hot bath and some alone time at this point. "I just got out of a shitty relationship back home, so everyone can cool their jets about making this official. Let's get something straight —just because a man fucks me doesn't mean he *owns* me."

He quietly observed me, as if trying to solve a puzzle. "We are not *men*, Herculeia. And you are our mate."

I swallowed hard. I'd dated possessive guys before, but this was feeling like my dark mafia book boyfriends had come to life. While my body was 1000% on board with more monster orgies and fated mates, the rest of me was vaguely wondering if I needed a stronger sense of self-preservation. To be honest, *not* having a bigger problem with the craziness bothered me more than anything.

Don't tell me I'm one of those TSTL heroines...

Noticing I was dangerously close to inviting hottie hind into the tub with me confirmed I needed space to think. Twisting my ring, I forced myself to politely thank Krysos for helping me before waving him off. He obeyed without complaint, but just before he closed the bathroom door, I heard the urgent knocking from outside again, followed by Timyn loudly threatening whoever it was.

Imma let them deal with that.

Left in blessed silence, I processed my sexcapades of the past few days. I'd arrived here hesitant about sleeping around, but something about *these* men cranked my libido all the way up. Even though we'd only just met, there was more happening between us than just sex. The connection I felt with each of them was intense—and slightly concerning—but with everything I'd been through, it was hard to separate fact from fiction.

I tested the bath before lowering myself into the basin with a sigh of deep satisfaction. Existential crises aside, I was determined to make the most of the hot water and fancy soaps until I felt human again.

Because I'm the only human here...

My chaotic emotions immediately settled. As wild as this entire situation was, I needed to remember I wasn't dealing with humans. Everyone on this island was a mythological creature—some with murderous grudges and most being extremely dangerous. I couldn't expect them to behave with the same logic and restraint I was used to back home.

While my men were a little... obsessive, they hadn't harmed me. If anything, they were clearly trying their hardest not to crush me like a grape or tear me in half with their monster cocks. The whole 'mate' thing was a lot, but I appreciated how open they were being. As shocking as their confessions were, it was probably a leap of faith for them to admit their biological *need* to impregnate me, knowing it could scare me away.

I can't wait to hear what they think of my birth control shot...

Leaving that problem for Future Leia, I dried off and dressed before walking back into the bedroom. My men were gone, as were our travel packs, but before I could panic, I noticed a piece of paper with flowing script waiting for me on the bed. The note said they were meeting with Pholus, and I should wait for them by the fountain outside the main entrance.

By some miracle, I found my way there without getting lost. Sitting on the edge of the fountain, I took in the impressive water feature at its center—the brightly painted marble statue depicting a half-naked, terrified woman slung over the back of a bull as she was carried off.

"It's the Rape of Europa," an unfamiliar voice startled me and I whipped around to find a centaur standing nearby, impassively surveying the water feature. He was naked—of course—except for a straw hat on his head and a bandana around his neck.

This must be what passes for workwear around here.

It wasn't entirely clear if he was expecting me to reply, but I still racked my brain, digging deep to unearth the long-buried legend from my childhood. "Yeah, I remember that one... Zeus decided, in his Zeussy way, that he just had to have Europa. He turned into a bull and convinced her to climb onto his back before running off to make babies with her."

The centaur grunted, which I interpreted as approval of my thrilling retelling. "What a dumbass, though, right?" I continued my critique. "First, who climbs onto a bull? Also, Zeus was always turning himself into animals to entice human women. You would think word would've spread— like, don't ride cute creatures, ladies! You just might find yourself barefoot and preggers by a psychopath."

The centaur snapped his attention to me, suddenly *very* interested in interacting. "Yet you seem to be headed down the same path."

I crossed my arms and gave him a withering glare.

"What exactly do you mean by that? My men will be here any minute, so spit it out, cowboy."

Because you're mighty judgy for someone dressed like a Toy Story porn star.

He smiled like he had a secret, which made me clench my fist, wishing I could punch the expression right off his horsey face. "As with Zeus' bull, these 'men' of yours are more than what they seem. I don't simply mean that they're *inhuman*. There are reasons they were banished here —dooming all of us to share their fate."

"They don't remember how they got here," I growled, my anger rising at an alarming rate. This rando thinking he could insult *my* men was fiercely pissing me off, even as I stubbornly ignored the red flag being frantically waved in front of me.

"So they say," he shrugged, gaze drifting back to the statue. "But you should be prepared in case any untold truths come to light, *Herculeia.*" With that ominous statement, he produced a small velvet pouch from god knows where and dropped it in my lap before cantering away.

What the fuck was that about?

"Was Nessus bothering you, Water Lily?" Timyn was suddenly looming over me, blocking out the sun, his rows of jagged teeth on full display as he smiled wickedly. "Do you want me to eat him?"

Deeply unsettled by the centaur's warning, I stared back at the Hydra for a moment. "I... I think I'd like to get out of here now," I softly replied, suddenly unsure about everything.

I don't belong here.

Timyn's smile faded, his confused gaze sweeping over me before drifting to the statue above my head. An oddly detached expression passed over his face before he turned and called to the others to join us. I took advantage of his distraction to stand and walk away, so I could peek inside Nessus' pouch without him seeing.

I was grimly unsurprised to find another bronze obol waiting for me. Tucked in with the coin was a small glass vial full of deep red liquid—the skull and crossbones on the label implying the contents were deadly. A slip of paper was wrapped around the bottle, with the same handwriting from the note left in the bedroom.

"Dip your arrow/but do not touch/and be sure your aim is true."

Hiding the pouch in my hand, I accepted my travel pack from Ambrose and covertly slipped my newest gifts into the interior pocket with my growing collection of *obols*. I had no intention of touching the poison—and didn't even have an arrow—but the biggest question was *who* I would be aiming for.

If it's my men, do I really want to know?

20

KRYSOS

Leia was upset about something—her usual chatter noticeably absent as we journeyed to Julius' fortress on Mount Erymanthos. Ambrose and Timyn were filling the void with conversation, but my attention was solely on my mate, determined to draw the problem out of her somehow.

She can't hide from me.

The others told me how their stunted powers flared to life when Leia touched them—how they instinctively knew she was theirs. I couldn't say whether that happened during our first meeting, because my clumsy Fawn was too busy kicking my legs out from under me. However, when we were alone together before Symposium, my hind was snorting and scraping, wanting to leave its scent all over her.

Since I hadn't completely claimed her yet, I was in the unique position to view the situation more objectively than the others could. Leia had been quiet since we left the vineyard, twisting her ring as if deep in thought, and I assumed that idiot Nessus had said *something* to upset her.

Probably the same tired warning that we're 'dangerous.'

While this warning was entirely accurate, the memory of how Leia had eyed Timyn at the fountain—like she was *afraid* of him—was making my beast pace in agitation. Didn't she know he'd never hurt her? None of us would. Timyn and Ambrose would tear apart anyone who threatened her. They'd rip the entrails right out of their body and I would force the offender to eat them while they were still alive.

Surely she would find that romantic?

Many heroes had made the mistake of thinking of me as nothing more than a harmless deer. But I was a steed of Artemis, born of wind and war, and I could incinerate my opponent before they were done admiring my beauty. While I had no intention of hiding what I was from Leia— as Ambrose had foolishly attempted to do—I wondered if our 'otherness' was playing a part in her discomfort.

Thinking back, I realized Leia had been withdrawn since I left her in the bath. I didn't *think* she regretted our bacchanalian orgy—even slightly drunk on Dionysius' wine, Leia was clearly a willing participant—but maybe her pesky human inhibitions were sneaking up on her.

I suppose I could simply ask.

"Is something bothering you, Fawn?" I murmured, moving closer to better inhale her pleasing natural aroma, buried beneath the offensive soap she'd scrubbed herself with.

She startled at the question, but then glanced at the two men walking far ahead. "Well, I *have* been wondering..." she began, before pausing long enough that I suspected she was carefully choosing her words. "What happened between you and Ambrose?"

I was so surprised by the question, I almost stumbled

like a clumsy fawn myself. Before I could reply, she elaborated, "Is it because he and Timyn have..." She gestured vaguely and it took me a moment to understand what she was implying.

Such a human way of looking at things.

"No, Leia," I chuckled, enchanted by her concern. "You must remember, we've been stuck on this island for centuries. I think we've all fucked each other at this point."

She blushed as her scent perfumed the air, confirming the thought pleased her. "Oh, okay," she haltingly continued. "I only asked because Timyn was messing with Ambrose last night while we... well, he obviously knew which buttons to push so he'd freak out. I didn't know if it was because you two were *mates.*"

Overwhelming sadness washed over me. My relationship with Ambrose was tragically broken, despite how intensely I'd once cared for him. Even though she was asking, it didn't seem appropriate to burden Leia with my story just yet, so I focused on what I could answer.

"I don't actually know if two men *can* have a mate bond," I awkwardly replied, keeping my voice low so the others wouldn't overhear. My gaze drifted to where Ambrose was loudly laughing, his muscles rippling as he shoved Timyn in jest, his lustrous hair shining like it was made of sunlight itself.

"Mating is a biological instinct with us," I pointedly glanced at the woman at my side. "And as it's the females who carry our young—"

She cleared her throat. "Yeah... about that. Listen, I'm not looking to get knocked up anytime soon. I mean, how would that even work? We're not the same *species*... and I don't really *know* you guys. The reason you ended up here is still a little unclear, and my main goal is to get off this island, so..."

My vision tunneled as I realized *this* was closer to what had been bothering her—that her questions about Ambrose and me were merely a deflection.

"What are you gossiping about back there?" Timyn called from where they'd stopped next to an abandoned farmhouse, waiting for us to catch up. "Inquiring minds want to know."

More like nosey mates.

I sighed. While it would be disappointing for Leia to not feel the mate bond in return, it wouldn't keep the rest of us from our obsessions. As her mates, we were now attuned to her every movement and emotion, but it wasn't simply about impregnation. Her safety, happiness, and well-being were also our top priorities.

This would need to be carefully explained, because if Nessus planted doubt in Leia's mind, promises alone wouldn't prove our devotion. If we were still at the vineyard, I would find the centaur and wring his slippery neck until he told me every word of their conversation. For now, however, I simply needed to ensure the others thought everything was fine until I could fix things.

Two more psychotic mates won't help the situation.

"Leia was wondering why we were trudging along in human form," I replied, plastering on a wide grin I didn't fully feel. "When we could ride on a lion or Hydra and get there faster."

Both men stared at us with an amusing combination of offense and lust, as their distinct halves warred with each other. I wasn't being obtuse when I'd pointed out to Leia that we were not men. Just because we'd inhabited these bodies for centuries didn't change the fact we were nothing more than wolves in sheep's clothing.

Leia sharply glanced at me, no doubt noticing how I made a point not to share her concerns. I'd have to wait until we were alone again to continue explaining what mating meant for us.

Although if I get her to myself again, I'll want to solidify our bond...

Ambrose recovered first, replying with the candidness I used to love. "It depletes our energy to shift into our true forms—especially if we're away from our sources of power for too long. For Timyn, it's the lake of Lerna, and for Krysos, it's the Ceryneian valley, where Pholus' vineyard is located."

Leia nodded, taking it all in with a fascinating amount of acceptance. "What about yours, Ambrose? Is it your olive grove?"

My heart panged. A visceral memory of Ambrose tending to his olive trees in the early morning light combined with the terrible knowledge his home no longer existed. I eyed my former love warily, ready to divert the conversation from his trauma, if need be.

It appears I still care after all...

"My cave was destroyed in retaliation," he softly answered, readily baring his soul, to my utter surprise. "I haven't been able to access my lion for a long time. Not until you came along."

Leia paled, perhaps understanding how vital she was to us already. Then she straightened, lifting her chin with a fire in her eyes that I very much liked the look of. *"Who* destroyed it? And *why?"*

This time, Ambrose hesitated, and I pursed my lips,

annoyed he seemed ready to withhold information from our mate.

I expect better from you.

"Julius would be the better choice to explain the *why*, but as to *who* took my home from me..." He closely watched her reaction, even as he surprised me by elaborating. "It was our common enemy—the man who sent you here. Eurystheus."

21

LEIA

A rage flared up in me that was so intense I practically levitated. *"Eurystheus destroyed your home?!"* I shrieked, feeling every atom of my being ignite with an irrational thirst for revenge.

Who's the monster now?

Ambrose took a step back, his shocked gaze roaming over me as if he'd never seen me before. Krysos looked smugly satisfied, and Timyn seemed about ready to jump my bones, his pupils transforming into reptilian slits as he hungrily licked his lips.

No one was more surprised than me. I brought the heat when needed, but I could count on one hand the times I'd felt this wrathful before. Once was when my mother *forgot* my eighteenth birthday, and more recently when I'd walked in on Dylan cheating. Of course, this rage mixed with unimaginable grief when my dad burned to death in his own car.

Don't think about it.

"Yes... he did, " Ambrose slowly replied, as I twisted the ring on my finger so violently it left a mark. "Eurystheus demolished my cave until there was nothing left but a pile of rubble. I continued living nearby, hoping to still draw power from the location, but any magic that previously existed was gone."

He observed me for another moment before closing the distance between us to pull me into a hug, instantly diffusing me. "It's all right, Leia—it happened a long time ago." Respectful silence fell over the group as I cuddled into Ambrose's wall of man-muscle, slightly embarrassed that *he'd* felt the need to comfort *me*.

Krysos was closely watching our interaction again, the small smile on his lips erasing my lingering concerns. Even though I'd used it to redirect our conversation earlier, I was genuinely curious if he and Ambrose considered each other mates. It was easy to pick up on the history between those two—to feel how unfinished it was—and I didn't want to get in the middle of their relationship.

I mean, I do want to get in the middle, but...

"I'm sorry that asshat blew up your cave, Ambrose," I eloquently offered, refocusing on the topic at hand. "If I ever get near him, I'll punch him in the nuts for you."

"Mmm... you do wield quite a punch," Timyn purred in my ear as he and Krysos passed us to begin walking again. "Although, you *could* hit me harder next time, Water Lily."

Ambrose chuckled and tucked me under one of his tree trunk arms, guiding me to follow the others. I was thankful for his familiar calming energy, even if I didn't regret my outburst. The idea of anyone hurting my men apparently turned me into Scary Leia, which didn't seem to turn these men off one bit. In fact, I got the distinct impression she fit right in with present company.

She may also be needed to survive this island.

Shuddering, I recalled how creepily fixated on me the

centaurs were, and how outnumbered I was at the vineyard —as a woman and a human. They seemed just as angry as my men to be trapped here, but Nessus giving me another *obol,* along with a bottle of poison, was not a good sign.

Is Porn Cowboy working with Eurystheus?

I opened my mouth to tell Ambrose about the inappropriate gift—and how I kept finding *obols* everywhere we traveled—but promptly snapped it closed again. As infuriating as it was to listen to that horse-man talk shit about my men, I knew I had to humor the possibility his warning held a grain of truth.

Part of me vehemently rebelled against the idea of being afraid of my men. Sure, our forced proximity was probably to blame for their intensity and how I *thought* I felt about them, but worse things could happen. In the end, I needed to keep my eye on the prize—a way off this island. I couldn't keep getting attached to every Big Fat Greek Monster Peen that fell in my lap.

Or whose lap I fall into...

About an hour later, we reached a wall of boulders. I untangled myself from Ambrose to scale the pile, thankful for the loose tunic and leggings Krysos had rustled up for me this morning. While I looked like an extra from *Robin Hood: Men in Tights,* the outfit was way more appropriate for hiking than my dress.

Hopefully, I don't have to run away from any more wild beasts...

Timyn was waiting on the other side to help me down, and I gasped at the scene spread out before me. If I'd thought the Ceryneian valley was gorgeous, this vista absolutely took my breath away.

Fallow farmland led to a ridge dotted with low shrubs, reminding me of the southwest's high desert back home. Dilapidated stone walls snaked over the landscape, giving the scene a rustic vibe that briefly reminded me of my *lack* of technology and inability to document my journey. I quickly forgot about my phone again when I spotted a distant mountain looming behind the ridge, with craggy peaks dusted with snow disappearing into the clouds. The most prominent feature was an actual *castle* built into the rock face—looking exactly like an evil villain's lair.

I have a bad feeling about this.

"Is that... where we're going?" I swallowed, wondering what kind of man—*monster*—lived in such an imposing place.

"Yes, that's Julius' home," Timyn sniffed, clearly unimpressed. "His source of power is the entire mountain, so he decided to lurk up there like a gargoyle. Which is appropriate, since he's a broody asshole," he added, before turning his intense green eyes on me. "If you're still interested in a ride, I could be convinced to let you climb aboard."

My lips twisted in amusement. "I will take you up on that offer, although I *have* ridden you before."

He growled and crowded into my personal space, which I didn't mind one bit. "Yes, the sight of you bouncing on my cock was a vision I won't soon forget. Let's do that again."

Krysos made a noise that sounded suspiciously jealous. When I glanced over, he was pointedly not looking at us, while busying himself with his pack to prepare for the climb. I wanted to go to him immediately—to comfort him and possibly even things out. The skin underneath my mother's ring itched as I tried to process how in tune I seemed to be with his needs. With *all* of them. I knew I didn't owe sex to any of these men. But their unwavering confidence about our connection, along with my compulsion to agree it existed, was making it difficult to think straight.

It would help if they weren't so distractingly sexy.

All three of my men were naked when I returned to reality. Before I could comment, or take Timyn up on that ride he was offering, they each seamlessly transformed into their respective beasts.

Oh, right—that *ride.*

I'd already seen Ambrose's lion and Krysos' stag in the light of day, but Timyn's true form rendered me speechless. If I didn't know him—trust him—I'd be terrified. While it was easy to see why I'd mistaken him for a dragon during our late-night encounter, he was obviously something else entirely. The Hydra towered over me, like a shimmering green and purple brontosaurus, except instead of one long neck, he had *nine* that ended in lizard-like heads with very sharp teeth.

And very long tongues...

"Are you going to climb aboard?" Timyn purred in my head. *"Or are you busy wondering if you could take on more of my appendages?"*

I yelped as one of his tails curled around my waist, effortlessly lifting me into the air and gently depositing me on his upper back. It then slipped away to join two other tails in loading our packs onto a disgruntled lion and equally annoyed looking deer. Remembering how involved those nimble appendages had been on the beach, I forced myself to focus on finding something to hang on to while up here. Timyn's smooth scales lay flat against his skin, but I spotted a slightly raised ridge on his central neck—like an iguana's dorsal crest.

Giddy-up!

I straddled his neck, but the instant I grabbed hold of

the leathery crest, it popped up, like a sail catching wind, making me gasp. Worried I'd accidentally injured him, I let go, only to have the crest start undulating between my thighs, drawing a completely different noise out of me instead.

His wicked laugh echoed in my head, telling me he knew exactly what he was doing. *"Let's play a game, Leia. How many times can I make you come before we reach the top?"*

I opened my mouth to protest just as the Hydra lumbered forward. This forced me to focus all my energy on not falling off—knowing I was at Timyn's mercy with whatever dirty tricks he had up his scaly sleeve.

22

LEIA

Unfortunately for my vagina, the Hydra was successful in wringing *four* freaking orgasms out of me by the time we got to the top. To my credit, he got one of his tails and two of his heads—and their tongues—involved, so it was far from a fair fight.

No. More. Appendages.

I'd all but collapsed around his neck by the time we finally reached the oddly Gothic fortress built into the mountain. A wintery chill in the air, coupled with the shadows of impending dusk, made the building even more gloomy and imposing than it already was. Although a fur coat had been draped over me at some point, I was cranky and stiff from hanging onto a devilish Hydra for hours, and was looking forward to a warm welcome.

"What the fuck have you brought to my doorstep?"

He sounds nice.

Squinting in the fading light, all I could see around the girth of Timyn's neck was a massive man looming in the arched doorway. I couldn't make out his expression as he was backlit by torchlight and wearing what appeared to be a hooded cloak, but his displeasure was heard loud and clear.

"Julius, this is Herc... *Leia,*" Ambrose stepped forward, gloriously naked in human form once again. "And she is our—"

"Our mate," Krysos casually interrupted, nakedly strutting over to greet our host. "Although I haven't had the pleasure of marking her as mine. Yet."

Is this how they do introductions?

"You'll want to allow her some recovery time, Krysos," Timyn unhelpfully added, after setting me on the ground and shimmering back into his human form. "I kept our mate *extremely* satisfied during the climb up this godsforsaken rock, and judging by how wet my neck is, she may be spent for now."

"Really guys? *Really?*" I huffed, glaring daggers at all three of them, although judging by the heated stares I got in return, they were unrepentant.

Flustered, I turned to our host. "Hi! It's, uh, nice to meet you, Julius. Thank you for inviting... Oh, hmm. You probably weren't expecting us, were you? But hey, it's not like we could've *told* you we were coming, because—no phones! Actually, that's kind of the problem. See, I was shipwrecked here a few days ago, and I'm trying to figure out how to get off this island, since I can't contact anyone to let them know I'm alive. The guys thought you could help, sooo..."

Julius grunted noncommittally, not even bothering to reply before spinning on his heel and stomping back into his evil villain lair. No one else seemed put off by his behavior, which probably meant he was this grumpy all the time.

"I think he likes you, Water Lily," Timyn stage-whispered, practically shoving me through the door after our reluctant host. Krysos snorted as he followed, and Ambrose looked like he was also fighting a grin, which instantly relieved some of the tension I was feeling.

Despite the four orgasms.

"I suppose you'll be expecting dinner?" Julius' voice boomed through the cavernous space. I assume the question was rhetorical—not that I could actually *see* enough of our host to gauge his intentions. All he was giving us was his broad, fur cloak-covered back as he dismissively plowed ahead.

Choosing to match his energy, I ignored the question altogether and openly gawked at my surroundings instead. I religiously followed enough influencers to know a Notre Dame knockoff like this place didn't belong on a Greek island, but I allowed it. The craftsmanship of the vaulted woodwork, rich tapestries, and floor to ceiling stained glass filtering in the first rays of moonlight were hard not to appreciate. Even the golden wall sconces we passed were fancy—shaped to look like hands holding the torches aloft.

Human hands...

My eyes narrowed. Julius may not even *have* hands in his true form, so it was an odd choice of decor—unless he was being ironic, which I doubted, based on his lack of humor. Timyn implied Julius simply moved into this ready-made mansion, which sounded a lot like what Ambrose did with his Italian-style villa by the sea.

Again, I considered how *strange* it was for there to be an Italian villa here. The centaurs' vineyard seemed authentic to the location—and time period—of these legends come to life, but stylistic details were still off. It was almost as if someone were haphazardly decorating the island according to their moods and personal preferences, like a child rearranging their dollhouse.

Or playing god.

It was still a mystery to me why and how my men ended up here, and where Eurystheus fit into the whole thing. Ambrose said Julius would be best to explain certain things, so I decided to be brave, if only to break the silence.

"Who do you think built this place?" I called out, wanting answers, but also determined to *force* this man to acknowledge me.

I immediately regretted my decision. Julius abruptly stopped walking and spun to face us, somehow looking ten times more irritated than he'd sounded. In fact, he looked *enraged*. That might have been because he was scowling like I'd pissed in his cereal... while *missing an eyeball.*

His face was ruggedly handsome—because, of course—with thick eyebrows, cascading black hair, and a beard that would have looked right at home at a death metal show. His skin had a more sepia tone than the others, and I distractedly wondered how their human skin colors were determined, even as my stunned gaze drifted dangerously close to his eye area.

Don't you look at his missing eye... don't you fucking dare...

"You know full well who erected this structure, *human,*" he hissed, as I gaped at his empty eye socket like someone with a death wish.

Wait, what?

"Julius." Ambrose's voice held a warning tone as he grabbed my hand, either to show solidarity or to stop me from running. This only seemed to further irritate our irritable host, as Julius held up his hand to silence Ambrose before turning his back and continuing on his way.

"Speaking of *erections,* Julius," Timyn sang out as my stomach sank. "When's the last time you fucked anyone? You seem a little... *tense.*"

I braced for impact as Julius stopped in his tracks, but to

my surprise, his shoulders shook as if he were silently laughing. "If that's an offer, Hydra, I'll be sure to leave my door unlocked tonight," he called back before disappearing around a corner. "See you bastards at dinner."

"Lucky," Krysos murmured, earning him a self-satisfied smirk from Timyn and narrowed eyes from Ambrose. The hind met his former lover's gaze and shrugged, uncharacteristically awkward. "It's been a while since I was properly put on my hands and knees."

Lawdamercy.

My pussy practically overflowed at the thought of *that* scenario—which my men zeroed in on like the predators they were.

"Oh, no, no, no," I held up a hand, mimicking Julius' sassy gesture. "Food before fucking, and it better be cooked! On that note, can one of you ask the grumpy bear to *cook* my meat for me? I don't like it raw."

This earned me a round of laughs, as Timyn slung an arm around my shoulders and began leading me toward the stairs. "I promise to talk to him about how you prefer your meat. Although, you should know, Julius is not a bear."

"True, but he's definitely grumpy," Krysos cut in, as if sensing I was too tired and hangry to handle another big reveal at the moment. "Although I think he missed us."

"Yes, I think you're right," Ambrose softly replied. Stealing a glance at his stoic profile, I got the sense he meant *all* of them—that maybe they'd all been missing each other more than they wanted to admit.

23

LEIA

Dinner was not at all what I expected. Based on the grand Gothic architecture, I assumed we'd be eating in a lifeless medieval hall, at a banquet table so long we'd have to get up and walk to pass the salt.

Instead, we'd taken over a gaudy parlor room that Liberace would have considered extra. Renaissance paintings in ornate gold frames packed the walls and moonlight poured through arched stained glass windows. A cozy fire burned in a gigantic flagstone fireplace, warming us as we lounged on couches of brocade and velvet.

Food was already laid out when we arrived. The grazer in me was thrilled to find it was mostly one big mezze platter, with a side of raw meat for the guys. My bowl-cup was filled with the ubiquitous water and wine, and I finally understood the reason for its strange design, as I didn't spill a drop while lazily reclining.

No wonder Greece was famous for its great thinkers.

Our host was noticeably on-edge while he caught up with the other men, his one good eye on me as if I were about to steal the silver. Maybe Julius' panties were in a bunch—assuming that's what he wore under his toga—but if I had to guess, it was that my very existence was offensive to him.

His bowl-cup must be full of haterade.

"I have to admit, Ambrose," Julius drawled, shrewdly observing the other man. "It's surprising to see you here after my last several letters went unanswered. Don't tell me you're only taking an interest in our mission again because of a *woman.*"

"Yes, Julius, it *is* because of Leia," Ambrose sighed, already sounding exhausted by the conversation. "It seemed prudent to involve you, as she is the first *human* to appear on our shores since we were banished here. She somehow made it through the fog, with an *obol* under her tongue—a coin placed there by Eurystheus himself—"

Julius leaped to his feet, dramatically tossing his cup against the fireplace with a loud clatter. "You thought it prudent to bring an associate of Eurystheus to *my* house?! Must I remind you that man is the same burden on the earth who took everything from us—including my fucking eye!"

Triggered!

As if he could smell my judgment, Julius turned his piercing glare my way. "What's the plan, harlot? Did Eurystheus send you here to seduce us in these weaker forms? To finally finish us?"

I shrank against Timyn, who protectively pulled me into his lap. Krysos growled low in the corner, wisps of smoke curling from his nostrils like a dragon, reminding me he apparently breathed fire.

Ambrose stood with feline grace, the lion rippling over his skin the only sign of his barely contained anger. "You will not talk to my mate that way. She is as much a victim of Eurystheus as we all are."

"That remains to be seen," Julius snorted, clearly unconvinced, although he chilled out enough to no longer seem murderous. "Until then, to the crows with both of you!"

I frowned, having no clue what that archaic insult meant, but assuming it wasn't nice. Before I could retort, Julius swept away, with an annoyed-looking Ambrose hot on his heels. Krysos threw me a concerned glance, but Timyn waved him off, so the hind refocused on the contents of his bowl-cup and left us to each other.

"Didn't I tell you Julius was an asshole?" Timyn chuckled in my ear, cuddling me so tightly, I wondered if my cold-blooded monster was stealing my body heat.

I huffed a laugh. "Yeah, and I agree, he obviously needs to get laid! Maybe you *should* help the grumpster out with that 'tension' of his."

The Hydra stiffened beneath me—in more ways than one—before pushing away to better look at me. "You wouldn't *mind* if I went to Julius' bed tonight? Don't humans consider that... *cheating?*"

Although I'd been mostly teasing with my suggestion, I paused to seriously consider. These men had known each other for centuries and, as Krysos said, that inevitably resulted in plenty of fucking over the years. He'd made their friendships sound casual, but I bet most of their relationships went deeper than that. I couldn't imagine how alienating it must have been for my monsters to suddenly wake up as *men,* with no one else to relate to their experiences.

Except for each other.

"I actually *don't* see it as cheating," I murmured, surprising myself yet again. "You're not sneaking around, and your relationships existed long before I came along. It would be kind of ridiculous to expect you guys to throw away all that history just for me." I awkwardly cleared my throat. "Even if I'm supposedly your... mate."

Timyn roughly gripped my chin, forcing me to meet his intense gaze. "You *are* my mate, and I will see my *seed* dripping out of you again." I grumbled at his choice of words as he grinned mischievously. "You could join me tonight, Water Lily. There's always room for one more."

I barked a laugh. "Um, no. Not sure if you noticed, but Julius doesn't seem to be my biggest fan. I doubt he wants me anywhere near his bedroom."

"Oh, he just gets worked up. It's the whole..." Timyn dismissively gestured toward his face, "missing eyeball... thing. But you're right. It would be best if I did this alone—to sacrifice myself for the greater good."

Something tells me he doesn't see this as a hardship.

"Besides," he purred, throwing a sidelong glance at where Krysos was languidly draped over a chaise, sipping his wine. "Your talents would be better utilized elsewhere tonight."

"Why exactly are you leering at me, Hydra?" Krysos eyed us suspiciously.

"Because you're just so fucking pretty," Timyn clapped back before whispering in my head. *"Just get them both drunk and they'll be buried in each other's asses in no time. I bet they'd even let you watch."*

My thighs involuntarily squeezed together at the thought. "I think everyone here can drink me under the table," I stuttered in reply. "And that's saying a lot, because I used to be the queen of Thirsty Thursday."

Timyn smiled, his sharp teeth flashing. "You already

have a solution at your fingertips. Simply dip your ring in the wine, if you're worried about losing your head."

"My ring?" I muttered, twisting the familiar band on my finger, confused by his suggestion.

"Yes. It's amethyst, correct? Wealthy men used to drink from carved amethyst goblets, or mix in powdered amethyst with their wine. They believed the stone would keep them sober. *Amethystos:* Not intoxicated."

I absorbed this fascinating bit of new information. With how much my mother loved to torture me with history lessons, none of her lectures ever involved this ring, despite it being so precious to me. It was the only jewelry of hers I owned, but I couldn't seem to remember *when* she'd given it to me.

Knowing my mother, she doesn't remember it either.

Ambrose suddenly appeared in the doorway, looking like he'd emotionally been hit by a bus. I leaped off Timyn's lap, once again *compelled* to comfort one of my men.

"Aww, was the big angry bore mean to you?" I cooed, gently running my hands along his jawline, shivering at the feel of his skin under my fingertips.

He looked at me curiously for a moment before his face fell. "Julius has every right to be angry with *me*. It wasn't polite to show up unannounced, especially after ignoring his letters the way I did." Krysos made an exaggerated sound of surprise, which Ambrose pointedly ignored. "But everything's fine now, Siren. I explained *your* circumstances, and he no longer thinks you're plotting against us with Eurystheus. He'll be on his best behavior tomorrow, I promise."

Yeah, when pigs fly.

"Well, I'm going to ensure he is," Timyn lazily rose, stretching as if he were getting ready for a workout. "Our mate's given me permission to sacrifice myself for the old *bore* to take out his aggression on. Leia's all yours tonight —*both of yours."*

Krysos abruptly sat up to peer at Timyn in the dimly lit room. "Is that a fact?" he murmured before his gaze flickered to Ambrose, who was staring at me with bald hunger.

What am I getting myself into?

"Enjoy your evening, Leia," the Hydra smirked, tapping his ring finger. "Try to pace yourself."

"It's just a myth, you know!" I shouted after him as he practically skipped out of the room.

Of course the little shit needed to have the last word, wickedly chuckling in my head. *"Aren't we all, Herculeia? Aren't we all."*

24

AMBROSE

Everything about Leia commanded my attention. That smooth olive-toned skin of hers, the metal piercing glinting below her plump lower lip, the way she smelled like honey and tasted like sin itself. That she had seen our true forms and still allowed us to worship her, with our tongues and cocks, only confirmed she was my mate.

Our *mate*.

After Timyn left, Krysos joined us on the couch to drink, and Leia was now nestled in his arms, stretched out with her tattooed feet in my lap. I rubbed my thumb along her arches, admiring the various markings that turned this woman into a work of art. She said humans got tattoos for fun where—and when—she came from, and I enjoyed the glimpses of Leia's personality with each design she'd chosen.

Although the numbers on her wrist are still a mystery...

"It's getting hot in here," Krysos murmured. "We should take off our clothes."

For some reason, Leia thought this was hilarious,

drunkenly rolling off the couch into a giggling heap before hauling herself to her feet. Despite her odd reaction, she must have agreed with Krysos' suggestion. Swaying precariously, she hopped out of her leggings and clumsily pulled the tunic over her head, revealing her naked body in all its glory.

I growled low. My mate was absolute perfection, and it was all I could do not to take her to the floor, sink my fangs into her neck, and fuck her until she screamed. It was an ongoing struggle to behave myself, but she was a welcome distraction from the *other* deadly temptation in the room.

Since I'm dangerously close to taking him *to the floor as well.*

After hours of drinking, all my *kylix* had brought me was an unbearably frustrating awareness of Krysos' every move—and his every interaction with Leia. Knowing him, much of it was a performance to further antagonize me.

"Come here, Fawn," Krysos spoke in that effortlessly sensual way of his. "Let me taste you."

She only hesitated a moment before moving to stand in front of where Krysos reclined. He immediately grasped her thighs, yanking her closer so he could drag his tongue through her wetness. I echoed Leia's moan as my lion paced, desperate to pounce on either of them.

On both of them.

No doubt sensing my beast rising to the surface, Krysos glanced at me before shifting his gaze back to Leia. "Shall we make a wager?" He smirked, licking her wetness off of his lips. "Let's guess how much Ambrose can watch before he breaks."

Naughty devil.

"Mmm," Leia hummed, dropping her hands to the base

of his antlers and yanking hard enough that he hissed. "Bet. Except my money's on *you* breaking first."

Krysos gaped, his normally detached demeanor momentarily faltering, betraying his surprise. Before he could regain control over the situation, Leia straddled him —facing me—and I could have sworn she winked before addressing the hind over her shoulder again.

"I know you're dying to get inside me, Krysos," she purred, rubbing herself along his length, making both of us growl. "But I want Ambrose to help get me ready for you."

I'd thought my Golden Hind the master of taunting my beast—and the Hydra knew how to inflame me for personal gain. However, I feared it was my mate who was truly going to be the death of me.

I'm surrounded by devils.

Despite the power shift happening at the other end of the couch, Leia wasn't trying to dominate *me*. She simply continued to coat Krysos' cock in her slickness, raising and lowering herself as she peeked at me through long lashes— wordlessly begging me to take control of both of them.

With pleasure.

I set aside my *kylix* and crawled along the couch, feeling my lion ripple over my skin as I stalked my prey. Leia sharply inhaled, her human instinct for flight still strong, despite knowing she was safe with us. In contrast, Krysos defiantly lifted his chin, knowing I loved the chase most of all.

Upon reaching them, I hungrily took in the sight of my mate, bared and ready for me, shaking with need. I gently cupped her breast, lowering my head to teasingly nip the sensitive skin. She moaned as I laved her nipple with my lion's tongue, the hint of pain from the barbs causing her arousal to perfume the air.

"Ambrose," Krysos impatiently gritted out, as if to hurry me along.

Anger flared in my gut at his insolence. Yes, the original rift between Krysos and I was entirely my fault, but *he* was the one who refused to make amends. The hind acted as if he were mortally wounded by my actions, but I was the one continuing to pay the price. A single night of misspoken words had resulted in close to a century of me being deprived of the only creature on this island who'd made me feel whole.

Until now.

I gripped Leia's hips, holding her steady as I settled between her thighs, determined to deliver her first climax of the evening. She gasped as I began lapping at her folds, leaning back against Krysos to better angle her hips in offering, granting me full access to what was mine.

Good girl.

Krysos huffed, continuing to rub himself against her, probably hoping I'd lose my head and mindlessly include *him* in my efforts. With a snarl, I roughly shoved his cock aside, gripping him so tightly around the base that he yelped.

"You are not in control, Krysos," I growled up at him. "Despite what you may think, this cock still belongs to me. It will always belong to me. Leia may use you as she sees fit tonight, but you will not come until *I* say you can."

Leia anxiously whimpered, thrusting her needy cunt in my face until I gave her another long lick to settle her. Krysos was clenching his jaw, panting out more smoke, clearly warring with himself. His obsession with punishing me was all-consuming, but I knew he *needed* to submit—to be tamed by someone more dominating than him.

And I will bring him to heel.

I turned my attention back to Leia, nuzzling my face into her curls to better inhale her scent, bathing myself in it. Plunging my tongue into her cunt, I massaged her front wall, sliding my hand down until my thumb found her clit. She gasped as I circled the bundle of nerves, her hand falling to grip my hair, holding me tightly against her as if there was danger of me stopping.

Not until I'm dripping with you, Siren.

It didn't take long for her to cry out, soaking my face as she violently shuddered in Krysos' arms. I gently lapped her through the aftershocks, swallowing as much of her release as I could and marveling at how my body responded to it. When Eurystheus destroyed my cave, I thought I'd never feel the full power of my beast again. Leia somehow filled me with the same steady hum of completeness I used to feel every day as the Nemean Lion, and I realized just how precious she had already become to me.

My haven—my sanctuary.

My home.

After drinking my fill, I raised myself to my knees and curled my body around both of them, purring as I rubbed my cheek against Leia's. My lips brushed against Krysos' as I coated him in our combined scents, drawing a needy sound out of him that almost made me come.

"Ambrose…" he whined, his impending submission like music to my ears.

I squeezed harder with the hand still choking his cock, reminding him who his master was. Krysos released a ragged breath as he pressed his forehead to mine, his beautiful gray eyes shut tight.

"Please, " he begged, and I loosened my grip incrementally. "I need…"

Leia was panting between us, but she didn't intervene.

"Say it," I hissed, no longer interested in this dance that had gone on long enough. "You will say it or you get *nothing.*"

"I *need* to claim her," he sobbed, opening his eyes to desperately meet my gaze, finally ready to admit what I'd been aching to hear. "And I need *you* to reclaim me. Please..."

My lip curled in satisfaction.

It appears our mate won the wager after all.

25
LEIA

uck, YAS.

If I wasn't sandwiched between the rock-hard muscles of two incredibly tense hotties, I would have taken a bow. As it was, I could barely move, so an internal high-five in my honor would have to do.

Look at me, taking one for the team!

Despite Ambrose having just wrung a mind-blowing orgasm out of me with his textured cat-tongue, my body was vibrating for more. I'd thought Krysos' begging meant we were all on our way to threesome-town, but the guys were still glaring at each other over my shoulder while I became wetter and wetter.

Maybe they just need a little more encouragement?

"Ambrose," I cooed, putting on my best pout for Daddy. "Can Krysos claim me now, *please?* I'm ready..."

As expected, my big scary kitty immediately softened for me. "Of course, Leia," he replied, sweetly kissing me before releasing Krysos' dick and backing off from their angry boner standoff. "I'll gladly watch you ride him, but he's not allowed to come until you do. Twice more."

"Fuck," Krysos grumbled, as I spun my body to face him. "Try not to take all of me, or I won't last long."

I dropped my gaze to where his deer dong towered between us, shimmering in a gold that matched his antlers. My boy was worrying unnecessarily, as it was several inches longer than any cock I'd encountered before—from either man, monster, or toy box. There was no way in hell I was fitting his entire length inside me.

Not unless I want a nosebleed.

Forcing myself to focus on the task at hand, I lined myself up and began lowering my hips, holding onto his broad shoulders to control my descent. The instant he entered me, Krysos groaned, slapping his hands to my ass and squeezing so tightly I squeaked.

The casual-yet-obsessive way these men constantly touched me—grabbed handfuls of me—was a gift I didn't know I needed. I didn't require their validation to accept how I looked, but feeling like they were physically unable to resist my luscious bod sure as shit boosted my self-esteem.

A girl could definitely get used to this.

To be honest, I couldn't get enough of them either. Even knowing what beasts lurked beneath their skin, I felt weirdly safe with them—when they weren't unaliving me with orgasms. Besides how emotionally obsessive they were, their unique equipment made me wonder if I could ever be satisfied with boring humans again. Ambrose stretched me to my limit with his thickness—even before the barbs came into play—and Timyn's glorious ridges and lock still gave me pussy flutters to think about.

Never mind his nine tongues.

Krysos warned me he would become just as possessive as the others after 'claiming' me as his mate. The idea should have made me nervous, but I found myself eager to make it official—which didn't match my original plan of no-strings fucking.

Let's make that another problem for Future Leia to worry about.

Needing to touch more of him, I lightly caressed the velvety surface of Krysos' antlers with my fingers, hiding my smirk when he desperately moaned at the contact. This emboldened me to fully take the reins. Grabbing onto his antlers, I eased myself further down his impressive length, knowing I needed to be careful, despite the way my body was aching for him.

"Your cunt is addicting, Fawn," Krysos rasped, nuzzling against my chest. "I don't know how I can be expected to control myself, now that I'm inside you."

"You *will* control yourself," Ambrose's voice rumbled from the other end of the couch, reminding me who was really directing the action. "Your only purpose right now is to please our mate."

Krysos growled, but obediently slid his hands under my thighs to lend support, even as he battled his own instincts. There was something so incredibly *hot* about Ambrose commanding him for me—that they both agreed *my* pleasure was the number one priority.

"How does he feel, Siren?" Ambrose's breath tickled my ear, his sudden proximity making me shiver.

"So fucking good," I sighed, closing my eyes and tilting my head back so Ambrose could kiss me. As usual, he fully captured my mouth—his hot tongue sliding in as if he were devouring me, nipping my lips as I slowly rode the man beneath me.

A sharp lick of pain had me tearing my mouth away from Ambrose's, gasping in shock. Krysos was teasing my nipples with controlled puffs of flame before soothing away the hurt with his tongue. For a moment, I could only stare. That *fire* was turning me on, rather than terrifying me, only proved my libido had officially taken over for my brain.

"Do you want to come on my cock, Leia?" The hind smiled wickedly. "Is that what you want?"

"I want..." I stuttered, not knowing how I was expected to survive the sensations coursing through my body. "I want to come, and then I really, *really* want to watch Ambrose fuck you. I hope that's okay, I just—" my breath caught as Krysos angled his hips, forcing his cock to rub against my g-spot with every measured thrust.

"Of course, it's okay," he chuckled, licking his way up my neck and along my jaw, torturing me with every snap of his hips. Pulling back, he cocked his head, as if listening to something, before a smirk spread across his face. "I wish you could hear Timyn and Julius right now. Our Hydra won't be able to sit down tomorrow."

As if that delicious visual wasn't enough, Ambrose pressed his broad chest against my back and sank the tips of his fangs into my neck, sending me over the edge.

Oh, fuuuuuck!

I cried out as my orgasm ripped through me, shuddering uncontrollably, and all but collapsing in Krysos' arms afterward. For reasons I couldn't explain, I suddenly felt simultaneously cared for and deeply destroyed—inextricably connected to these men, even though I still barely knew them. Much to my horror, this strange cocktail of emotions caused a ragged sob to escape me, loudly echoing around the quiet room. "Sorry," I muttered, beyond embarrassed. "It's just..."

Why can't I get my shit together?

"It's because you feel it too," Krysos softly kissed my shoulder before moving his mouth to where Ambrose had bitten me, softly licking the wound. When I lifted my head to stare down at him in confusion, he shrugged, uncharacteristically unsure. "At least, I *hope* you do. You're our mate, which means we're your mates too, even if you don't fully understand what that means yet. How it means everything."

Before I could melt into a blubbery puddle at his words, Ambrose was wrapping me up in a soft blanket before lifting me off Krysos' lap and depositing me at the other end of the couch. "Don't worry about that now, Leia," he murmured, nipping my bottom lip, demanding I stay focused on the action. "Now tell me, how shall I fuck our hind for you?"

That'll do it!

My gaze darted between the two men, excited and nervous to be put in charge. As my heart rate settled, I realized Ambrose wasn't simply talking dirty. He *needed* me to take control—they both did—so that neither would have to get their hearts involved.

Not on my watch, dudes.

Kicking the blankets off my overheated body, I spread my legs, shamelessly abusing my pussy power. "I want you to fuck him so hard you forget your human names." I licked my lips, noticing how they both tracked the hand I'd dropped over my clit. "But mostly, I want you to fuck him in the way you both *need* it to happen."

Ambrose narrowed his eyes at me, but didn't argue before grabbing Krysos by the antler and roughly tossing him to the floor. I gasped and sat up, but Ambrose had already pounced, covering the other man's body with his much larger one and plunging his cock into Krysos' ass with no warning.

Or lube...

The hind shouted, but I glimpsed pure pleasure in his expression before Ambrose shoved his beautiful face down onto the hardwood floor. "That was for putting Timyn's cock in your mouth in front of me." Another violent thrust. "And this is for denying me what's mine—what belongs to *me.*"

"Fuck!" Krysos twisted his head to the side, gasping for air. "Forgive me."

Tension vibrated over Ambrose's muscular form as he buried his cock deep inside Krysos and held himself there. *"You* belong to me," he hissed in the other man's ear, gripping his blond hair so tightly his knuckles turned white. "Say it."

"I belong to you," Krysos choked out, his hands scrambling for purchase on the floor. "Only you."

"Wrong," Ambrose barked, although he loosened his grip and began to move, setting a punishing rhythm. "You also belong to Leia. From now on, you can play the brat out there as much as you want, but in the bedroom, you exist only for *our* pleasure. Do you understand?"

I was rapt with attention, my pussy pulsing in time with every slap of Ambrose's hips against Krysos' ass. In fact, I was so worked up, I could probably come just from watching these two together.

Ambrose delivered another cruel thrust, clearly displeased at being kept waiting. "I understand!" Krysos yelped. "Yes!"

"Yes, *what?*" Ambrose growled, curling his body so his elongated fangs hovered directly over the hind's neck, telling me exactly what was coming next.

"Yes, *Master,*" Krysos sobbed, just as Ambrose pierced his skin, clamping down and drawing a howl out of the other man that I felt in my core. In fact, my core felt it so strongly, another surprise orgasm thundered in, with liquid spraying out of me to soak the floor in front of the action.

Oh my gawd, whyyyyy?!

My cheeks heated as both men momentarily froze, staring at the soggy evidence while I died inside.

"What a lucky little hind," Ambrose chuckled low, yanking Krysos up to all fours. "That's two for our mate. Now lick it up."

I gaped as Ambrose shoved Krysos' face into the puddle, my jaw dropping even further when the hind moaned and eagerly set to work cleaning up my mess.

And now, I identify as a hardwood floor in an oddly Gothic palace.

Once he finished, Ambrose began jackhammering into Krysos again, showing no mercy. Unable to stay away, I slid off the couch and crawled closer, until I was kneeling beside them, my gaze glued on Krysos' bouncing golden dick, temptingly dripping with precum. Sensing what I wanted, Ambrose immediately sat back on his heels and hauled the other man into his lap. He held him in place with one clawed hand on his throat and the other restraining his wrists behind his back—offering Krysos' cock to me like a tasty gift.

Don't mind if I do.

"Oh, fuck," Krysos croaked, as I bent my head and lightly licked the v under his crown, making him twitch.

"Our plaything is allowed to come now, right?" I cooed, circling his girth with both hands to hold him steady.

Ambrose hummed in agreement, and I swallowed him down, noticing my lion snapping his hips just enough to set the rhythm without choking me. I could only take about half Krysos' length, but it wasn't long before he was help-lessly grunting, thrusting into my mouth like he hadn't been allowed to with my pussy. He groaned like he was in pain, and the taste of his cum shooting down my throat a moment later made my basement flood all over again.

As soon as I moved out of the way, Ambrose withdrew and unceremoniously tossed a still-shuddering Krysos to the floor. Flipping him onto his back, Ambrose held him down by the throat before stroking himself to finish all over the other man's face.

Stick a fork in me, I'm done.

"Mine," Ambrose repeated, although his voice was softer, almost inaudible beneath the adorably contented purring. Then—because my pussy hadn't clenched enough for one night—he lowered his head and began gently lapping up his own cum.

"Yours," Krysos replied, eyes closing as he sighed happily. "Always."

Deciding I needed to lie down, I retreated to my snuggly blanket on the couch, giving my men the space they needed to reconnect while I drifted off to sleep.

26

LEIA

Waking up glued to monsters was nothing new, but opening my eyes to Krysos' sleeping face inches away from mine would never get old.

He really is so fucking pretty...

"Oh good, you're awake," Timyn's smiling face—complete with razor-sharp teeth—suddenly appeared over the hind's shoulder.

"Shit!" I hissed, clutching my chest to calm my racing heart. "How could you even tell?"

He cocked his head, staring at me with reptilian pupils for a good ten seconds before he finally blinked. "I was listening to you breathe, and your breathing changed."

That's not super creepy or anything.

"However," he continued, trailing a finger down Krysos' bare arm and getting sleepily batted away. "Word around the campfire is this morsel's off the menu again—thanks to *your* skillful meddling. I figured I'd steal some cuddles while his owner's away."

I snorted and sat up, helping myself to a cup of water on the bedside table, no doubt thoughtfully left there by the owner in question. "Where *is* Ambrose?" I looked around the spacious bedroom that *someone* had carried me to last night. The decor had a distinct Tudor flavor to it, with dark wood, tufted velvet furnishings, and a massive canopy bed big enough for multiple monsters. I half expected Henry VIII to prance in and demand a beheading.

Or just plain ol' head, knowing this crew.

Spotting a pile of clothing thrown over a chaise, I rose and helped myself to a white, goddess-cut dress that was a less see-through version of my ruined nightgown and some boots that were two sizes too big. Yanking the dress over my head, I hurriedly finger-brushed my hair, wondering *who* was tasked with dressing-the-human this time. All my beauty supplies were lost at sea, but I actually preferred my less complicated daily regime. The only items I truly missed were my Ancient Olive products, and for that, I could always dip into Ambrose's olive oil stash if need be.

Assuming we don't use it all for... cooking.

"Ambrose is with Julius, planning a war," Timyn finally replied, sliding off the bed to stand and languidly stretch. "In the war room."

I gaped at him for a second before annoyance coursed through me. "Why the fuck didn't they wait for the rest of us?" I huffed. "The whole reason we climbed this mountain was to discuss what to do about Eurystheus. I'm as ready as the rest of you to kick his ass."

Timyn grimaced, probably sensing he was in danger. "Well... I was involved in the discussion until they told me to ask if the hind wanted to join."

"No," Krysos curtly snipped before rolling onto his stomach and ignoring us once again.

Timyn cleared his throat and glanced at me warily. "But

they said nothing about you..." he trailed off, looking mighty scared for a 50-foot lake monster.

Why do men?

"Take me to the war room," I gritted out, in no mood to be excluded because I owned a vagina. I'd suffered through countless meetings at Auracle, where every woman who wasn't considered fuckable was talked over like she didn't exist. I had no intention of letting that nonsense be the norm here.

"Please don't be mad, Water Lily," Timyn begged, draping his arm over my shoulder and guiding me out the door. "We're just not used to women being around, and the ones we've encountered in the past have been, well, *helpless.*"

I took several deep breaths before deciding *not* to lecture the Hydra on the misconceptions of a patriarchal society. My monsters may be over-protective, but they'd also shown a willingness to learn, so the best thing would be to *show* them how capable I was.

Plus, Timyn appeared to be walking with a limp, which earned him some sympathy.

"Rough night?" I smirked as he steered me down a dank, torch-lit hallway that seemed to burrow deeper into the mountain.

He sighed dreamily. "Mmm, yessss... so deliciously painful." A beat of silence followed before he thoughtfully added, "We don't feel pain in our true forms, Leia—at least, not how humans do. When Heracles 'defeated' me, I was simply sent into a temporary sleep while I regenerated for the next hero. A hero who never came."

Understanding washed over me. "Ohhh, so *that's* how you guys knew this wasn't the underworld—and that I wasn't dead. *You* can't die!"

Timyn nodded, pressing his lips into a grim line. "Not in our true forms, no, but I assume we could like this. We certainly can be injured, as you've seen with Julius and his sexy missing eyeball."

I barked a laugh that echoed off the stone walls. "Please tell me you've told him how sexy his empty eye socket is."

My Hydra rewarded me with a toothy smile. "As if there were any doubt! Although," he eyed me shrewdly. "Our *bore* might appreciate the compliment more coming from you... in bed, that is."

"Timyn!" I playfully shoved him away. "You know that grump hates me. But seriously, I already have *three* of you—that's enough for me to handle, trust."

Timyn stopped walking and grabbed my shoulders, forcing me to face him for an odd moment of seriousness. "There are *twelve* of us, Herculeia." He swept an assessing gaze down my body. "You should... *prepare* yourself."

TWELVE?!

Before I could reply, he dramatically kicked open the wooden door to my right and dragged me inside. I immediately knew this was the 'war room,' as the walls were covered with ancient armor and weaponry. Plus, a battle-worn, extremely sour man was standing next to a roaring fire, glaring at me with his good eye.

"Timyn, are you *trying* to anger me?" Julius shifted his judgmental gaze to the Hydra.

"Maaaaaybe," Timyn mischievously replied, plopping down in an ornate wooden chair and gesturing for me to take the next one over. "Krysos wasn't interested, per usual, but Leia insisted on joining us. Frankly, I was terrified to say no."

The ghost of a smile twitched under Julius' beard, but

he quickly buried the hint of humor. "Fine," he growled, still only addressing Timyn. "She is permitted to *observe*."

Oh, take several seats!

"Julius!" Ambrose's scolding tone rang out as he appeared in the doorway with a tray of food. Setting it on the table in front of us, he poured me a cup of water before bending down to rub his cheek against mine. "Don't allow him to bully you, Siren," he whispered in my ear. "Speak plainly, as you are entitled to do."

As if his verbal support wasn't enough to make me teary, he then brushed his fingertips over my wrist tattoo. Ambrose had no way of knowing the numbers inked there were the date my dad died, but his touch reminded me I'd once had someone who was *always* in my corner.

I have a right to be here.

"I'll be doing more than *observing* these discussions," I raised my voice, careful to keep my tone steady. "Since I'm the one who recently interacted with Eurystheus and made it through the fog." I was sweating on the inside when Julius finally shifted his gaze to me again, but he simply nodded once in reply.

"Well done," Ambrose nipped my earlobe before backing off to sit next to me. Thanks to my recently unlocked praise kink, his words caused wetness to immediately blossom between my thighs—which Timyn drew attention to with a deeply satisfied inhale.

Talk about putting a damper on my Boss Bitch vibes.

Julius pushed away from the mantle and stalked to a seat of his own. While I gathered my thoughts, I noticed the chairs—all *twelve* of them—were arranged around the table in a circle, which was unexpectedly diplomatic. I'd assumed Julius was the leader here, but as he was still waiting for me to speak, it seemed all opinions were given airtime here.

"Ok," I faltered, unaccustomed to such undivided attention during a meeting. "I'm going to assume the others have filled you in on how I got here... the shipwreck and the *obol* from Eurystheus." Ambrose nodded in confirmation, so I continued, "But what I haven't told any of you is that I keep finding coins at every location we've stopped so far."

Although I was trying to come clean, I still didn't share how Pornstar Centaur gave me a bottle of poison with the last *obol*. I felt bad, but I still didn't know what to make of the warning—and poetic-sounding prophecy—Nessus included with his chilling gift.

"Interesting," Julius stroked his metalhead beard, narrowing his gaze at me in a way I did not like the look of one bit. "It's almost as if Eurystheus is leaving *payment* for you as his accomplice. Are you sure you're telling us everything you know?"

"Listen, jackhole," I leaped to my feet, which annoyingly didn't make me any taller than he was still seated. "Eurystheus might be using me, but it's without my knowledge or consent. And since none of you have bothered to tell me the whole story of *why* you ended up here, I'm still in the fucking dark about how to help figure this out. So don't you dare come for *me* about sharing information— not unless you're about to start talking yourselves."

The streets have been unleashed, motherfucker!

Julius' eyes widened in shock before pure fury clouded his expression. "You will not come into *my* house and speak to me in such a manner, girl. Who *raised* you?"

Oh no, he didn't.

I dug my nails into my tattooed wrist so hard I bled, even as I held his gaze. "A better man than you," was all I said, before I strode from the room with my head held high.

27

JULIUS

"*Must* you be so unpleasant to our mate, Julius?"

I openly rolled my eyes at Ambrose's inane question. All three idiots had been babbling non-stop about this *human* being their mate, and I'd had enough. We were legendary beasts, created by the gods themselves. We weren't supposed to mate with humans, much less have mates at all.

By Ares, most of us are the only one of our kind!

"You better not have scared my Water Lily away," Timyn pouted, like the brat he was. "She's already promised to make dragon babies with me."

"You're not a fucking dragon!" I shouted, staunchly ignoring the random twinge in my gut at the thought of Leia, round with child.

"Well, *she* thinks I am," he sniffed, haughtily turning his attention back to his wine. "And Leia finds dragons sexy."

Thoroughly exasperated, I reached for the *amphora* to pour myself another cup, questioning why I hadn't locked the door yesterday when this rabble showed up. The opportunity to bring Eurystheus to his knees had been too tempting to resist, of course, and I'd have been a fool not to recognize this human's role in achieving that.

However, we still needed to plan our next moves strategically, and not be distracted by temporary trysts. There was absolutely no reason for me to humor the current conversation, or to care if one of these bastards impregnated a random human who'd washed ashore.

Especially one as unpleasant as her.

"Leia has every right to be angry," Ambrose murmured, somehow able to read my thoughts *and* ignore the delusional Hydra. "None of us have told her everything we know about why we're here." He sighed before looking at me with such a desperate expression, I already knew I'd do whatever it took to wipe it off his face. "Could *you* please go find her and try to explain what little we know?"

"Me?!" I scoffed, almost dropping my *kylix* in astonishment. "You honestly think that girl wants to see *my* ugly face right now?"

"She thinks your missing eye is sexy too," Timyn smirked across the table.

Before I could respond to *that* ridiculous statement, Ambrose continued. "You hurt her, Julius—a *woman* we all deeply care about. Someone you could care for too if you stopped behaving like a *kataratos* swine."

My beast bristled at the grave insult, but logically, I knew my friend was simply ensuring his point was made. Swallowing the rest of my wine, I slammed my *kylix* down on the table and sighed heavily.

"Fine, I'll track her down," I snarled. "Mostly because I don't need her sniffing around my fortress, unattended."

Ambrose's lip twitched. "As if you haven't already been... *tracking* her."

Timyn snorted, and I shot the Hydra a withering glare

before trudging from the room. Yes, my sense of smell was unmatched, but I wouldn't waste my talent on inhaling the rancid funk of some watery tart who...

Ah, fuck.

The instant I stepped into the hallway, I knew exactly where Leia had run off to, as every inch of my *home* was polluted with her tantalizingly earthy musk. Her scent had been clouding my brain ever since she'd arrived, contributing to my foul mood. Incredibly annoyed, I stomped toward my private study, wondering why in Zeus' name she'd wandered there, of all places.

Why couldn't one of them simply chain her up, like any other pet?

A girl—a *woman*—was the last thing we needed right now. If a human had to wash ashore, a man would have been more useful, and nicer to look at. Leia was all curves and soft flesh, nothing like what an ideal specimen should be. There was barely any muscle definition covering her fragile bones, so how exactly she could help...

WHY DOES SHE SMELL SO FUCKING GOOD?!

Suppressing a groan, I flung open the door of my study to find Leia sitting at my desk, calmly rifling through the drawers like she was the lady of the manor.

"What exactly are you doing?" I growled, looming over her for maximum intimidation. She smelled like godsdamn *truffles*, which made it extremely difficult to remain angry when all I wanted to do was drop to my knees and lick her.

"Pissing you off with my existence, obviously," she sweetly replied, not even sparing me a glance as she opened another drawer and stuck her filthy paws inside.

Deep breaths, Julius...

Fuck, I'm unable to take deep breaths right now!

Remembering I was supposed to be *nice*, I gritted my

teeth and tried again, softening my tone. "Are you looking for something in particular?"

That got her attention. Leia paused, suspiciously glaring up at me in a way that was infuriatingly alluring. "I'm looking for any proof that you're not a bunch of psychopaths planning on roasting me over the fire when you're done with me."

I laughed despite myself, begrudgingly amused by her spirit. "Silly human," I smiled, allowing my curved tusks to elongate until they scraped against my cheekbones. "We don't cook our meat before eating it."

She arched a brow at the sight, but didn't flinch. "Well, that's a handy party trick. Paired with the..." she gestured toward her eye. "It's a good look on you."

"Yes," my smirk grew larger. "Timyn told me you find this..." I pointed at my empty eye socket. *"Sexy."*

"What?!" she shrieked, abruptly standing. She stomped across the room, her tiny hands balled into useless fists as she continued to rant. "I never said... *ooooh,* that naughty Hydra needs a good spanking!"

To my horror, the mental image of Timyn on the receiving end of Leia's palm had my cock twitching beneath my robes. I was suddenly grateful the others insisted we all wear some sort of clothing while she was around—to be less barbaric, apparently.

Pretending to be human is so tedious.

"The letters..." she mused, turning to face me again, done with her latest hysterics. "I recognized your dark blue stationery over there. The pile of unopened letters on Ambrose's desk must have been from you."

Sighing, I sank into one of the velvet tufted chairs in front of the fireplace, motioning that she should take the other. "Yes, that's correct, and I'm not surprised he stopped opening them. In his prime, Ambrose was as fierce an opponent as I'd ever seen, but something *broke* inside of him the day his cave was destroyed by Eurystheus—something vital. Even those of us still connected to our sources of power choose to remain in our human forms most of the time, to conserve energy for if we're attacked. Ambrose has been stuck for centuries... until you came along, that is." I shrewdly observed her reaction to my statement, but her furrowed brow relayed nothing but confusion.

She doesn't know about the effect she has?

Deciding to leave *that* subject for another day, I refocused on my assignment. "While it was troubling to witness how easily Ambrose gave up the fight, I admittedly can't imagine how it would feel to have something like that taken from me—to feel so incomplete. The loss must have been almost unbearable."

Leia nodded, swallowing hard as she stared into the empty fireplace, oddly quiet. "I understand, in a way," she finally replied, before clearing her throat. "Eurystheus also took something from you—"

I laughed bitterly. "It's just an eye, Leia, although it was a novel experience to be injured at all. What angered me more was the coward sending someone else to do the deed. Eurystheus heard of our plan to demand an audience with the gods—to convince them to reverse their decree. Ambrose disarmed the assassin before they could finish me, and his home was destroyed because of it. By the time we licked our wounds and regrouped, our one chance for arranging that audience had mysteriously... disappeared."

Leia was staring down at her lap, her delicate fingers trailing over a set of fresh scratches on her wrist. My nostrils flared when I realized she'd injured herself, feeling irrationally compelled to lick her wounds.

Sorceress!

"I know you're not happy about sharing information with me," she rasped, meeting my gaze again with fierce determination in her expression. "And I get it, because I don't trust easily either. But you *have* to tell me why you're here. Please. Why did the gods decide you all needed to be banished to this island? I... I *need* to know why I feel like this..."

She was clutching her stomach now, as if it were physically painful for her questions to go unanswered. Hera knew why, but I was suddenly desperate to earn her trust— to tell her everything she wanted to know. Exhaling slowly, I harshly reminded myself that Leia's allegiances were still unknown, despite her claims of Eurystheus being her enemy.

A pawn doesn't always know the end game.

"Why do you care?" I growled, disregarding my promise to Ambrose to play nice. "So you can figure out how to abandon my idiotically smitten friends and return to your human world with no regard for the destruction you'll leave behind?" To my disgust, I found I didn't relish the idea as much as I thought I would.

"No," she vehemently shook her head, leaning forward to grip my forearm. Her touch sent a jolt of energy through me that made my hair stand on end and my stomach sink. "I want to help you get your revenge and then escape along with me."

28

LEIA

Julius may have reacted to my heroic declaration with pure shock, but I was equally surprised. Sure, I'd been casually enjoying my monster dong buffet while waiting to see if they could help get me off this rock, but now the thought of abandoning them made me stabby.

And Eurystheus is a stab-worthy target.

"Wh... what exactly would *you* be able to accomplish?" Julius sputtered. "You're only a—"

"Don't you *dare* say I'm only a *woman!*" I growled, leaning further into his personal space to give him a firm jab in the chest.

"I was going to say *human,*" Julius scrunched his nose in disgust before clearing his throat. "Let's continue this discussion outside. I... need some air." Abruptly standing, he grabbed a random fur draped over the arm of his chair and tossed it at my face before racing from the room, looking like he was struggling to breathe.

Do I stink or something?

Discreetly sniffing my pits as I slung the fur over my

shoulders, I hurried after him, determined to get answers, once and for all. Instead of heading toward the front entrance, Julius led me down a darkened hallway ending at a worn wooden door. Flinging it open, he revealed a court-yard walled in by sheer cliffs on three sides, with a thick evergreen forest at the far end.

He took a deep inhale of brisk air before turning to face me. "Very well, Leia. I will take you at your word that you wish to help, but if you betray us, I will gut you myself." Julius paused to literally stink-eye me. Singular. "Now, you wanted to know *why* we were banished here?"

"Was it for casually threatening to gut someone?" I sweetly cooed, feeling a thrill of satisfaction when his lips twitched under his bushy beard. Obviously wanting to hide the fact he found me hilarious, Julius spun on his heel and began striding across the courtyard, leaving me to race after him.

"Disemboweling so-called heroes was what we were created to do, by the most murderous beings of us all. The gods," he scoffed. "The scandalous truth is that we were exiled here because we were no longer 'needed,' and since we can't be killed in our true forms..." Julius broadly gestured to the towering stone surrounding us. "We were penned up like animals instead, forsaken and forgotten."

I frowned. "But where does Eurystheus fit into this? I thought he was just some creepy dude I crossed paths with, not someone with the power to magically send you all here. But if he's the same Eurystheus from legend, then he was the king who assigned Heracles his Twelve Labors..."

"There are twelve of us, Herculeia."

I trailed off, my mouth going dry as I realized my ending up on the island might not have been an accident. If Eurys-

theus somehow masterminded an island prison for mythological creatures, then it was possible he was smart enough
to figure out who I was, despite my attempts to fool him
with false information.

Your full name was on the cruise tickets, dumbass.

Something told me he knew my name prior to
purchasing my spare ticket. It was probably also safe to
assume every one of our encounters was premeditated—
starting when he met me at the airport and ending with
him throwing me overboard. Julius' suspicions that I was
sent here to harm them didn't seem so far-fetched now,
although I still didn't know how anyone expected *me* to
defeat a pack of invincible monsters.

I'm just a girl from New York City who loves cupcakes!

Oblivious to my impending panic attack and butter-
cream frosting withdrawal, Julius solemnly nodded.
"Eurystheus was merely a human in his time, and an unimpressive one at that. Yet he earned immortality through the
favor of the gods. He convinced Olympus that our existence
reflected unfavorably on them—that if we continued to
fulfill the purpose *they* had originally given us, their reputations would suffer."

*"The only trends I follow are those directly related to the
reputations of my clients."*

I'd ignored Eurystheus' comment when we'd first met,
brushing it off as silly small talk. Now I realized he'd been
speaking the language of public relations and damage
control—a language I spoke fluently, thanks to my years at
Auracle. If his clients were *the gods,* of course he'd want to
keep them happy. Otherwise, they'd probably smite his
ass.

We need to fight fire with fire.

"What you guys have here is an image problem," I

seamlessly transitioned into account manager mode, excited to flex my skills and actually help. "If you want the gods to consider an appeal to your sentence, you need to first revamp your brand."

Julius stopped walking so fast I stumbled into him. "What the fuck are you talking about?" he snapped.

I sighed. "Listen, you're literally monsters of... various kinds," I pointed at his prominent tusks, still unsure *what* he was, but oddly intrigued. "It probably didn't take much for Eurystheus to *de*humanize you with a nasty smear campaign. I say we counter with some positive press of our own—to show Olympus you're not dangerous threats needing to be penned up."

Now he was looking at me like I had nine heads. "But we *are* dangerous, Leia."

"That's not the point!" I threw my hands in the air. "We just need to prove you can be tamed. Look how the guys are with me. Ambrose is a big purring kitty cat, Timyn is a 50-foot golden retriever, and Krysos is just a sweet li'l cinnamon roll. *You* try to act like a big grumpy bear, but I bet you like to cuddle."

Julius grimaced. "I'm afraid you've misunderstood..."

I huffed in exasperation. Planting my hands on my hips, I prepared to educate this dense pile of man-muscle, when a voice I knew well roared across the courtyard.

"Step away from my mate, Erymanthian! She is fertile and I mean to fill her with my seed!"

Krysos?

"As if on cue," Julius muttered, sighing as he turned to face his opponent.

I followed his gaze to find my sweet cinnamon roll looking more like an angry sourdough bun swinging a very long baguette. Krysos was glaring daggers at Julius across the courtyard, his true form flickering over his naked body as he angrily paced. The velvet on his antlers was hanging off in bloody strips, but when I took a step in the hind's direction, Julius roughly grabbed my arm.

"You need to *run,* foolish girl," he snarled, shoving me behind him as plumes of smoke began seeping out of Krysos' nostrils, puffing in time with his animalistic grunts.

"I'm not gonna run from my... from *him!*" I hissed, unable to stop my gaze from landing on Julius' toned ass, when he dropped his robes.

Julius kept his gaze locked on Krysos as he replied. "But you should run from me."

An icy chill that had nothing to do with our altitude filled my veins as my survival instincts finally kicked in. I hurriedly backed away as Julius' body contorted and shifted, just like Ambrose in the vineyard. This time, instead of an armored lion, an enormous wild boar appeared before me, scraping the flagstones with his hooves as he bristled, readying to attack.

Well, that explains the tusks.

Krysos burst into the full glory of his Golden Hind just as I turned tail and raced for the tree line. The ground shook as the two behemoths slammed into each other—the clash of antlers and tusks mixing with roars of fury and pain. It physically *hurt* to leave them behind, but I didn't slow down until I was deep inside the dark recesses of the forest. Only when the sounds of battle had grown faint did I finally stop, collapsing against the trunk of an ancient evergreen as I caught my breath.

This PR campaign is going to be trickier than I thought...

I closed my eyes, allowing the silence of the surrounding forest to calm my racing heart. A twig snapped beside me the instant I realized the woods were a little too quiet.

"There you are, little wanderer," a familiar voice made my blood turn to ice in my veins. "It's time for us to have a chat."

29
LEIA

"*Get the fuck away fromph...*" I started to yell, before a large hand slapped itself over my mouth, successfully cutting off my words.

Something sharp pressed into my ribs as Eurystheus tutted scoldingly. "Now, now, we've come so far together already. It would be a shame for me to have to start over with another expendable human. Especially when you're just so perfect, *Herculeia*."

Well, that confirms he knew my name.

Eurystheus stepped into my line of vision, somehow looking immaculately dressed in his suit, despite being at the top of a remote mountain on a mystical island. I glared at him, annoyed that the creeper got the drop on me, even though he probably materialized out of thin air with his gods-granted powers.

Yet he's threatening me with a regular ol' knife...

Realizing he couldn't kill me with the snap of his fingers made me relax somewhat. Eurystheus removed his hand from my mouth—even as he gave me a look that told me to behave. Mostly, I obeyed because I didn't want his grubby hand on my face again. I also assumed he would 1000% stab me and start over if need be. He may see me as expendable, but he'd gone through the trouble of getting me onto this island, so I needed to convince him he'd made the right investment.

Plus, he seems like the type to launch into an evil villain monologue, if prompted...

"I don't know why I'm here," I stuck a waver in my tone, shooting a fearful glance back the way I came for dramatic effect. "And I really want to go home. Just tell me what you want me to do, and I'll do it. I... I need to get away from them."

He stared at me like he was looking into my soul, but I held his gaze like a pro. I even threw in a pathetic sniffle to sell it better, hoping my PR pitch to Julius had been far enough away from the woods to stay private. At the thought of my guys back there, possibly trampling each other to death, my breath genuinely caught. That reaction was apparently enough to convince Eurystheus to talk.

"This is the deal, Herculeia," he coldly replied, finally moving his knife away from my kidneys. "You are to continue doing exactly what you've been doing—getting close to the twelve. While you don't need to *fuck* these animals, it appears to be helping them grow more attached to you." He gave me a judgy once-over, as if what I did with my body was any of his business. "So, carry on." Another judgmental sniff before he narrowed his eyes at something rustling in the bushes.

I frowned. "Why does it matter if they get close to me? What are you... *we* trying to achieve?"

A slender woman suddenly appeared from the dense undergrowth, her slate and moss-toned skin and hair resembling camouflage beneath the thick canopy. Eurys-

theus didn't seem at all surprised by her random appearance, and continued the conversation as if a naked nymph
wasn't standing next to him.

"Why, little wanderer," he scoffed at my question.
"We're trying to *kill* them."

"Kill them," the woman repeated, startling me with her
ominous input.

"Okay..." There was no faking the waver in my voice this
time. The thought of anyone hurting my men made my
anxiety skyrocket as that uncontrollable rage threatened to
surface again. "How do you expect me to help?"

"Help," the woman whispered, and something in her
tone had me snapping my attention to her face again. She
was standing where Eurystheus couldn't see her face,
including the pleading look in her eye.

Is she being held against her will?

Again, Eurystheus didn't acknowledge her remarks,
although his jaw ticked the slightest bit, betraying his
annoyance. "As I said, you are to simply continue doing
what you're doing—weakening them with your presence.
Carry on with fucking your monsters."

"Your monsters," the woman gasped, almost like the
words hurt, and Eurystheus finally spun to face her.

"Is there a reason you're here, Echo?" he snapped. "We
have nothing further to discuss. You failed in *your* mission
and, therefore, lost your chance to leave this island. Go back
to whatever hole you crawled out of, and be thankful I'm
not sending you to Hades, where you belong."

"Where... belong," she choked out, sinking to the
ground in a sobbing heap, and I realized she was Echo. This
legendary mountain nymph was cursed by Hera to repeat
the words of others, as a punishment for trying to distract
the goddess from one of Zeus' many affairs.

Guess she never heard about 'sisters before misters.'

"Speaking of *failure,* Herculeia," Eurystheus observed me with mild distaste, as if I were nothing but a rat that crawled out of the sewer for a slice. "If *you* fail, you will not only never leave this island, but I will kill you myself. Any further questions, *human?"*

What the FUCK?!

I was so stunned by his blatant threat, all I could do was gape in reply. There was absolutely no way I would willingly help him—especially to hurt my men. I would bet that even if I did what he wanted, he'd still dump me in the ocean instead of sending me home.

Deciding the conversation was over, Eurystheus shot us both withering glances as he spun on his heel and headed deeper into the forest. I saw him pull an object out of his pocket, and a single ray of sunlight caught on its metallic surface before he melted into the shadows completely.

This left me alone with the weeping Oread. "Hey," I crouched down and awkwardly patted her head, stifling a gasp to discover her hair was actually moss. "Um, I know you can't actually tell me much, but if I ask you some yes or no questions, can you at least nod or shake your head?" She raised her gaze to meet mine, nodding sorrowfully.

I considered my options. Eurystheus said she was no longer working with him, but the fact she had in the past automatically made her suspicious. Regardless, I needed to find out what Eurystheus had tasked her with, knowing how desperate she was to escape the island.

Was her assignment the same as mine?

With this unpleasant thought in my head, I hesitantly asked, "Echo, this mission Eurystheus gave you... did it involve getting close to the monsters here? The Nemean Lion, the Hydra, the Golden Hind or the..." My eyes widened as I realized who Julius was, living up here on Mount Erymanthos. "The Erymanthian Boar."

"The Erymanthian Boar," Echo *echoed,* as she nodded in confirmation.

All the betrayal from the Dylan-and-Jasmine situation came rushing to the surface. Tears clouded my vision and my guts twisted as I imagined this attractive, mossy babe in bed with *my* monsters. Echo had probably been commanded to weaken my men in the same way, but I refused to blame the other woman here. I'd only been on this island for a handful of days. I couldn't imagine the mental state of someone who'd been trapped here for centuries.

What anyone might agree to under those circumstances...

My men, however, were firmly on Team Not Eurystheus, with no illusions of escape. This meant no one had forced them to stick their dicks in a cursed, practically mute mountain nymph who had no other options.

"I think we've all fucked each other at this point."

My rational brain knew I had no right to be pissed off at my men for sleeping with someone else before me—especially as I'd already declared that fucking each other was fine. Unfortunately for them, I wasn't feeling very rational at the moment.

And I still haven't gotten to stab anyone.

Angrily swiping the back of my hand across my face to dry my tears, I stood and forced myself to calm down, determined not to show any weakness.

I was so fired up, I almost tripped over Echo, momentarily forgetting there was another traumatized woman present. "Uh... do you have somewhere to go? Would you like to come with me to Julius' fortress?"

Pure panic washed over her features. "Julius' fortress!"

she yelped, vehemently shaking her head as she scrambled to her feet, backing away from me.

Oh, shit.

My jumbled thoughts cleared with the chilling realization that my monsters may have done something very, *very* bad to this woman. It sounded eerily similar to what Krysos seemed about to do had Julius not stepped in.

"We are *dangerous, Leia..."*

The frightened Oread ran off before I could get more information out of her. My breath caught when I spotted another obol gleaming from beneath the leaf litter where she'd fallen, and I grimly grabbed the coin. Gathering the fur wrap around my shoulders, I slowly made my way back to the fortress, unsure if I was headed away from danger or toward it.

30
KRYSOS

I'd been a fool to think I could remain objective when it came to Leia. I thought I understood how the mate bond would affect me, but I barely remembered what happened in the courtyard. Her scent had clouded my reason, my vision turning red until all I registered was a rival male standing between me and what was mine.

It was lucky Julius was there to intervene, and his boar sparred with my hind long enough for Leia to escape into the forest.

To escape from *me.*

"Shouldn't one of us go after her?" Timyn was pacing the room, two of his Hydra heads towering over his human one, hissing at me every time he passed.

"Mmm, she hasn't gone far," Julius hummed from where he casually leaned near the open window, scenting the breeze. Unlike me, he seemed energized from our fight, looked only slightly worse for wear after our monstrous beasts clashed in the courtyard.

He probably needed the outlet...

Suddenly, he straightened and peered suspiciously

toward the forest. "There's someone else out there with her." Julius took a long inhale, his expression turning murderous. "Oread."

Ambrose growled beneath me, the threatening vibration doing little to settle my nerves. I whimpered, and he immediately turned his attention back to where I lay in his lap, his expression strained as he carefully removed pieces of tattered velvet from my antlers.

More evidence I'd lost control.

"Why would I behave that way?" I whispered, burying my face against him as much as my antlers allowed, incredibly ashamed of myself.

"It wasn't *you,* my heart," Ambrose soothed, causing tears to sting the corners of my eyes. While I was grateful that our rift had been mended—thanks to Leia—the thought of never sharing her again broke something deep inside of me.

"But it *was* me... and I have no excuse," I rasped. "It's not even the correct time of year for the rut. Everything was perfect last night, with the three of us together."

Ambrose sharply inhaled before muttering a curse. "It's not your fault, Krysos. It's mine. I didn't allow you to finish breeding her."

At the thought of filling Leia with my seed, my whimpering morphed into a snarl—my vision tunneling again until Ambrose gripped the back of my neck, instantly settling me.

What is happening to me?

"How fascinating that the mere *thought* of her calls to the hind," Julius nonchalantly chuckled. Suddenly, I wished I'd landed more blows before he'd subdued me earlier.

"The effect Leia has on *all* of us is inescapable, and you're next, Erymanthian," Ambrose retorted, ever ready to protect me. "Tell me—why did you feel the need to defend her, as your *boar,* no less? Perhaps you were also staking a claim on your mate?"

Julius' jaw ticked, but he ignored the accusation. "The girl is the key to taking down Eurystheus once and for all. Why would I allow Krysos to gore her to death—either with his antlers or his cock?"

I howled in despair. "He's right! I'm no better than an animal. She'll never let me near her again."

"Oh, I think she will." Timyn kneeled beside the couch, his Hydra heads retreating as his more human side took pity on me. "Our mate is a very forgiving little treat."

Julius snorted, moving away from the window to take a seat at his desk. "So you say. Your little treat is currently stomping across the courtyard, and she doesn't look in the forgiving mood. "

Four terrifying beasts tensed, holding our collective breath as we heard Leia stalk down the hallway in our direction. The instant she flung open the door, I threw myself onto the floor in supplication, praying she'd either forgive me for my mistake, or punish me.

"All right, boys, we all need to have a little cha...*holy shit, Krysos!* I almost stepped on you. Why the fuck are you on the floor?"

I deserve to be stepped on.

"Our Golden Hind is embarrassed because he behaved *exactly like the animal he is,*" Julius huffed. "However, perhaps everyone learned a lesson today. Seeing as you barely made it out of there unscathed, *now* do you understand how dangerous we are, silly girl?"

I apprehensively peeked up at Leia, waiting for her to agree—to tell us she rightfully deserved humans in her bed instead of monsters who only knew how to mindlessly rut.

Don't think about the rut... don't think about the...

To my surprise, she simply shrugged, although her nonchalance seemed unnatural. "Mmm, *I* can handle you maniacs, but it would be a different story if I wasn't given the choice."

Confused by Leia's insinuation, I sat back on my knees to better observe her. I may have crossed a line, but the others respected her wishes in the bedroom, and Leia always seemed an enthusiastic participant.

Although, now I'm questioning my judgment.

"I made a new friend out there in the woods," she continued, and I grimaced, unease pooling in my gut. "You know, when I was on the run from men who can't control their dicks." Although her biting comment was clearly meant for me, Leia scrutinized each of us as if we were equally guilty.

Julius loudly sighed, drawing her attention to him. "Cease playing games and simply state *who* you are speaking of."

"A mountain nymph. Goes by the name of Echo," Leia replied, crossing her arms over her chest and meeting Julius' glare with an impressive amount of dominance. "She was upset, so I offered for her to come back here with me, but it was almost like she was *afraid* to. Any idea why?"

Ambrose, Timyn, and I froze as the tension in the room increased exponentially. We all knew damn well who Echo was—and why she wouldn't want to set foot near this fortress—but this was Julius' story to tell.

Assuming he'll even want to share it.

"I can't imagine," Julius replied icily. "However, I am interested to learn what *your* connection with the Oread is."

"Siren," Ambrose cut in, eyeing Julius warily. "Why don't you go sit with Timyn?"

"Ooh yes, do that," Timyn smirked, plopping into a velvet armchair and patting his lap invitingly. "My Hydra misses feeling your flesh on mine."

Leia obeyed, even as she continued to unwisely taunt the boar. "What's the matter, Julius? Do you and Echo have a history you don't want me to know about?"

"Water Lily..." Timyn cautioned, curling his body protectively around her as scales flickered over his skin, his reptilian eyes on the boar.

With a brazenness that only made me desire her more, my mate wiggled out of his hold—leaning forward to maintain eye contact with the seething man seated behind his desk. "What did you do to her, Julius?"

Wrong question, Fawn.

I braced for Julius' explosive anger. Instead of replying, he reached for some stationery on his desk and began writing, his anger a palpable thing.

Unaware of the dangerous game she was playing, Leia laughed bitterly. "It's funny how men get real quiet when they're called out for bad behavior. You'd think with how long you've all been around, you'd know a thing or two about how to treat women."

Timyn scoffed. "Why would we know anything about women?" When she twisted in his lap to meet his gaze, he shrugged. "As you know, there aren't many on this island with us, and before that, well... we weren't exactly considered eligible bachelors for willing maidens."

"*Willing* being the key word here, guys," Leia sniffed, turning back around to judgmentally fix her gorgeous honey-brown eyes on me, causing me to dip my head in shame.

How is she ever going to trust me again?

"Leia," Ambrose gently addressed her, although I

sensed his words were for my benefit as well. "Krysos was at the mercy of his hind, consumed by the biological *need* to mate. Not that it excuses how he frightened you," he quickly added. "But based on our similar experience, I guarantee he wouldn't have hurt you. We are attuned to you now. *Your* pleasure and comfort take precedence over everything. You will always have the power to decide what does or doesn't happen between us, despite our primal needs."

I emphatically nodded in agreement, realizing my hind would have backed off completely had he sensed any discomfort or genuine fear in our mate.

Even if a taste of fear would be delicious...

"So, all I have to do is tell you to stop?" Leia asked.

My cock instantly hardened, and Timyn released an audible groan. "Oh, *fuck.* Say it again."

Julius swore under his breath, but continued writing, the rapid scratch of his quill the only sound in the room as we all focused on getting our beasts back under control.

Ambrose cleared his throat. "That may not be the best choice of words. Our automatic response to any sign of weakness is predatory, which is why Timyn told you *not* to run from me in the vineyard. Yet, I assure you, even as I gave chase, I truly wasn't intending to eat you."

"At least not in *that* way," Timyn whispered, and I glanced up to find him slowly thrusting against Leia, softly kissing her neck, making my hind ache to do the same.

Leia reached back to absently run her fingers through his hair, as if unconsciously urging him on. "But Julius told me to run in the courtyard—"

"Yes, but he did so while purposefully facing *away* from you, lest his boar respond," I dared to speak, carefully watching as understanding washed over Leia's face.

"Oh," she whispered, and I had to stifle a groan of my own as her scent filled the room, implying the chase didn't bother her quite as much as she let on. Her expression turned grim as she addressed Julius once again. "Is *that* what happened with Echo? Did she tell you to stop and you—"

Julius' head snapped up, a look of pure horror on his face. "Is *that* what you think of me? That I would be capable of—" He abruptly stopped, slowly blowing out a breath before turning to address Ambrose. "I'll see if Gaia's messenger is available to get these letters out tonight. It would be far better for the remaining eight to know we're recruiting them before we arrive on foot." Standing, he hastily gathered the correspondence and swept past us to exit the room, pointedly not looking at Leia.

Our mate stared at the doorway, her brow furrowed with a mix of confusion and annoyance on her face. A long silence passed before Ambrose spoke again. "Echo took his eye, Leia. She feigned camaraderie so she could get close to Julius while he was in human form, although they were never more than acquaintances. Luckily, I was there to intervene, so she couldn't finish him. After a bit of... torture..."

He paused to gauge Leia's reaction, but she simply pressed her lips together and nodded. "Keep going," was all she said.

Ambrose nodded once in reply. "We discovered she'd been working for Eurystheus, and was coerced into attacking Julius in exchange for a way off of the island. Regardless, the only reason she's still alive is that we *can't* kill the Oread in her true form—the only form she has here, unlike us."

"Well, we could have killed her with my poisonous

blood," Timyn murmured. "But I was indisposed at the time. Perhaps we should bottle it up for such occasions?"

"Fuck, I am *such* an asshole," Leia's voice cracked, and I rushed to her side, kneeling at her feet to comfortingly wrap my arms around her waist.

Please don't reject me.

To my relief, she allowed my touch, even as she gently caressed the base of my battered antler with her thumb, offering me reassurance in return.

"You are not an asshole," Ambrose approached, dropping to his knees on her other side. "This sort of miscommunication is bound to happen, simply because of how fundamentally different we are. While we look like men, we are not human. The wide variety of emotion we experience in these forms don't always make sense to us, even after all this time. In fact, we've had misunderstandings of our own... ones that have been quite painful for everyone involved."

He met my gaze over Leia's lap, the regret in his expression making me roughly grab his face to deliver a kiss—one that hopefully conveyed everything I still couldn't speak aloud.

I forgive you.

I love you.

I would die without you.

Leia patiently waited, as if understanding the importance of this moment. After we separated, she softly replied, "So maybe we should all try to use our words from now on—like actual humans. That includes me." She released a shaky breath. "On that note, I should probably tell you... when I was in the forest, I ran into Eurystheus."

31
LEIA

Apparently, telling your monster boyfriends their enemy cornered you in the forest meant they would immediately spring into murderous action. I tried to explain that Eurystheus was long gone, but Ambrose, Timyn, and Krysos insisted on running off as a pack to track him down, anyway. It didn't take long for me to grow restless while sitting alone in Julius' office, so I decided to poke around the fortress some more.

And maybe find a boar to poke while I'm at it.

To be honest, I felt terrible for accusing Julius of assaulting Echo. Now that my blind rage had settled, I could acknowledge my men wouldn't do something like that, despite Krysos' alpha-boner declaration in the court-yard. They were monsters, but they weren't *bad guys*... aside from torturing traitorous mountain nymphs and acciden-tally-on-purpose killing centaurs with their poisonous blood.

A shiver danced down my spine as I recalled Eurys-theus' threat to my life. While I mentioned that part of the conversation to my men, I left out how he thought I would somehow be able to 'weaken' them with my presence. We already had enough to worry about with convincing the gods to let us off the island. Plus, I assumed as long as I *appeared* to be following Eurystheus' plan, he'd leave me alone.

So why add more reasons for them to fly off the handle?

At the moment, I was totally focused on my overwhelming *need* to find Julius and make things right. Apologies weren't easy for me, but if I was going to attempt to communicate better, then I should probably set aside my pride and take accountability for my actions, too.

Look at me, self-improving and shit.

As if led by an invisible guide, my feet carried me to a stone staircase on the opposite side of the fortress. I slowly ascended the darkened turret, somehow instinctively knowing Julius would be lurking at the top when I got there.

My money had been on him either pensively brooding or spinning straw into gold. Instead, I found him standing on a small balcony with an enormous *eagle* perched on his arm. An eagle he appeared to be *talking* to. The bird suddenly flapped its wings, hovering so Julius could slide a stack of blue envelopes into its talons before it took off into the fading evening light.

That was a totally normal occurrence.

"Since you stomped out of the war room before we could get your input, I suppose I should fill you in now," Julius grumbled, still facing away from me. I bristled but held my tongue, knowing he didn't have to fill me in at all. "Those letters are for eight allies we'll be journeying to meet, setting out tomorrow morning. It shouldn't be difficult to recruit them to our cause, as they are fellow monsters cursed to be men by Eurystheus' schemes. Interestingly, they were also associated with Heracles' Twelve Labors, because yes," he finally turned around, "I am aware your full name is Herculeia."

Suddenly overwhelmed by the enormity of our situation, my shoulders slumped, my entire body deflating with an exhaustion that was bone deep. "I don't know what to think of this, Julius," I sighed. "So what if my Greek history-obsessed mother named me Herculeia? Why would that inspire Eurystheus to send *me* here? I'm no one."

To my surprise, Julius gestured for me to join him. My shoulder pressed against his arm as I squeezed onto the awkwardly small balcony, the sensation of his skin on mine making me gasp and sway precariously.

"Easy, girl," he quickly wrapped his tree trunk arm around me, pulling me close. "Now that you've seen my true form, you know I wouldn't be able to fly down after you if you fell. Only Zephyr could manage that."

I assumed Zephyr was one of the eight, but didn't have the energy to remember which Labor involved a flying whateverthefuck. My libido, however, still had enough juice to wonder if I'd feel the same instant connection with the others as I had with Ambrose, Timyn, Krysos... and even Julius.

Yeah, yeah, I wanna bang the boar—so sue me.

I already knew this grumpy-ass man cuddling me was mine, and I wasn't opposed to the idea at all. "Mmm, you may not fly, but you have other fancy features working for you," I teased, snuggling closer, making him adorably tense. "Like those sexy tusks and even sexier battle wound."

"Don't toy with me, Leia," he warned, which only made me want to tease him even more. "I will not be made a fool."

I twisted my body so I could gape at him in shock. "You

think I'm kidding?!" I squawked—mortally offended by the idea. Wrestling my hands free, I reached up and rested my palms on his cheeks, smiling at the feel of his beard scratching the pads of my fingers. "I want to *see* you."

Julius grimly stared down at me, even as his tusks slowly emerged from beneath his bottom lip, curling upward. I gently caressed them with my thumbs, noticing his Adam's apple bobbing as he swallowed hard at the contact.

"You don't find me... hideous and frightening?" he furrowed his brow, accentuating what had been taken from him.

Fury pulsed in my chest. If I'd known Echo was to blame for half-blinding Julius, I would have snatched Eurystheus' knife and stabbed her myself—repeatedly until she bled out on the forest floor.

Jesus, that was dark.

"No, I don't," I laughed nervously, banishing my momentary psychotic episode. "I mean, don't get me wrong. If you were coming for me in the dark in full boar beast mode, I might run, but..."

I trailed off as Julius' pupils dilated. "Would you, now?" His voice came out as an odd growl, making me rub my thighs together, which caused his nostrils to flare.

There may be enough room on this balcony to...

Julius abruptly shook his head and redirected our conversation. "Tell me more about your idea to sway the gods—by working on our... brand." He cleared his throat, sounding like he was doing his best to breathe through his mouth.

I blinked, slightly dazed by his manly proximity. "Oh, um, okay. So, a common tactic for inspiring positive press is philanthropy. What if you guys did some good deeds around the island? You know, while we figure out the whole revenge-and-escape thing? It might make you look... *nicer* in the eyes of the gods until we can officially plead your case."

Julius thoughtfully stroked his beard as he looked out over the landscape far below us. I followed his gaze and gasped. The natural beauty of the island repeatedly took my breath away, but this view was downright majestic. Fertile farmland and rolling hills dotted with rock formations stretched to the horizon, with the setting sun casting a pinkish hue over everything. I saw rural farmhouses and tiny villages in the distance, which reminded me more creatures than just my guys were stuck here.

Why were they all banished together?

It didn't sound like the others were being punished for anything specific. And obviously some of them—definitely Echo and possibly the centaur Nessus—were working for Eurystheus, albeit under duress.

"Well, our first destination is near the Augean stables," Julius mused, bringing my attention back to our conversation. "They haven't been cleaned since Heracles rerouted the Alpheus and Peneus rivers during his fifth Labor, although there was more to the story than that." He slyly glanced down at me, smiling like he had a secret. "Perhaps that could be our first good deed?"

I groaned. The Augean stables were filled with 3,000 immortal cows and their immortal poop. According to the legend, Eurystheus assigned this particular Labor to Heracles as extra punishment for literally slaying the first four. It wasn't possible to look heroic while shoveling shit. Luckily, we wouldn't have to complete it in a single day, like Heracles did. But I didn't want to think about how long it was going to take, and how gross it would be.

Since I doubt any of us can reroute one river, let alone two.

As much as I tried to simply enjoy the stunning vista and the hot bod pressed against me, my thoughts inevitably drifted. It wasn't my phone I thought of, but our enemy. Julius had described Eurystheus as an unimpressive coward, and as the myth of Heracles' Twelve Labors came back to me, I realized that reputation was probably accurate.

After killing his wife and children in a fit of god-induced madness, Heracles visited the Oracle of Delphi for guidance. It was there he learned he would be pardoned and granted immortality after serving his cousin, King Eurystheus, in whatever way the king saw fit. Unlike Heracles, Eurystheus was a run-of-the-mill human who never got his hands dirty. So being given the opportunity to lord power over his more famous family member really blew his petty toga up. Our hero prevailed in the end, completing each supposedly impossible Labor, which made the king look like an idiot.

What would Eurystheus gain from killing my monsters now?

I may not yet have figured out how the original Labors related to our current situation, but I knew one thing for sure. If the former king was still trying to mess with my guys—to kill them, even—that meant he considered them a threat. Knowing we were on our way to amass a small army of man-monsters to foil his plan sent another shiver down my spine. Only this time, it was full of dark pleasure.

We'll show him exactly how afraid of us he should be.

32

JULIUS

I t had been physically painful to leave Leia with Ambrose, Timyn, and Krysos last night before returning to my room alone. I tried to ignore what they were doing in there, but the thick stone walls of my fortress were no match for my hearing.

Or my sense of smell.

Leia had apparently encountered Eurystheus in the forest yesterday—a threat she chose not to share with me. When the others returned from the hunt, half-crazed with unfulfilled bloodlust, I surrendered her to their care. The only way to soothe their beasts at that point was to breed their mate—filling her with seed, repeatedly, all fucking night long.

I'll sleep when I'm dead, I suppose.

I was consumed with the same insatiable need to protect Leia, but it didn't matter. She didn't see me as one of her mates, so I needed to find an alternative outlet for my raging testosterone.

War is always a good choice.

My focus needed to be on our mission anyway, not on a human turned monster-mate who smelled like dinner and dessert. I'd always been the tactician of this endless campaign—it's what I did best. It was vital for me to plan for every plausible scenario, assuming the others would still be willing to help us.

If they haven't completely gone mad, that is.

"Soooo, these eight men... monsters we're going to find..." Leia suddenly appeared at my side, startling me from my thoughts. "Are they all various animals, too?"

I snorted, irritable from my lack of sleep and unrequited yearnings. "Why does it matter to you? Are you the *Potnia Theron* of this island?"

Timyn howled with laughter. "Oh, Leia is definitely Queen of the Animals! Or at least, an animal herself, judging by last night's activities."

Leia flushed red, which only caused me to picture her in the throes of passion. "Shut your mouth, you overgrown lake snake!" she hissed, giving the Hydra an impressively well-placed punch on the arm.

"Hit me again, Water Lily," Timyn groaned, making Leia squeal as one of his tails burst from beneath his toga to wrap around her waist. "If you make me bleed, I'll give you a treat."

I rolled my eyes as Leia made some nonsensical comment about craving 'cupcakes,' although the appearance of Timyn's tail intrigued me. Of course, we'd taken our true forms to descend my mountain, but generally kept our beasts dormant when away from our power sources. The Hydra being so careless with his appendages was noteworthy.

I wonder...

Seeing that everyone else was distracted by conversation, I discreetly experimented with unleashing some of my own features, curious if I'd feel the usual energetic drain. To my surprise, I felt *stronger* for having done so, as if a piece of Mount Erymanthos had come along with me on our journey.

"Ohhhh, I like when his tusks come out," Leia whispered in Timyn's ear, inspiring him to flash his own fangs and pretend to bite her. Wiggling herself free from his tail, she approached me again, oblivious to my volatile mood as she boldly grabbed my forearm.

I grunted in surprise as my bones abruptly began contorting to accommodate my boar. Leia jumped backward, which caused me to abruptly shift back into my human form—leaving me off-kilter and concerned that I'd frightened her.

What is happening to me?!

"I'm sorry," I muttered contritely, before remembering I was angry at her for reasons I didn't want to examine.

"No! It's okay," she soothed, moving closer again, although she didn't touch me this time. "You don't scare me, although I have to admit, I used to have recurring nightmares about wild boars as a kid—"

"Recurring dreams?" Ambrose's gaze was now riveted on Leia. "That sounds almost like premonitions." He pointedly glanced at Krysos, and I realized the lion was harboring a theory he hadn't yet shared with me.

Why is everyone keeping secrets lately?

She laughed, waving a hand dismissively. "I wouldn't call them *premonitions* unless Julius is planning on chasing me through the snow anytime soon."

I had to physically stifle a groan. It wasn't an exaggeration when the others urged Leia not to do *anything* that could spur our beasts into predatory action. Just the thought of her running from me, of her fighting me off...

Timyn shot me a knowing look before focusing on Leia. "What about lake snakes? Any dreams about me?"

She frowned and stumbled over a divot in the farmland we were traversing. "I... maybe, now that you mention it. And I just remembered this weird dream I had while napping on the deck of the cruise ship. There was a coin with a crazy design of some dude wearing a lion pelt over his head like—"

"The Nemean Lion," Ambrose snorted. "Yes, that was Alexander the Great's infamous mint. He insisted he was a descendent of Heracles, so showing my pelt on the coin 'confirmed' the rumor. Regardless of his ancestral claims, Heracles is the *only* hero who ever defeated me—any of us, really. That is, until you came along." Like the saccharine romantic he was, Ambrose placed his hand over his heart before pinning Leia with a meaningful look.

I'm not at all jealous.

Instead of appearing sufficiently wooed, Leia looked almost nervous as she chewed her bottom lip. "I don't even know *how* I would defeat you guys."

Before I could clarify what she meant by that odd statement, Krysos interrupted. "Why exactly are we headed toward the Augean stables, Julius? I would prefer not to commence this journey covered in dung."

"Leia had an idea," I coldly replied, unimpressed with his haughty tone. The Golden Hind was one of the few with a direct connection to the gods, which he often reminded us of. I couldn't help noticing Artemis had yet to appear and grant us pardon, so his supposed favor wasn't benefitting us.

That being said, Krysos *had* proved himself useful when

he coaxed Ambrose out of his misery over his seemingly permanent human form, and I was pleased they had reunited.

Not that I would tell them that.

I gestured toward Leia, indicating she should elaborate on her plan, but the girl simply gaped at me. "You want *me* to explain my idea to everyone?" She eyed me suspiciously, as if that weren't exactly what I was implying.

"Yes, Leia," I sighed, annoyed by her hesitation. "It was *your* idea, and you are an equal party here, so speak plainly —and quickly, before the hind starts whining again."

To my continued exasperation, *tears* welled up in her not-at-all-beautiful brown eyes. "Thank you, Julius. Where I come from, men rarely invite me to speak."

We all froze and stared at her with varying degrees of surprise and rage. "Who are these men?" Timyn hissed, scales flickering over his skin as his eyes narrowed into reptilian slits. "We will kill them all."

Leia barked a laugh. "Well, I'm not gonna encourage mass genocide, so don't worry about it. Okay," she collected herself, straightening her shoulders before addressing the others. "Julius told me how Eurystheus convinced the gods to contain you on this island—because of how dangerous you are. I thought if we could show Olympus you can play nice, maybe they'll let you plead your case?"

"Nice?" Krysos muttered, understandably confused by the concept.

"Yes," Leia nodded, speaking slowly. "Like doing good deeds around the island while we're out here. Julius mentioned we'd be near the Augean stables, and I'm sure the locals would appreciate thousands of years of cow shit being cleaned up..." she trailed off before turning to me in concern. "Um, the next guy on our list isn't some half-cow creature, is he?"

Timyn smirked. "No, you spicy monster-fucker, the cows in the stables are simply immortal cows, not cow-people. That would just be weird."

"Agreed," Krysos sniffed, squinting at Leia. "Save that bovine lust for the Cretan Bull, Fawn."

Leia grabbed my arm, shrinking against me as if for support or protection, which pleased my beast immensely. "Is the Cretan Bull a... minotaur?"

"In a way," Ambrose absently replied, shielding his eyes against the midday sun, peering toward the nearby river before turning to me. "Well, we were calling on Vann anyway, and as *he* is the one who diverted the Alpheus and Peneus rivers for Heracles—"

"Peneus," Timyn snickered.

"Wait, wait, wait," Leia cut in. "Heracles didn't divert the rivers with his godlike strength? How did that Labor even count then?"

Ambrose smiled indulgently at her. "Ah, but that Labor *didn't* count—albeit for entirely different reasons. Originally there were Ten Labors, but Eurystheus added two because of Heracles' misconduct."

"By misconduct, you mean *cheating*," Timyn grumbled. "It was only because he had his brat nephew with him that he bested me. I would wager Vann lost to Heracles in a game of knucklebones, and that's why he helped with the rivers. On that note, you should know Vann isn't speaking to me at the moment, the sore loser. So, perhaps we should send our Water Lily to charm him with her voluptuous curves?"

I pinched the bridge of my nose. It had been centuries since all twelve of us were together, and the thought of adding *more* noise to my daily existence gave me a headache. Ambrose was correct, however, in that we were planning to call on Vann anyway, so why not recruit him first with a Herculean task?

With Herculeia being the perfect bait to lure him out of his lair.

33
LEIA

During my time at Auracle, I'd dreamed up some pretty ridiculous publicity stunts for my marketing clients. None ever involved me wearing a raggedy, see-through nightgown while standing on a jagged rock a half-mile out to sea.

The wind had picked up since Timyn left me here, and the spray from the waves was chilling me to my bones, despite the warm sun beating on my back. While the Hydra had given me a ride out here, I couldn't remember *who* decided I should be the one coaxing this Vann person from the ocean.

Not a person...

I froze, realizing I hadn't bothered asking what kind of monster I was dealing with here. For all I knew, he was a fish-faced sea slug or a killer whale.

Moby Dick.

My snicker was abruptly cut short when something *moved* across the surface of the water, far enough away for me to think I'd imagined it. A splash to my left made me flinch, but peering into the waves, all I saw was foam and reflected sunlight.

"Vann?" I hesitantly called out, suddenly questioning my life choices. "Will you come out where I can see you, please? I have a message from—"

I yelped as something violently smacked against the opposite side of my rock—shaking the secure perch like the tassels on a burlesque dancer's ta-tas. If whatever was circling me could do *that,* then I was in way over my head. My body started involuntarily shuddering, and I crouched low to avoid being tossed into the roiling sea. Remembering how Eurystheus threw me overboard did not help the current situation, and soon enough, my breaths became labored as a low-grade panic attack took over.

Oh shit. I'm not supposed to show any fear.

As soon as I recognized my mistake, a goddamn *tentacle* shot out of the water, curling around my waist and yanking me off my perch. I sucked in a breath before I hit the water, although the force of the impact caused my vision to momentarily white out.

When the spots faded, I frantically looked around in the near-darkness. All I could see was a murky blur of bubbles and the large appendage stretching away to connect with whatever this creature was. The tentacle kept winding around me, even as we moved, tightly coiling until almost every inch of me was contained, including my eyes.

Knowing I was about to die caused a strange sense of calm to wash over me. I'd always loved the sea—it was why I had the underwater scene tattooed on my bicep—and even in my last moments, I refused to allow anyone to take that away from me. My thoughts grew hazy as I ran out of air, and I randomly wondered how my monsters would react to this unprovoked attack.

Maybe Vann will show up and save me...

Even though I knew it was stupid, I opened my still-uncovered mouth—choosing my death instead of waiting to see if I was about to become squid chow. To my surprise, cold lips pressed against mine, blocking the incoming flow of water to breathe oxygen into my burning lungs. I panicked, but then I felt a forked tongue against mine, and heard a familiar dulcet tone in my head.

"Shh... I'm here, Water Lily."

The tentacle restraining me uncoiled until I could open my eyes again. Timyn's human face was pressed against mine, but out of the corner of my eye, I saw the rest of my Hydra facing off against what was definitely a giant squid. Instead of battling they were... *arguing,* with Timyn's eight remaining heads in lake snake form, snapping irritably at the other monster, as if scolding him. Meanwhile, the squid looked like it was pouting, with two of its enormous arms petulantly crossed over what would be its chest.

What the fuck is happening?

The tentacle unceremoniously released me, but before I could fall to the depths, I felt one of Timyn's tails collect me, securing my mouth on his as we moved through the water again. My adrenaline plummeted—my hot tears immediately washed away by the salty sea as I wrapped my arms tightly around Timyn's human neck.

"You're all right, Leia. Vann was just frightened."

Wait. What?

Before I could process that *Vann* was the giant squid—and the squid was afraid of *me*—we were breaching the surface. Timyn gently laid me on the rocky beach, and I opened my eyes to find three other worked-up men huffing and stalking and stomping around.

"We shouldn't have sent her out there! What *possessed* you to even suggest it?"

"Must I remind you that you agreed to the plan? How would I know Vann would react that way?"

"Where is he?! I will *kill* that fucking Kraken."

Kraken?!

"He thought she was a Gorgon, hence the *over*reaction," Timyn calmly cut in, back to his human form and deliciously wet. In fact, my entire body was vibrating with the need to plaster myself to him—to reconnect with *all* of them, skin-to-skin.

Is this that mate bond they kept talking about?

"Ah, yes," Ambrose thoughtfully hummed, even as he eyed me hungrily, his nostrils flaring. "I feared the same when I first found Leia on the beach. It's her green hair that confused me."

I huffed and got to my feet, attempting to discreetly shake the sand out of my ass crack. "Humans dye their hair for *fun* where I come from, just like how we get piercings and tattoos. It's because we enjoy—"

"The pain?" Timyn asked hopefully, his vibrant green eyes raking over me with interest. At this point, being practically naked in front of them felt normal—even as Julius looked everywhere *except* at me—but I still appreciated how much they admired my body.

Exactly how I am.

"We do it because we enjoy expressing ourselves and our uniqueness." I pressed against Timyn with a satisfied sigh, feeling like a piece of me had snapped into place. Another wave of gratitude washed over me to acknowledge he'd valiantly rescued me—even if my kidnapper was just a salty friend of his. "Thank you for saving my life, my brave lake snake. That was very heroic of you."

Instead of replying with his usual teasing innuendos, Timyn actually *blushed* and frantically waved away the compliment. "Oh, none of that nonsense, Leia. I—*we*—will always save you, but, uh... we *can't* be heroes, you see."

I took a step back, furrowing my brow. "What do you mean? *Anyone* can be a hero."

"Not us," Ambrose shook his head, smiling sadly. "We exist so *others* can prove their mettle—to make heroes out of worthy men."

Well, that's some bullshit.

Before I could get on my soapbox, someone cleared their throat on the shore behind me. I spun to find another ridiculously handsome man, awkwardly kicking at the pebbles beneath his feet while refusing to meet anyone's gaze. His almost white-blond hair reflected the sunlight, the swimmer's build of his naked body suggesting this must be the infamous *Vann* who'd almost drowned me at sea.

That and the fact his dick was a freakin' tentacle.

34
VANN

Well, that was embarrassing.

To my credit, it *had* been a while since I'd seen a Gorgon, and the human's green hair looked oddly snake-like as it danced in the ocean breeze. The others could be displeased by my actions, but everyone knew the severed head of Medusa was used to turn the sea monster Cetus to stone, and I wasn't interested in suffering the same fate.

I don't even belong here, for Rán's sake.

It was simply bad timing that I'd drifted down from the North for a visit when these foreign deities trapped us all here for eternity. One would think the 'all-seeing' gods would've looked closer before indiscriminately corralling everyone with impenetrable fog.

Release the Kraken!

I couldn't help wondering if the reason I'd been lumped in with these animals was because of the part I played in Heracles' Fifth Labor. Boredom was why I agreed to help the demigod in the first place, and now I was being asked for a repeat performance.

As if I have nothing better to do than reroute Grecian rivers.

"Why do the Augean stables need to be cleaned again?" I frowned at Julius as we stood apart from the others near the shoreline. "That human king Augeas is long dead— killed by Heracles himself, if I remember correctly—so who cares if some immortal cows are dirty?"

Julius sighed with the exhaustion of a thousand lives. "Because our... *their* mate, Leia, wants us to perform helpful tasks to improve our reputation, and possibly be freed. I told her we could fit in a few good deeds around our true mission of defeating Eurystheus. On that note, I assume you received my latest letter?"

There was much to unpack here. However, when given the choice, I always chose chaos. "You almost said 'our' mate, didn't you? Is she not also *yours?*"

The boar gave me a look worthy of a Gorgon before gritting out, "No, I am not sharing her bed as the others are. Now if we could discuss—"

"Do you think she'd be interested in sharing her bed with *me?*" I interrupted. My gaze drifted to the curvy morsel sunning herself on a boulder with the Hydra, drying the useless scrap of fabric she wore. Now that the storm had settled, I felt *drawn* to her—like a beacon of light on a rocky cliff. "She keeps stealing glances at me."

"Well, your cock is out, and it looks like a tentacle, so I'm guessing it's morbid curiosity," he deadpanned. "We brought you a toga to cover up with—"

"Why do I need to cover up?" I interrupted again, mostly to redirect my thoughts *away* from the possessive need to stuff the tentacle in question deep inside everyone else's mate.

All my tentacles, really.

Julius pinched the bridge of his nose. "Because wearing

human clothing is what we do now, apparently." He brusquely gestured at his own Spartan-esque clothing, his boar visibly flickering over his skin in agitation, much to my surprise.

So far from Mount Erymanthos too...

Recognizing what was truly vexing him, I allowed my gaze to appreciatively track down his muscular chest, landing on what I knew lay beneath his toga. "You shouldn't deprive the lovely nymph over there of your greatest assets. *Both* are quite enjoyable to experience, you know."

"Can we stop talking about our cocks?!" Julius snapped, drawing a snicker from the crowd farther down the beach.

Teasing Julius is as much fun as capsizing whaling vessels!

I broadly grinned. "And disappoint our audience with pesky plot?" My smile faded as my gaze wandered to Leia again, as if compelled. "Very well, I will divert the rivers again, if that's what *she* desires. Perhaps it will make up for our... misunderstanding at sea?"

He thoughtfully hummed. "Perhaps. Leia has proven to be very forgiving of our more monstrous qualities. Her mother is a Greek historian, so she has more knowledge of our legends than most, but it's still worth noting how easily she's accepted us... *them,* despite being human herself."

Despite how unaffected he pretended to be, I easily picked up on the desire radiating from the man before me. I couldn't blame him. I'd barely been around Leia for an hour and my beast already wanted to claim her, but our boar was his own worst enemy at times.

Nothing like a gentleman's wager to loosen him up.

Allowing a tentacle to slide out from my back, I curled it around Julius' waist and yanked him closer. He growled at our sudden proximity, but his dilating pupil betrayed his body's reaction to mine.

"Let's play, Erymanthian," I whispered. "Which of us hideous monsters can tempt the little nymph first, considering our unique... *assets?*"

He stopped scowling to scoff incredulously, his gaze roaming over me. "You are not hideous and you know it."

I peered over his shoulder to find Leia sitting up, watching our exchange with interest—even as she eyed my tentacle warily. Timyn was staring too, and I shot that lousy cheat a glare before turning my attention back to Julius.

"Not in this form, perhaps, but just imagine her reaction to us in our full glory. How her heart would race, how her terror would flavor the air as she ran from us. Think of how your boar would relentlessly pursue her. Exhausting her with the chase until you took what was yours... breeding her over and over."

Julius was clenching his fists so tightly his knuckles were white, his body shuddering as the beast fought to break free. "What is the point of this, Vann? Why goad me when we have a greater mission to focus on?"

I abruptly released my hold on him, noticing my tentacle instinctively reach for Leia before I drew it back. Her flinch did not go unnoticed, along with her subsequent arousal, but I had to agree with Julius. There were more pressing issues at hand. Backing away until my feet were submerged in the ocean, I began unleashing my tentacles, one after the other, as my body began to contort into my true form. Interestingly enough, the change felt less draining than usual, but I assumed it was thanks to my recent taste of terror.

Which was most delicious.

"I'll meet the rest of you at the stables!" I called out, mostly for Leia's benefit, since the others would have no problem hearing me if I whispered. "And you," I addressed Julius as I continued to retreat into the depths. "I expect you to give me a worthy challenge. Loosen up and let that beast out already, before you burst a blood vessel."

———

Rerouting the Alpheus and Peneus rivers was easier this time, which was odd. When Heracles convinced me to do it originally, I'd been at the peak of my power, not stunted as I was now. Then again, nothing about our entrapment made sense to me, including why real-world landmarks like these rivers existed here at all.

Walking around the now pristine stables, I found the group gazing out to the valley and farmland beyond. Something twisted in my chest as I observed them—that odd *pull* from Leia again, but also the unexpected gathering of monsters I'd almost come to think of as *friends*.

Although, Timyn can go fuck himself...

I hadn't answered Julius about whether I'd received his letter. Of course, I had, although I tried my best to ignore it when it first arrived. It wasn't the first passionate declaration our tactician had sent, but the idea of us banding together again had proved tempting enough for me to leave my lair. When we existed as our original legends, we were solitary beasts whose only purpose was to be terrifying foes to those brave enough to face us.

Including scantily clad women resembling Gorgons.

Obviously, I'd frightened Leia by dragging her underwater, but she didn't seem scared now. Turning to face me, her pleasing face broke into a wide grin, and she met me halfway as I moved to join the group.

"Thank you, Vann," she shyly spoke, the sound of my name on her lips making my Kraken preen. "Julius thinks if we can get one of Gaia's eagles to spread the word of our deed to the gods—"

She abruptly stopped talking as the others began reacting to something rapidly approaching by air. I squinted as it neared, frowning when I realized it was *not* an eagle, but a man riding a chariot pulled by dragons with a sheaf of wheat in his arms. My Kraken flexed beneath the surface—ready to fight, despite being so far inland—but it settled again as the others visibly relaxed.

"Ho there, Triptolemus!" Ambrose called out a name which meant nothing to me. "What brings you down from Olympus?"

That was fast.

The man reined in his dragons so that he hovered above us, clearly still too important to land upon our lowly soil. "Farmers in this area have suffered from poor crops due to groundwater contamination for years. It appears cleaning the Augean stables may have solved the problem, so I am here to spread grain over the land once again."

"Well, isn't that nice of you," I sneered, drawing the divine being's attention to me. "Yet, you couldn't be bothered to solve the problem yourself? Do the inhabitants of this island mean nothing to those lording on high?"

It was foolish to invoke godly wrath, but being trapped here for so long had made me cagey. Again, I readied to attack or defend, but Triptolemus did nothing more than softly smile. "Norseman, you must understand how immutable the hierarchy of the gods can be. I was merely a priest of Demeter in my lifetime, taught agriculture by the goddess herself so I could pass the knowledge along to mortals. I assure you, I am not the only divine being aware of your plight. However, the twelve Olympians were swayed into believing every creature here should be left on this island."

"But *I* don't belong here!" I shouted, daring Demeter herself to come down and smite me in defense of her priest. "And I would assume this *human* doesn't either." I gestured at Leia, even as the other monsters glared at me, no doubt displeased at the implication *they* deserved this fate.

None of this is my problem.

Triptolemus cocked his head at Leia, as if considering her. "I wouldn't say that, Kraken. Our greater purpose can take time to make itself known." After delivering this infuriatingly vague statement, he shifted his gaze back to me. "I will mention this deed to Demeter, although I cannot promise it will achieve anything. Might I suggest visiting the nearest Oracle for guidance instead?" Without waiting for a reply, he snapped the reins, spurring his scaly steeds into whisking his chariot away to the farmland below.

"When are you going to accept that you're stuck here with us, *calamari?*" Timyn teased, unable to resist poking me for long.

"When you stop cheating at knucklebones, lake snake," I hissed in return.

"*Ohmygawd,* you call him lake snake too?" Leia cackled, hooking her arm through mine, causing my heart rate to inexplicably increase. "You know, I actually thought he was a dragon when I first saw him," she whispered conspiratorially.

"I assume Timyn was more than happy to encourage that misconception," I laughed, smiling down at her and staunchly ignoring the Hydra's indignant huff. "Of course, *now* you've seen actual dragons," I pointed in the direction the chariot had flown off. "And if Julius is successful in tracking down the others, you'll be meeting one of the largest ones soon enough."

Leia's honey-brown eyes widened, her grip on my arm tightening as her body aromatically reacted to the thought of adding another monster to her stable. Julius narrowed his good eye at me, the beast in him finally rising to my earlier challenge, much to my delight.

May the best monster win.

35
LEIA

As if it wasn't surreal enough to be collecting a harem of mythical monsters, we'd had our first visit from an actual demigod.

If I still had my phone, my selfie game would be on point.

I vaguely remembered Triptolemus from the legend of Hades and Persephone. It was during Demeter's quest to rescue her daughter from the underworld that she met Triptolemus and taught him agriculture to benefit humanity.

It was weird that these random legends were coming back to me now. Sure, my mother loved to flex her knowledge, but her visits home were rare—especially after the divorce—and it wasn't like we sat for *hours* discussing the Eleusinian Mysteries, or anything.

At least, not that I remember.

I absently tapped my latest *obol* against my ring, choosing to ignore the fact I'd discovered it *stuck to my ass* after my wild ride with the Kraken. At this point, I wasn't even fazed that coins for the dead kept popping up on my travels—it almost felt like a treasure hunt.

If I could have an obol for every guy I bag...

"Isn't there an Oracle dedicated to Artemis atop Mount Taygetus?"

I was snapped out of my thoughts by Julius' super hot, gravelly voice. For a moment, I panicked, thinking he was asking *me* about the Oracle, until I saw his focus was on the Golden Hind.

Krysos nodded as he walked beside Ambrose—holding the other man's hand, because they *wanted to unalive me with their cuteness*. "There once was, although the nymph serving as its priestess, Taygete, hasn't been seen since Echo's failed attack on Julius."

I frowned. I'd thought most of the creatures here couldn't actually die, despite Eurystheus' obsession with killing my guys off. Sure, he randomly thought *I* could somehow weaken them, but I'd assumed that was just his evil villain delusions. He must know they were only vulnerable in their human forms, and I doubted anyone could get the jump on them again after the Echo incident. I thought about how the Oread's punishment was to continue being trapped here. If I failed—at whatever I was supposed to be doing—would Eurystheus actually follow through on his threat to *kill* me?

This does not bode well.

"Have others disappeared from the island?" I hesitantly asked, extremely concerned about not only myself, but all my monsters—including the ones I hadn't met yet. "I thought you all just existed here... for eternity."

Ambrose shrugged. "We do. Although it *was* odd for Taygete to be trapped here in the first place. No other priestesses—especially those capable of powerful visions— have been seen here since the beginning. The nymph was a favorite of Artemis, however, so perhaps that's why she was allowed to leave—"

"I was a favorite of Artemis too," the hind sulked, earning him an annoyed sound from Julius.

"And *I* thought I was a favorite of Hades, since the lake of Lerna is an entrance to the underworld," Timyn dramatically sniffled before winking at me. "Or maybe that old dog just liked my muscles."

"Has anyone ever told you that you're a bunch of imbeciles?" Vann suddenly piped in, startling me into releasing his arm. It had felt so natural to latch onto him as we walked, I'd completely forgotten the attempted drowning from earlier.

All it takes to distract me is a tentacle dick and nice forearms.

Julius threw a heavy arm over my shoulders and pulled me out of the Kraken's reach. Vann narrowed his stormy blue eyes at my grumpy protector, but didn't comment on the possessive display before refocusing on the conversation.

"Imbeciles," he repeated, in case anyone missed the insult the first time. "Your enemy cut you off from Olympus. Why would he trap anyone here with a direct connection to the gods?" The glares of the other monsters slowly faded as we all realized Vann was speaking facts.

Salty facts.... but facts, nonetheless.

Julius thoughtfully hummed. "A fair point. Perhaps a stop at the Oracle of Taygetus would prove fruitful. Since there's no prophetess to communicate with the gods for us, we'll simply sacrifice the hind on the altar. That should get Artemis' attention."

"I beg your fucking pardon?" Krysos hissed as Ambrose growled.

Glancing up at Julius in alarm, I saw his lips twitching under his beard, reminding me the abrasive monster had a sense of humor hidden beneath his gruff exterior. When I secretly smiled at him in return, he flinched in surprise, so I added a reassuring little squeeze on the arm before diving in to mediate the man-drama.

"Visiting the Oracle can't hurt, and no, we won't need to sacrifice *anyone*," I laughed. "My mother has overseen excavations at Delphi for decades and it was a lot of smoke and mirrors. Countless studies have revealed that the 'divine visions' the *Pythia* received were probably thanks to hallucinogenic gasses floating up from cracks in the earth below the stool she sat on. Maybe Krysos can get high and make a call to Artemis?"

The guys all responded with various displays of agreement and encouragement, which made me teary. True, it was a novelty that men were listening to my opinion, but it was more than that. Feeling unconditionally supported was something I'd only experienced with a few people in my life. Iola was one of them, but my biggest cheerleader had always been my dad.

I miss him so much.

"What is it, Truffle? Why are you crying?" Julius' rough voice was gentle as he murmured down at me.

"It's just..." I cleared my throat, determined to get a hold of myself. "I was just thinking about someone I haven't seen in a while."

Distress flickered over Julius' face before he buried it. "We'll get you home, somehow, I promise. You don't deserve to be trapped here with us."

Maybe I want to be...

I banished the thought. My family and friends were probably sick with worry—if they weren't already mourning my death. I needed to get back to them and my life. I couldn't be running off to live with 5-12 hot monsters on a cursed island, no matter how good the sex was.

"Is no one going to comment on how Julius just called Herculeia a *truffle?!*" Timyn cackled, wildly waving his hands in the air. "If I had a heart, I fear I would swoon."

"You have a heart, you fucking lake snake," Julius growled, earning him a satisfied chuckle from Vann. This made me wonder if the competitiveness I sensed between the two of them was more about lighting a fire under my boar's backside than anything.

Dudes are so weird.

"Okay, so it's settled—we're off to the Oracle of Taygetus!" I loudly declared, realizing Julius needed saving before they all ganged up on him for being adorable. I then waited until we were all walking again to add, keeping my voice low. "And you can call me *'Truffle'* anytime you want, big guy."

He didn't reply, but I spied his beard twitching again, only the slightest bit.

36
LEIA

My men took their true forms again when we reached the base of Mount Taygetus. I hadn't expected Vann to let his Kraken out for the climb, but now I could say I'd witnessed a giant squid scaling a mountain.

All I'm asking is what those tentacles do?

I still didn't fully understand *how* they'd been turned into humans—and by whom—but watching their bodies change from men to monsters was awe-inspiring.

And kind of gross, to be honest.

We'd stopped for the evening, so the guys could recharge while I ate. Our plan was to hit the summit by the light of the full moon, so our 'weak human eyes' could see better. Now that my monsters were out of the closet, I thought they'd chow down in front of me. Apparently, they didn't need to eat often, even in this form. It was almost like their skin suits were exactly that—a thin veneer covering of magic that only added to their dichotomy. As fascinating as I found them, I was secretly thankful to *not* be watching them rip into raw flesh.

Of course, the bowl-cups are still generously overflowing all around.

"Does it... *hurt* when you change forms?" I mumbled around a mouthful of unknown wild game I refused to think too hard about.

Our resident masochist answered. "Not how you think, Water Lily. I'd call it *uncomfortable,* but the change happens so quickly, I barely notice it anymore." Timyn pressed his lips together, his serious expression making me realize this was a touchy subject. "It took a while to get used to this human form."

My appetite was gone, so I set aside my mystery meat. "I'm so sorry Eurystheus did this to all of you. I can't imagine how *violated* you must have felt. Not only to wake up on this island, but to be physically... altered."

"It was disorienting at first," Krysos murmured as he took a dainty sip of wine. "But we didn't yet possess the self-awareness to feel anything besides confusion and fear. We were still primitive back then, and our initial reactions were mostly focused on survival alone."

"As we wandered, we located our power sources, as well as others suffering the same fate," Julius gruffly added. "Things became easier to bear after that."

Because they found each other.

"And we picked up the language from the more advanced creatures fairly quickly," Ambrose added, leaning forward to poke the campfire with a gnarled stick. "I was initially surprised you could communicate with me, Leia, as the dialect we speak probably isn't common nowadays. However, with your mother being a Greek historian, I suppose it's not that strange."

"Mmm..." I hummed, scrunching my nose. "It's a little weird, to be honest. My mother tried to force-feed me a lot of info, but I can't say I was fluent in anything besides New Yorker before coming here. Yet, you all seem to have no trouble understanding me, either. Including the 'Norseman' over there," I waggled a finger at Vann. "What language are *you* speaking, sailor?"

The Kraken smirked before nonchalantly shrugging. "When in Greece..." I noticed the others shooting him confused looks, but I let it go, wanting to learn more about my monsters' pasts.

"Okay, how did you get your names?" I asked, snuggling closer to Julius—for warmth, but also because my pussy had been singing the boar mating song for *hours* at this point.

"Most chose their own names, but some of us gave them to each other as gifts," Ambrose replied. He grabbed Krysos' hand again, brushing the hind's knuckles against his lips in the softest kiss. "Gifts that were most appreciated, even when some of us stubbornly —and hurtfully—refused to accept our fate." Turning to me, he elaborated. "One night in the vineyard, I told Krysos I only cared about finding a way back to my true form and my old life. That I considered everything else to be temporary. I have regretted nothing more than those hurtful words."

Oof... that sounds familiar...

Krysos shrugged, although I could tell he was soaking in Ambrose's repentance like an expensive spa treatment. "Oh, my pride was injured more than anything, you drunk. Besides, it's not as if we couldn't fuck each other in beast form, if it came to that."

I sharply inhaled, imagining that exact scenario and deciding I fully supported it. My pussy must have subsequently sent out a bat signal, as every monster in attendance snapped their attention to me, the air growing thick with rising tension.

"Oh, by Thor's hammer, can someone please *breed* her already!" Vann groaned, reaching beneath his toga to not-so-subtly adjust his *tentacle peen*. "If one of you won't, I will happily stuff every orifice until she's satisfied."

I would be okay with that.

As if sensing I was less than one bowl-cup away from climbing aboard the S.S. Kraken, Julius growled and yanked me closer. Vann simply laughed and raised a challenging brow, but neither monster spoke or carried me off into the woods, caveman-style, like I was hoping.

It's time to take matters into my own hands.

Wiggling out of Julius' grasp, I stood—unsteadily—before removing my fur coat and *peplos* as sexily as I could, given my half-drunken state. Everyone's attention was fixed on me, but I focused on Julius alone. "I'm going to run now. If you catch me, you can fuck me however you want. But if I make it back here, it's anyone's game."

Check-mate, big guy.

Julius gaped at me in astonishment, but before he could reply, I turned and ran into the surrounding forest, bare-ass naked except for my boots. There were a few inches of snow on the ground, but I had my adrenaline—and horniness—to keep me warm.

A deafening roar rang out from the campsite, followed by scattered whoops and the vibration of hooves pounding the ground. Suddenly, I wondered if this had been a good idea.

"Definitely a good idea." -Sincerely, Leia's pussy.

I screamed as something *big* crashed through the undergrowth behind me, terrifyingly close, and I panicked before veering sharply to the right. Unfortunately, that route brought me face to face with a wall of icy granite, with nothing but massive pines blocking any other potential escape routes.

Looks like I'm fucked.

A loud chuff, and the feel of hot breath on the back of my neck had me slowly turning, anticipation lighting my nerves on fire. Of course, I *wanted* to be caught. But it was one thing to crave a grumpy metalhead human, and quite another to be facing down a massive boar like I was Princess Mononoke.

I stumbled backward as the beast advanced, my hand gripping a gigantic icicle on the wall behind me for balance. Julius-the-boar stopped with his snout inches away from my very hard nipples. His nostrils flared, dredging up some random trivia that pigs and boars could register scents up to seven miles away and 25 feet underground.

Like truffles...

The boar cocked its head at me, as if gauging my reaction to his proximity. My chest was heaving as my adrenaline settled, but my emotions were definitely leaning more towards desire than fear, even when faced with a monster.

Especially when faced with a monster.

This monster in particular.

Before I could verbalize this sentiment, Julius began backing away, probably wrongfully assuming I'd changed my mind.

Oh, no you don't.

I grabbed hold of his tusks, making him snort in surprise, but it halted his retreat. My fingers barely touched around the hard circumference, and my thoughts wandered to how girthy other parts of him might be.

"Don't even *think* of leaving me out here unsatisfied," I growled, earning me another chuff. "I want this, Julius, and

I want *you,* in all your grumpy-assed, sexy-tusked, and even sexier missing eyeball glory. I want to know you. And right now, I want to know what surprises you're hiding under your proverbial toga."

Julius' toga was long gone, but from this angle, I couldn't see what he was packing below the pelt. All I knew was Timyn could barely walk the next day after being in his bed, and the anticipation was killing me.

Since my boar was *still* hesitating, I threw down the ace up my sleeve, uncaring that I was playing dirty. "Please, Julius," I begged, putting on my poutiest pout. "I need you to *breed* me."

37
LEIA

Apparently the 'B word' was all it took to unlock Julius' chastity belt. He snarled like an unholy demon and used my grip on his tusks to toss me to the ground.

"Fuck!" I yelped as my back hit the ice-crusted snow, quickly propping myself up on my elbows to better glare at him. My scolding instantly evaporated as Julius nosed open my legs and licked a wide swath up my center—his tongue so large, both my inner thighs were soaked from a single pass.

The Hydra may have some competition.

I moaned as he continued past my stomach, coating each breast in saliva before moving his attention to my neck. He repeated the motion, never lingering long enough in one place. I soon realized this action was more about marking me as his than giving me the release I desperately needed.

Grasping his tusks again, I attempted to shove the enormous boar down toward my throbbing center. I knew I was no match for his strength, but my pussy had its own heartbeat. If I didn't get off soon, I was turning into a wild beast myself.

Julius' tusks shrank in my hold as he morphed back into human form, although he kept them out for maximum hotness.

Who's playing dirty now?

"What's the matter?" he darkly chuckled, sitting back on his heels with a shit-eating grin on his face. "Is my little monster *slut* not getting what she wants?"

Excuse you, sir?

"Okay, but who do you think you're talking to, calling me a..." The words died on my lips as my gaze landed on his cock.

His *two* cocks.

As expected, the main attraction was a two-hander, thick and veiny, but his secondary cock confused me at first glance. It was skinnier, protruding from the underside of the other to extend past it in length, and ribbed like a chain of anal beads. Just as I realized it would make an excellent back door knocker, it *moved*—spiraling around Julius' main cock to add texture and thickness.

"I... I want..." I stuttered, my brain no longer able to compute.

"Mmm, I know what you want," Julius hummed, giving his cocks—plural—a rough stroke. Copious amounts of precum were leaking out of both tips, and he spread it around as the bonus one uncoiled itself once again. "Now get on your fucking hands and knees and present yourself to me."

Yes, sir, right away, sir!

I flipped myself over, scrambling to my hands and knees and waving my ass in the chilly air like a cat in heat, which was accurate. My pussy had taken over central operations.

All I wanted—all I *needed* was Julius and his double-dong buried inside me.

"Good girl," he murmured, and I melted under the praise. My body was so overheated, I barely registered the snow beneath me as I lowered my forehead to the earth, panting as I waited for him to take me. I gasped as thick fingers swept down my ass and through my folds, dipping inside to stretch me while I unapologetically ground myself against his hand.

"So wet already," Julius' rumbling voice was in my ear as he curled his enormous body over mine. "Will you take all of me, Herculeia? Will you be my good little slut?"

"Yessss," I whined, practically sobbing with need. Normally, I would never allow someone to talk to me like this, but right now, I was here for it. "I want all of you. I want to be your slut, Julius, pleeeeease."

He chuckled again and licked a wet trail up my neck as he eased his main cock into me. The stretch was almost too much, but the bumps of his second dick hopped over my clit the deeper he went, triggering more wetness as my legs began to shake. With one final grunt, Julius bottomed out, his ribbed cock slapping my clit, sending me hurtling into a surprise climax. I was still shaking when he hauled me up into his lap, pinning my wrists behind my back and tightly looping his other arm across my stomach.

"You have such a needy little cunt," he rasped, tusks scraping against my neck as he snapped his hips upward, making me squeak. "We could take turns fucking you all day—filling you with our seed until it poured out of you— and you'd still never be satisfied."

I whimpered, too overstimulated to reply. My body was immobilized in Julius' hold, impaled on his cock, with my next orgasm alarmingly close as I was violently bounced on his lap. I felt uncomfortably full, but all I wanted was for him to keep filling me.

Breeding me.

As if sensing I was close, Julius reached down and positioned his bonus cock so that on the next descent, it slid inside me, along with the first. I cried out as the ridges hammered my g-spot, writhing in his arms through my second climax. He took pity on me this time, slowing his thrusts while I came down from my latest little death.

I sleep now...

"By Olympus, why do you feel so fucking good?" he hissed in my ear. The slight hitch in his voice made me realize my stoic man wasn't as unaffected as he pretended to be.

Abruptly releasing my wrists, he grabbed my waist and effortlessly lifted me off his cocks before spinning me to face him. Reaching behind me, he notched his smaller cock against my asshole, guiding it into me as I sank onto him again. I choked on a breath, my body instinctively tensing from the intrusion before I remembered to bear down and exhale. Even with how wet I was, it was an effort to take all of him in both holes.

Quitters never win!

Determined to share some of my discomfort, I dug my nails deep into Julius' neck. He shuddered, his eyes momentarily closing as he blissfully sighed. When he opened them again, something was different. There was a predatory glint in his expression I'd never seen before, one that made me again question if running had been wise.

"Tell me to stop," he rasped, popping another natural-born anal bead into my ass.

"I don't want you to," I murmured, struggling to understand what he was saying over all the sensations coursing through me. "I told you, I *want* you to fuck me."

He growled again—the sound edging toward inhuman. "Oh, I'm still going to fuck you. But you're going to tell me to stop, and you're going to mean it."

Fuck.

My brain switched back to lucidity the same instant I felt Julius *expanding* inside me, his true form flickering over his skin as he began to shift.

"Julius, *STOP!*" I shouted, panicking as I attempted to shove myself away before he ripped me in two. "I can't... I can't take you like that!" He responded by slamming me down on both cocks, holding my waist in an iron grip as he mercilessly thrust from below.

"You will take it," he snarled, ignoring my screams and the fists pounding against his chest. "You're my *mate,* which means you were made to take my cocks—to milk my seed. You are *mine.*"

I was full to the point of pain, tears blurring my vision as I sobbed, but my body still opened for him. My rational side did not like this game. But there was a much louder—more untamed—part that was enjoying it immensely.

Julius' hips stuttered, his grunts more animal than human. All I could do was hang on for dear life as yet another orgasm pulled me under. I gasped for air as he emptied inside me with a low, satiated groan—our combined release dripping out of me even with his half-shifted dicks still stuffed inside.

Thankfully, Julius immediately returned all of his parts to human scale before sliding out of me. The searing pain of the stretch faded to a dull ache as he rested his forehead against mine, clearly needing a rest himself. I collapsed against him, allowing my breathing to return to normal as I processed what had happened and how I felt about it.

Who have I become?

It took me a few seconds to realize Julius was shaking, although I quickly realized it was with silent laughter.

"You fucking asshole," I hissed, punching him in his broad chest with all I had, which accomplished nothing but make him laugh harder.

Gripping my chin in his large hand, he pulled me in for a surprisingly sweet kiss, his tusks gently gliding across my lips. "You liked it, my little Truffle," he smirked before standing with me still in his arms. "Come. Let's return to the fire. I'm sure one—or more—of the others will fuck you if you still hunger for monster cock."

Huffing, I buried my face against his chest. I refused to let it show that I *did* like it, and *was* considering whether I was up for another round with a different fancy peen. Or four.

Probably not.

Maybe.

"You're still an asshole," I mumbled against his skin, although there was little bite behind my words.

He chuckled and began carrying me back toward the campsite. "And you're still a slut." He gazed down at me in a way that made my chest feel tight. *"My* slut."

Yes, sir.

38
TIMYN

Having our mate along for the adventure certainly made the journey more enjoyable than usual. It wasn't simply that she smelled fantastic and took our cocks so nicely—although that *was* a perk. The positive influence my Water Lily had on everyone around her was noticeable. She'd mended the rift between Ambrose and Krysos, and given Julius something other than mindless revenge to focus on. Vann was mostly behaving himself, and even I felt less murderous than usual.

Then again, we haven't seen any centaurs in a while.

Leia was riding my Hydra for the last leg of our climb to the top of Mount Taygetus. I could have caressed her into coming all over me again, but she'd only just recently survived our big boar, so I left her alone—at least physically.

"So, which of Julius' cocks is your favorite? If you had to pick."

She laughed, and I decided the throaty sound was one

of my favorite things. "You know damn well that's an impossible choice," she whispered in one of my ears, as if the others wouldn't overhear. "But you called it, Timyn. I am *definitely* a monster-fucker, and proud of it."

"You and me both."

The air was unexpectedly pleasant at this altitude, warming my cold blood, which I assumed meant we were close to the mystical summit. Leia mentioned the Oracles were fueled by vapors from the earth, and I knew firsthand how balmy the climate deep underground was—guarding the gates of Hades as I once did, along with Cerberus.

Speaking of multiple appendages.

"Hydra, I will give you anything you want in exchange for a ride back down this godsforsaken rock."

I inwardly chuckled as Vann's voice echoed in my head. As a fellow water dweller, he also possessed the ability to communicate in this way. Although he'd been noticeably *un*communicative, ever since I beat him at knucklebones, fair and square.

"You know I love it when you ride me, Kraken. A fair trade would be you letting me watch while you stuff our mate full of your more enjoyable attributes."

My perfectly reasonable request was met with thick silence, punctuated by a withering glare from the Kraken as he lumbered by. Regardless, I fully expected him to agree in the end, if only to protect his sensitive little tentacles from the rocky terrain.

"Oh, look—we're here!" Leia exclaimed, oblivious to her future role in my deep-sea fantasies.

I glanced around, taking in what was a rather unimpressive Oracle. The summit was flat and rocky, with only a few windswept shrubs for greenery. Nothing remained of the seemingly modest temple, besides a few crumbling columns and the tall, golden stool of the missing prophetess propped up on the cracked foundation.

Moving us safely away from the edge, I wrapped a tail around Leia's deliciously thick waist and gently lowered her to the ground before shifting into my human form. Once again, I noticed how easy the transition was. Instead of feeling drained by embodying my Hydra for such a stretch, I was oddly energized. With absolutely nothing to base my theory on, I decided it was Leia's doing, simply because she was everything that was wonderful in the world.

Look at me, showing my soft underbelly...

Gross.

"How can I be expected to command the attention of Artemis," Krysos pouted to Ambrose as the other man petted him like a golden-antlered dog. "The last time the goddess appeared was when I was captured by Heracles. That was only because she thought he meant to kill me."

"So we'll toss you off the mountain and see if that gets the Lady's attention," Julius shrugged. This earned him a snicker from Vann and a very enticing glare from Leia.

Ambrose also scowled, which wasn't nearly as cute. He then turned to our mate with a hopeful expression. "Siren, perhaps you could assist Krysos? You seem to be quite knowledgeable about the process and mentioned you've experienced visions yourself."

Leia choked on air. "I wouldn't call my random, usually indigestion-fueled dreams 'visions,' Ambrose."

"Did you not say you'd repeatedly dreamt of a wild boar chasing you through the snow?" a smug-looking Julius interrupted.

"Yeah, but those dreams never ended like..." Leia trailed off, blushing and fanning herself in the humid air while the rest of us tried to hide our smirks. Our human mate didn't realize they *hadn't* been far enough away last night for our sharp hearing to miss out on the action.

It sounded like they had fun.

"Okay, fine! I'll help Krysos connect with his feminine side, or whatever," Leia mumbled, adorably flustered. She steered the hind toward the uneven temple steps before pointing at the stool. "Go sit on the tripod. See how it's positioned over the cracks in the foundation? That's where the priestess receives her visions from the fumes."

We all waited as Krysos climbed up to perch on the stool, looking simultaneously graceful and awkward, which was oddly endearing. The Golden Hind liked to play the role of haughty prince, but I'd witnessed him at his lowest—when I was equally defeated.

He was the first creature I found after waking up as a man. Even without a way to communicate, we'd somehow recognized each other for who we truly were, and formed an immediate bond over our shared affliction. It took weeks of misadventure together to stumble upon Ambrose and the others, and longer still to piece together the gravity of our collective situation. I still didn't fully understand why the twelve of us had been cursed to human forms—on top of our banishment from civilization.

And why do we still have access to our sources of power?

Shaking my head, I refocused on our two stand-in priestesses, determined to show moral support. Krysos cleared his throat before calling out to the heavens, "Artemis, daughter of Zeus and Leto, goddess of the moon and the hunt—"

"*Potnia Theron!*" I loudly whispered in his head,

reminding him of her most primal role—which was appropriate, given the circumstances.

He nodded once in my direction before adding, "Mistress of Animals, please set aside your golden bow and arrow to hear your hind's humble plea."

"Humble," Vann scoffed, earning him a chuckle from Julius in return.

Get a room, you two.

Krysos paused, presumably to allow the goddess to answer. When nothing happened for several minutes, the hind pursed his lips and looked to Leia for guidance.

"It's okay," she soothed, lifting her skirt to climb the steps and join him. "Maybe we shouldn't be asking Artemis at all, considering she's one of the twelve Olympians who agreed to trap you all here. Triptolemus said others were aware of the situation. How about we try a more general appeal and see who answers?"

The hind nodded in agreement, even as disappointment flashed over his features. I wasn't a hugger, but *good gods!* I wanted to squeeze the sad look off his pretty face before Ambrose fucked the pain away.

What is with all these... emotions lately?

Leia must have felt a similar compulsion, as she quickly closed the distance between them, reaching for the back of Krysos' stool to steady herself on the uneven ground.

I didn't know which happened first. Her hand touched the tripod, and the mountain shook, knocking the rest of us to the ground. The cracks in the temple foundation widened—the gaping fissures emitting clouds of vapor so thick, I lost sight of everyone around me.

Then I heard Leia scream.

My Hydra half-burst out of my skin, instinctively needing to protect my mate. The others were experiencing the same reaction, judging by the panicked growls muffled by the choking fog. As quickly as it appeared, the vapors dissipated, revealing my worst nightmare. The golden stool remained upright in the ruins, but the temple now stood empty—devoid of hind or human.

Krysos and Leia were gone.

39
LEIA

When I opened my eyes again, the first thing I noticed was my heart still beating. The second was that a row of massive columns loomed above me, harshly reflecting the moonlight.

I thought the temple columns were on the ground...

Blowing out a breath, I sat up and attempted to reconstruct what happened in my mind. The last thing I remembered was feeling a *jolt* when I touched the tripod, similar to when I touched an *obol,* or my men. What followed was a fractured jumble of noise and chaos as I fell down into an endless pit, screaming with lungs clouded by the scent of laurel.

I must have imagined the fall. Because here I was, at the top of Mount Taygetus, with my feet on solid ground.

With my ass on it, anyway.

I rose to stand, slowly blinking as I took in the strange scenery. The temple foundation had somehow expanded 200 feet, and now featured the various remains of walled partitions surrounding several indentations, overgrown by weeds. Squinting beyond the columns, I saw what looked like an entire campus of ruins, sloping down the grassy mountain-side above and below the eerily familiar building I stood in.

Why does it look like I'm in Apollo's Temple at the Oracle of Delphi?

"Finally! It took you long enough to arrive, Herculeia. I swear, since birth, you've never respected my time."

Is that... my mother?

Sure enough, Dr. Alcmene Hatzi-Loukanis was briskly striding toward me. She was dressed in her usual Indiana Jones archeologist getup, despite it being the middle of the fucking night.

I must have hit my head harder than I thought.

"It's good to see you too, mama," I muttered, brushing the dust off my *peplos*. "Even if you are only a figment of my traumatized imagination. I guess all that therapy you paid for growing up didn't cure my inevitable psychosis, hmm?" I suddenly panicked, worried *this* was reality and my time with my men had been a dream. Then I felt the delicious ache between my legs from Julius and sighed in relief.

Even if that just makes being here *more confusing.*

As if anything in my life makes sense lately.

My mother snorted as she came to a stop in front of me and crossed her arms. "While this conversation may seem implausible, I assure you, your presence here is very real—at least on an ethereal level. Now, we have much to discuss before you re-inhabit your body on the island."

"Whoa, whoa, whoa!" I shouted, frantically waving my hands in front of me to slow down the force of nature that was Alcmene. "You *know* which island I'm on? As in, you could send a helicopter to airlift me the fuck out of there?"

"Don't be ridiculous," my mother rolled her eyes, as if *that* was the part of this conversation worth judging. "If I were to rescue you—which I'm uncertain I *could* without primordial help—then you wouldn't be able to fulfill your destiny. So, stop being dramatic, and tell me how things are progressing with your monsters."

I steadied myself on a low wall as I grew lightheaded. My ring had twisted on my finger, and the amethyst digging into my palm grounded me as I calmed my racing heart.

Okay, deep breaths, Leia.

Despite what my mother was implying, my existence here felt pretty fucking corporeal, if the night air chilling my very sweaty body was any sign. That I could *mentally teleport* was more than I could handle, so I focused on what I knew to be real. The memory of my men's skin against mine was real, like a permanent brand on my soul that pulsed with a life of its own.

They are real.

"You... know about my men?" I haltingly asked, unsure where to even start with all the questions crowding my brain.

"They are not *men!*" My mother threw up her hands, exasperated by my existence, as usual. "That is the entire point. Did you hit your head out on the island, child? Your lack of basic comprehension is extremely inconvenient at the moment."

Did I seriously astral project myself to Delphi just so my mother could berate me?

"Excuse me if I'm taking up too much of your precious time while I process all of this *very new information*," I hissed, having officially lost the last fuck I had to give. "How about you spit out whatever all-important prophecy you know? Then we can return to only communicating once every five years, per the terms of our non-existent relationship."

My mother actually *flinched* at my words, which surprised me more than the rest of this ridiculousness combined. "It was necessary for me to keep my distance, Herculeia," she replied, uncharacteristically contrite. "I tried to pass along enough basic history to give you a foundation, but I couldn't risk *you* knowing too much about where you fit into it, lest you give yourself away. If your existence was discovered when you were young, you would have been killed—or had your powers stripped—like the others before you."

Killed?!

She smoothly continued, as if my entire life wasn't crumbling into dust, like an ancient Doric column. "Maturing into adulthood meant you could handle yourself and any men—monsters—who came along. It is vitally important that you stay the course, Herculeia. Collect all twelve of the monsters cursed as men and bring them to their knees before you. Their weakness is your strength. Only then will you wield enough power to rewrite history."

Bring them to their knees?

Rewrite history?!

Where is my bowl-cup when I need it..?

"BISH! Where the *fuck* have you been?" An equally familiar voice snapped my attention away from the doomsday boomer spitting nonsense. I gaped to find *Iola* of all people stomping over the uneven terrain. Her velour loungewear implied *she* at least had been in bed at this hour —probably in the contractor's trailer behind her, nestled among the ruins.

"I've been shipwrecked on a fucking island, which apparently isn't news to anyone!" My voice cracked, my fragile composure slipping in the presence of my supposed best friend. "Are either of you even *pretending* to look for me? How could you leave me on that island—leave *us* out there—knowing damn well that I'm still alive?"

Iola's frantic gaze skittered between us. "What the hell is she talking about, Auntie Meanie? You *knew* where she was this whole time?!" My mother simply pursed her lips, back to her usual cool detachment and apparently uninterested in continuing the conversation in my niece's presence.

Because why not leave me hanging?

Closing the distance between us, Iola continued to babble. "I didn't know, I swear! Those random olive oil clients of yours offered to fly me out here via email, but they never picked me up at the airport, so I had no choice but to call Head Hoebaggler over there to come get me. The police or coast guard or whatever *claim* they've been looking for your cruise ship, but nothing has been found. It's like you just *vanished!*" Tears streamed down her face as she reached for my wrist. "I thought you were fucking dead—" She choked on her words as her fingers passed right through me, as if I were nothing more than a ghost.

How can I be in two places at once?

Furious beyond words, I turned my attention back to the person who was clearly to blame. My mother knew where I was, who I was with, and my supposed 'destiny.' She also apparently knew I was capable of whatever freaky deaky magical bullshit was going on here. I opened my mouth to finally give her the piece of my mind I'd been holding back for nearly three decades, but I quickly snapped it closed. All at once, I realized something chilling.

If I have these abilities, then they came from somewhere.

Or someone...

The stranger I *thought* was my mother cocked her head, as if hearing something whispered on the breeze. "They're calling you back, Herculeia," she nonchalantly replied, like *that* was a normal thing to say.

Part of me wanted to stay and comfort Iola, who was obviously losing her shit, but the solidness of my body was fading. "Who is calling me back?" I rasped, tears pricking my eyes. Some unknown force was insistently pulling me under, and I was too exhausted to fight it.

My mother knowingly smirked. "The Fates."

I heard Iola scream—saw her wildly reach for me again —but her anguished face disappeared. The smell of burning laurel and sulfur permeated my nostrils as my surroundings blurred into nothingness.

When my vision returned, I gasped to find myself flat on my back again with an enormous bird peering down at me from inches away. It was sleek, like an oversized falcon, with ochre-colored feathers that were tinged red—almost as if they were stained....

...with blood.

The bird's beady eyes brightened at seeing me awake, the bronze edges of its metallic beak scraping as it seemed to smile down at me.

"Well, hello, human," it squawked, a drop of what was *definitely* blood falling from its mouth to splash upon my cheek. "Don't you look *delicious.*"

40
KRYSOS

"If you hurt my mate, I will melt the feathers and flesh from your body," I growled at the bird looming over Leia's shivering form. "And the others will gladly take over once you've bled enough for me."

Zephyr cocked his head, as if considering whether a bite of Leia was worth our collective wrath. Luckily, he backed away, and I immediately rushed to my mate's side, thanking the gods she was free from the trance she'd been under.

Please don't leave me like that again.

When the earth swallowed Leia, I didn't have time to think. My only instinct had been to leap into the chasm after her, praying I could shift to my hind quickly enough to take the brunt of our fall. There was a chance I'd fail and die on impact, but protecting her was more important than my insignificant life.

The vapors were thick and suffocating as we fell, yet they also somehow *slowed* our descent—gently depositing us at the bottom, like invisible hands. The instant we landed, I blindly reached for Leia, relieved she was breathing and relatively unscathed. Only then did I discover she was trapped in a comatose state, similar to what an Oracle priestess experienced.

Could she be a..?

I couldn't help considering Vann's blunt observation— that any creature with a direct connection to Olympus would *not* have been left here for us to utilize. Growling under my breath, I weathered this latest blow to what little faith I had left, while a tiny piece of me sparked with hope.

"Can someone fucking answer me down there?" Julius' booming voice called down from far above. "Is Leia alive?"

"And Krysos?" Ambrose added, most likely panicking more than he was letting on.

Zephyr sighed heavily as he fully transitioned into his human form. Razor-sharp feathers morphed into smooth, ochre skin, and beady eyes into mesmerizingly black irises flecked with bronze. Even I could admit he was a visually appealing man in this form.

If he wasn't absolutely terrifying.

"All this fuss for a *human,*" he murmured with an exasperated glance skyward. "And you won't even let me have a taste."

"Might I add, you are not allowed to *eat* the human, you vulture!" One of the Hydra's heads snaked through the crack in the earth to shoot Zephyr a judgmental look.

Leia crawled into my arms, still shaking from our experience, and wherever her mind had traveled to. "He's not... really going to eat me, is he, Krysos?"

Our rescuer's hungry gaze drifted to her again, and I tightened my hold. While we were lucky Zephyr had appeared to offer his assistance, I refused to hand Leia over to him. The Stymphalian Birds were well known to feast on humans—back when they still existed among us. While

Zephyr may have been forced to adopt a new diet here, I knew firsthand how tempting our mate was.

In every way.

"You will carry us out of here—*together*," I commanded, hoping my concern for Leia was buried deep enough that he couldn't feed off of it as well.

When he simply stared at me, head cocked and eyes unblinking, I desperately added, "Leia is a rare *prophetess*, able to communicate with the gods. She wishes to help us escape this island."

"I'm not a—" Leia began, but I squeezed her so hard she choked on her words.

"Well, why didn't you say so," Zephyr grinned, his charming smile a deceptive facade. "Olympus knows, Artemis seems to have forgotten about her *pets*, hmm, my Golden Hind?"

I gritted my teeth and nodded in annoyed solidarity. The birds of Stymphalia were raised by Ares for war, but they were also favorites of Artemis, along with me and my fellow hinds. I wasn't special in the grand scheme of things, but it was a mighty blow to realize my goddess had no interest in showing me favor ever again.

We truly have been forsaken.

"Can we... get out of here.. please?" Leia's voice was uncharacteristically meek, causing me to sharply glance down at her again. Her eyes darted around, like a cornered animal looking to escape.

Something tells me it has nothing to do with the voracious bird in our midst.

Kneeling, I shifted into my hind, so Leia could climb onto my back. Once she was secure, Zephyr transformed into his bird, caging her in with his body while digging his talons into my flanks to lift us both to freedom. The pain was more irritating than anything—and I knew I'd heal quickly—but blood was soon pouring off of me.

As we rose from the fissure, I noticed most of the others were still in human form, except for Ambrose, who was pacing and moaning as the Nemean Lion. The instant we came into view, he let out a deafening roar, causing Zephyr to wisely drop us on the ground so he could pounce, unobstructed. He frantically lapped at my wounds, his barbed tongue covering Leia as well, in his efforts to ensure we were all right.

Oh, you big, stupid animal.

Even after my injuries were healed, he showed no sign of stopping, so I took my human form and threw my arms around his enormous head.

"We are *fine*, Ambrose," I chuckled, scratching behind his ears in the way that made him purr. "All you're accomplishing now is making us both extremely wet."

He huffed and morphed into a human himself. "I thought I'd lost you," he mumbled into the crook of my neck, clearly in no hurry to release us from under the weight of his massive body. "My mates."

"*Leia* is fine," I insisted, wanting to get off this mountain before it opened up again. I also couldn't shake the feeling that something *unsettling* had happened to Leia during her vision.

Where did you go, Fawn?

Ambrose finally moved and helped both of us to our feet, although he didn't grant us more physical space until Julius forcibly shoved him aside.

"What happened down there, girl?" the boar gruffly demanded, although I saw his gaze running over her body, checking for injuries. "Timyn said it seemed as if you touching Taygete's stool caused all of this. Were you contacted by Olympus? Did a vision come to you?"

We all turned to Leia, and I was horrified to see her plump bottom lip trembling, the piercing below it catching the light of the rising sun. "I... I somehow ended up in the Temple of Apollo at Delphi, with my *mother*—"

"Apollo?" Timyn crossed his arms, scoffing dismissively. "The temple at Delphi belongs to *Gaia*—our ancestral earth mother—everybody knows that."

"Why is it crying?" Zephyr cocked his head, staring at Leia as if she were a butterfly pinned to a board for his perusal.

Enough!

A battle-worthy rage overtook me—my mate's comfort being the only thing that mattered. "Stand down, all of you!" I barked, silencing the rabble. "Leia needs to *rest,* not be pestered to death. We should get her somewhere more comfortable."

Zephyr snorted, clearly unimpressed with my display. "You won't get very far taking the usual routes." When we all looked at him expectantly, he shrugged. *"That's* what I came here to tell you, before this 'rescue-the-human' thing took precedence. The Foloi Forest is aflame. It started about an hour ago and looks to be burning to the ground."

"WHAT?!" Julius shouted, rounding on the bird. "How did that happen? No. Don't answer that. It's clear this is just another one of Eurystheus' games."

Vann made a sound of disapproval, drawing my attention his way. The Kraken rarely joined our discussions—content with his self-appointed role of *outsider*—but I wished he would weigh in at the moment.

The squid's smarter than he looks.

"Pholus and his centaurs are already fighting the fire,

alongside the nymphs who live there," Zephyr yawned, absently picking at a talon. "I assume he's concerned the flames might reach his precious vineyard."

Julius furrowed his brow. "The vineyard is miles away. How did he get there so fast?" He shook his head, waving a dismissive hand before turning to Leia. "Well, Truffle, perhaps this could be another one of those 'good deeds' of yours—"

"NO!" Leia yelped, startling me—all of us—with the vehemence of her outburst.

"Is there a problem, Herculeia?" Vann was watching her closely, although I glimpsed an unexpected glimmer of concern in his usually cool expression.

Leia swallowed hard, her gorgeous gaze fixed on the ground. "I don't like fire. It's how my dad... died."

Oh, Fawn...

"All right, that's it," I snipped, shooing everyone toward the path back down the mountain. "Our mate *needs* to recuperate. Vann, your grotto is the closest sanctuary—can we bring her there?" The Kraken distractedly nodded before sweeping his gaze out over the farmland we'd recently saved.

A few minutes of commotion followed, as Julius instructed Zephyr to fly ahead to the remaining six. He was already convinced the fire was an attack by Eurystheus, and wanted confirmation that our former allies would join our cause in the face of this latest grievance. The rest of us would hole up in Vann's grotto while Leia recovered, assessing this recent development and planning our next steps.

Our mate was bundled in furs and handed off to Timyn for the journey down the mountain. I shifted into my hind, but noticed Vann was still deep in thought, making no move to transition into his Kraken.

He caught me watching him just as the Hydra's tail wrapped around his waist. "Dragons." was all he said before being lifted to ride alongside the one human who mattered more than twelve curses combined.

41
LEIA

Normally, I would hate being treated like I could break, but it seemed like a real possibility at the moment. I numbly watched as my men bustled around Vann's grotto, taking turns clumsily preparing me food and giving me plenty of comfort and cuddles.

Although I don't deserve any of it.

My gaze drifted to the water lapping against the stone slab of the main living area, lit from below by phosphorescent algae. This unearthly glow lit up the craggy stone of the entire cavern, giving the place a nightclub atmosphere while illuminating my monsters like neon gods. If I'd been in a better mood, I may have amused myself with imagining which angles of this rave-cave would produce the most Instagram-worthy lifestyle shots. Instead, I was more focused on the dire circumstances of the last several days.

My, how my priorities have changed...

I couldn't decide which newest bombshell was the worst. Discovering I had the power to mentally travel between Oracles, Eurystheus threatening my men with my existence, or my *mother* casually masterminding my entire life.

How much has she kept from me?

Ambrose plopped down beside me on the ridiculous number of floor pillows a Kraken apparently needed for land-based lounging. "You're still upset, Leia," he observed in that completely non-judgmental way of his, pulling me into his lap. "How can we help?"

I bit my lip so I wouldn't start crying again. I'd already shared a little about my weird trip to Delphi, but just like with my run-in with Eurystheus, I purposefully omitted details. With Eurystheus, I didn't want my men freaking out over what sounded like a delusional, evil plan. After what happened at the Oracle, however, I wondered if the real danger was actually me.

"Bring all twelve monsters to their knees. Use their weakness as your strength."

My breathing started coming in quick gasps as sweat broke out over my skin. "I need some air," I mumbled, clawing my way out of Ambrose's arms and quickly heading for the exit, tripping over a few pillows on my way.

The narrow path I took hugged the cavern wall, the bluish water lapping at my bare feet as it overflowed from the pool running alongside. I was overheating in the balmy air, shedding layers as I went, and after rounding the corner, I paused to rest my forehead against the damp stone.

What should I do?

"Care for a swim, my little mystical nymph?"

I spun to find Vann lounging against a large rock in the middle of the pool. He was naked from the waist up, with his hands clasped behind his head. He may have also been naked *below* the waist, but that half of him was obscured by the glowing water.

Including that tentacle peen...

Spying movement beneath the waves, I stepped closer, only to stumble backward again when one of his *regular* tentacles surfaced. It stretched, seeming to reach for me before soundlessly disappearing beneath the water again.

"Sorry," he smirked, not looking sorry at all. "Sometimes they have a mind of their own."

"You can't... control them?" I asked, crouching down to test the water temperature, considering his invitation.

Anything to distract myself.

He chuckled low, drawing my attention back to them. "Oh, I *can,* trust me. There are many things I can do with all of my... appendages."

I swallowed hard, thinking of the most interesting appendage of all. At this point, I'd experienced fancy monster accessories, but something about *tentacles* felt alien to me.

Not that I'm opposed to being probed.

Timyn abruptly broke through the surface—right between Vann's legs. "Water Lily!" he exclaimed with a radiant smile, unbothered that I'd probably just caught him giving an underwater blowie. "Have you come to play?"

"I was actually going to get some air on the beach," I stuttered, rising to my feet again. "And I don't want to interrupt you guys."

Timyn scoffed. "Oh, hush. You know I love to share and be shared. Now take off that ridiculous human clothing and come frolic with us. Unleash your inner Nereid!"

I stifled a smile. Timyn had big golden retriever energy —if the dog was a piranha known for ruthlessly ripping its enemies to shreds. There were definitely moments when it was painfully obvious my men and I were not the same species, but sometimes, they were the kindest, sweetest little killer puppy-fish ever.

And I'm the asshole who's been betraying them.

"What's troubling you, Leia?" I yelped in surprise as Vann suddenly appeared directly in front of me, like a fucking water ninja. "Something is causing you deep distress. I can *feel* it."

HE KNOWS!

"Don't look so terrified, Leia," Timyn laughed, loudly splashing over to join the Kraken at the edge of the pool. "Vann simply picks up on vibrations—as do I, to a lesser extent—and you seem very *low* right now." He smirked up at me, running a finger over the top of my foot. "Can we help raise your *vibrations?*"

Cheeky lake snake.

I chewed my lip, undecided. Escaping to the beach had sounded necessary for survival a few minutes ago. Now, I very much wanted to float around in the witchy blue water with two hot-bod mermen.

"We can make you feel everything and *nothing,*" Vann whispered, his words coiling around me like steam, lulling me into complacency with exactly what I needed to hear. Part of me *knew* either he or Timyn were using mind tricks to relax me, but I didn't care. I trusted them—even if I didn't deserve their trust in return. Firmly under their spell, I dreamily pulled my *peplos* over my head and cast it aside.

One of Timyn's tails wrapped around my waist and lowered me into his arms, half-submerged in the warm water. I vaguely wondered if the algae affected the temperature before banishing the frivolous thought from my mind, determined to be completely present.

Give me everything and nothing.

I gasped as I felt Timyn rub the head of his cock through my folds, his tail still holding me up as I hooked my ankles behind his back, urging him inside me.

"Please," was all I could say, and he smiled, guiding himself in. I slid halfway down his ridged dragon dick before he stopped me, either to collect himself, or to wait for permission before locking me in with his spurs again.

The answer is always yes, dude.

"*Fuuuck...* This. Cunt," he gritted his teeth before ghosting his lips over mine. "I've never felt anything as perfect as you, Leia."

"Careful, you're making me jealous," Vann drifted toward us, looking larger than usual as more tentacles slid from his back to surround the two of us, caging us in. "Is she hot and wet, Timyn? Is her cunt pulsing around your cock like she wants to milk every last drop of your seed?"

I guess I don't mind the S-word anymore...

Vann positioned himself behind the Hydra, curling himself around the other man before murmuring in his ear. "Does she feel as good inside as you do?"

Timyn tensed, his eyes rolling backward as he moaned. My brain fizzled as if an oversized toaster had just been dropped into our pond, suddenly realizing the man fucking me was taking a tentacle up the ass.

I'm having major FOMO, right now.

"Tell me how it feels," I whispered, cupping Timyn's handsome face in my hands, bringing his awareness back to me. My breath caught as he growled and pushed himself in deeper, still minding his spurs, even as he was clearly skirting the edge of sexy beast mode.

"It feels like... like being sucked on from the *inside*. It's incredible," he rasped, his irises now slits as those mesmerizing green and purple scales began decorating his skin. "Although, I have to say, your pretty little cunt is still better."

"Naughty Hydra," Vann rewarded his sass with a deep thrust before meeting my gaze over Timyn's shoulder. I noticed *his* irises were now *rectangles,* which was wild. "Give me your hand, Leia."

Like a good monster fucker, I held up my hand, curious what he'd do. With unexpected gentleness, Vann ran a tentacle across my palm, allowing me to feel the texture as he slowly trailed it over my skin. As I explored him, his individual suckers gripped my fingertips, closing around them with enough pull that I gasped.

I am buying what he's selling.

"Suck on her nipples, Vann," Timyn choked out, apparently still lucid enough to suggest the best idea ever.

Instead of diving in, the Kraken held my gaze. "Is that what you want, Leia? You want to feel me tasting you, inside and out?" Everything these men said sounded dirty, even while they were being admirably concerned about consent, but I forced myself to focus on his question.

I was no stranger to anal, but I'd never taken two men at the same time before. Never mind the monster cocks and other fancy appendages. This would be a level of trust I hadn't even reached with Dylan.

But he wasn't them.

"I want you everywhere... just like you're doing to him," I breathed. I was nervous while still feeling more sure of this than anything else in my life. "But you'd better go slow. I'm not the seasoned monster whore *Timyn* is."

Both men laughed before Vann did *something* that turned Timyn's into a groan. My Hydra thrusted deeper, the ridges on his thick cock twisting over my g-spot in a way that had me seeing stars.

I wanted him to lock me onto his spurs again, but no matter how much I wiggled and bounced—no matter how much I could tell he wanted it too—he kept stopping me from reaching the base.

"Timyn," I finally whimpered, "Why won't you..?"

"I'm not the one in charge, Water Lily."

Oh.

My gaze drifted to where Vann was looming over both of us. He was still expanding, looking more and more like the giant sea monster still lurking beneath the surface. He wrapped a tentacle around my back before curling it over my chest—the flexing appendage holding me steady while he positioned himself. Two large suckers lined up with my nipples, then latched on like vacuum seals.

"Vann!" I squeaked, tightening my thighs around Timyn's waist, making him shut his eyes, growling in frustrated pleasure. Most men didn't know what to do with a woman's breasts, besides poke at them. This was like a direct line from my nipples to my clit, and Vann was communicating like a pro.

The Kraken was watching my face with an intensity that would have freaked me out normally. "I love how responsive you are," he purred. "I wonder how much more of me you can take."

It's the moment of truth.

My mouth dropped open as I felt another tentacle slide under the curve of my ass, heading for deeper waters. Two more spread me open as the first squeezed its way inside. I tensed, even though there was no discomfort besides an increasing sense of *fullness*. Just like Timyn's cock, Vann's appendages seemed to secrete their own lube, which was handy for playing in the water.

I whimpered from the sensations, causing Timyn's vibrant green eyes to flutter open again. "Shall I help you relax, my love?"

Tears pricked my eyelids. Being impaled on dragon dick while a mythical squid shoved his tentacle into my ass shouldn't have been a sweet moment, but here we were. That was the heady juxtaposition of these men. We often had startlingly different ways of processing things, but they were genuinely focused on *me*—on my comfort and care— with a level of attentiveness I'd never experienced before.

Which is making my decision so much harder.

Forcing myself to stop thinking about the future, I nodded. Timyn unfurled his wicked tongue, extending it until it reached my clit—curling around the bundle of nerves before *starting to vibrate.* A helpless wail poured from my throat as waves of pleasure ripped through me like electric shocks, making me convulse around Timyn's cock. Vann took the opportunity to stuff the tentacle in my ass deeper, drawing out my orgasm until I thought I might faint.

Two more heads tore from my Hydra's shoulders as his handsome face morphed into the same reptilian one I'd first encountered at the lake of Lerna. His fingers were painfully digging into my thighs, each thrust inching closer to locking me on his dick, but *still* he deferred to Vann's unspoken authority.

Please, please, please.

As if hearing my plea, the Kraken chuckled and looped two more of his tentacles over my shoulders, slamming me down onto the spurs waiting between my thighs. Timyn snarled and began to rut as my vision went hazy, and all I registered, besides the feel of him stretching me, was Vann's silky voice permeating my semi-consciousness.

"Fill our mate with your seed, Hydra. I want her soaking wet for me."

42

VANN

Mine.

Both of them were mine. However, the burning desire to claim Leia completely made it clear my beast was answering a much greater call than simply wanting to fuck.

Although, we will be fucking as well.

If I hadn't been so focused on drowning her when we first met, I may have noticed the all-consuming need to protect alongside the desire to breed. It took observing how the others responded to Leia to realize there were larger forces at play here. Mating for life had never felt necessary before, especially as our basic needs were being met. It was far too coincidental that we all were drawn to the same woman.

"Water Lily," Timyn gasped as he rutted into our mate with a desperation I'd never witnessed from him before. "Your little moans are delectable. Do you enjoy being stuffed by both of us?" I rewarded the Hydra for speaking out loud—twisting the tentacle in Leia's ass so he could feel it caressing his cock through her inner walls.

"Yes! So fucking much. I... I think I'm gonna come again," Leia panted, yelping when I gave her luscious nipples a firm tug with my suckers. "Oh, fuck, Vann... whatever you're doing back there, don't stop. Don't... ahhhh!"

Wait until she works her way up to three *tentacles...*

Like Timyn.

Leia shuddered and writhed, wildly clawing at both of us while she came undone. Timyn growled—an inhuman sound that had my cock aching—and erratically thrust, chasing his release. He tightened around me and pumped our mate full of seed, prompting her fertile body to further perfume the air, driving me mad.

I must have her.

Withdrawing my tentacles from everyone, I unceremoniously tossed the Hydra aside, possessively gathering Leia's limp form against me before propelling us to deeper, darker waters.

"Oh, I had a lovely time as well, Vann!" Timyn called, dragging himself to the edge of the pool with a laughing groan. "So nice of you to send me off with a Viking Funeral, you salty fish."

Mine.

"Vann?" Leia's voice held a note of concern that made me slow my mindless pace. "You're not dunking me underwater again, are you?"

I chuckled. "No, *Aelfmaer,* but I'm done sharing, at least for now. I want you all to myself."

"I'm your little mystical nymph, hmm?" she dreamily hummed, confirming my suspicions that she understood more languages than Ancient Greek. I gently laid her on the soft moss blanketing the sloping cavern shore at this end, knowing she'd be comfortable—despite the near darkness.

"Couldn't you have just told Timyn to go join the others in your pillow fortress? I can barely see over here."

You won't want to see what's about to happen.

"Leia," I gritted out as my true form took over. Dozens of tentacles were now erupting from my spine, readying to strike—preparing to capture our prey. "Before my beast takes over, tell me if you truly want this. If you don't, I will immediately call Timyn to come get you."

Although I may still fight him for you.

My advanced eyesight allowed me to clearly see her sit up and blindly reach for me. She ran her hands over the already thick and rubbery skin of my chest, but didn't pull back in horror at the texture, much to my surprise.

"You don't have to hide from me, Vann," she murmured, almost wistfully. "I know what you are, and I still want you."

My Kraken practically exploded out of me, but I held him back, determined to maintain as much of my humanoid features as possible. It was one thing for Leia to whisper sweet words of acceptance. It was quite another to face a monster who had taken down countless vessels.

"Beautiful human," I purred, my voice distorted as parts of me continued to rearrange. "Are you sure you're not afraid of me?"

Maybe a little?

Leia laughed, a most enjoyable sound. "Let's call it a healthy dose of caution. But I *want* to know how that tentacle dick feels. So come ashore, sailor."

Two of my tentacles dove for my mate, wrapping around her thighs and roughly spreading her open. Timyn's seed was still dripping out of her, so I easily plunged in with one smooth stroke. She gasped at the no doubt foreign sensation. After all, most cocks weren't prehensile and covered with suckers on all sides.

Most also don't have tentacles of their own.

"Holy *shit,*" she choked out, her delicate hands scrabbling for purchase on my slippery skin. As much as I craved her touch, I preferred my prey immobilized as I feasted, so two more tentacles snatched her wrists, slamming her back down against the moss. Leia tried her best to wiggle and buck, but I only coiled tighter, reveling in the taste of her skin, her cunt... her inevitable human *fear.*

So incredibly delicious.

As much as she claimed not to care about my beast, her survival instincts were going haywire, her pheromones ripe with building terror at the realization that she was in the clutches of a very dangerous predator.

"What... *ohmygawd,* what *is* that?" she shrieked, as two feeding tentacles shot from the end of my cock to hook into the plush inner walls of her channel—ensuring she wouldn't dislodge me until I was done claiming her.

Breeding her.

"You're mine," I snarled, feeling my cock burrowing deeper, pushing past where any man—or monster—had been before. "You will take my seed, and carry my spawn, and you will *never* leave my side."

"Vann, I can't... it hurts!" she was sobbing now, and I leaned forward to lick the tears from her smooth skin, drinking in her anguish. Beneath the thin layer of terror and pain was a bottomless ocean of desire, so I continued to burrow, marveling at how well her body took me.

"You wanted monsters, Herculeia," I chuckled. "Just be thankful you can't *see* what's fucking you."

"But I want to... oh, *fuck,* I'm coming again!" she screamed, writhing like a worm on a hook, with no hope of escape. I threw my head back, howling in ecstasy as her quivering channel tightened around me, milking my cock with glorious pulses until she'd sucked me dry.

I was so focused on coaxing my Kraken to retreat that it took a moment to realize Leia was softly crying, which deeply troubled me. I quickly released her wrists and thighs from my grasp and gathered her in my human arms. It would be another minute before I could retract my cock's feeding tentacles, but I needed to ensure she was all right.

"Was that... *not* pleasurable?" I hesitantly asked, suddenly self-conscious about how my breeding methods may differ from hers.

"I don't *want* to leave your side," she blubbered against my chest. Her sudden anxiety caused my animal instincts to roar to life, which only sparked the need to claim her all over again.

Keep this up and we won't ever leave this pool.

"Why concern yourself with that?" I asked, tamping down my urge to fight or fuck. I gently ran a hand through her green hair, admiring how soft it was. *Everything* about her was soft—soft and perfect. "You belong with me, with *us*. It's fate." She stiffened in my arms, most likely because I was finally extracting my cock, followed by a satisfying deluge of seed.

"What makes you think this is fate?" Leia quietly asked, gazing up at me with a sadness I couldn't explain. "How do you know I'm not just part of your curse?"

What an odd question.

I was so thrown off, I could do nothing but propel us back to the brighter end of the cavern. Helping her climb out of the pool near her discarded dress. I scrambled for what to say. It seemed so obvious to me—so unquestionable that she was ours. There was no reason to believe it was a curse.

"The tattoo on your bicep has a giant squid on it that looks like me," I mumbled, my sizable brain apparently choosing *this* moment to be ineloquent.

Since when do I not have an intelligent answer?

She froze with the *peplos* pulled halfway over her head, so I couldn't see her face. By the time she'd emerged from the fabric, I suspected she'd buried whatever emotion had briefly flared up. "The idea for it came to me in a dream," she flatly replied. There was a grim set to her mouth that seemed incongruent with her usually cheerful demeanor.

"That only proves my theory," I smiled as I hoisted myself out of the pool, determined to make her happy again. "You've mentioned dreams that featured us before. Then you had a prophetic vision at the Oracle—" I abruptly stopped talking as she stumbled backward, her gaze darting toward the cave entrance.

Do all humans behave like they want to run after copulation?

"Come, Leia," I soothed, pulling her against me and smirking when her hungry gaze dropped to my cock again. "Let's rejoin the others. I'm sure they would all appreciate the opportunity to enjoy your company before we have to leave for our journey."

"Yes, let's do that," she murmured, allowing me to lead her back to my 'pillow fortress.' "Before we have to go."

––––––

When I awoke hours later, Leia was gone.

I forced myself not to panic, as shifting into my Kraken would crush the other men sprawled among the cushions.

She'd probably wandered off to 'break the seal,' as she referred to the act of urinating. I barely understood most of the slang coming from her tempting mouth, although she oddly understood the Old Norse I spoke on occasion. We would have time to learn each other's customs, now that we were mated.

I wonder what year *it is in the outside world?*

Leia's pack and furs were still with the rest of our supplies, and I frowned, realizing she'd be cold on the beach this early in the morning. I extracted myself from the pile of limbs as carefully as possible, determined to steal more alone time with my mate before the others joined us.

Julius murmured in his sleep, wrapping his enormous arms around a pillow, now that he no longer had me to cuddle with. Timyn had wormed his way *between* Ambrose and Krysos—a presumptuous choice destined to be noticed as soon as the Nemean Lion awoke. The punishment would most likely be Ambrose's cock in the Hydra's ass, which was probably the goal.

He truly is a 'monster whore.'

Grabbing the fur coat, I slipped away, nimbly navigating my grotto's slippery path to arrive on the beach. I didn't see Leia anywhere, but spotted her footprints in the sand, headed for a large cluster of boulders at the far end. My gaze drifted seaward to one of the larger rock formations, where my mate had first called for me, like the *Aelfmaer* she was.

Or a Siren, as Ambrose aptly named her.

I followed her footsteps, appreciating the damp sand under my bare feet. Land travel *was* easier in human form—a silver lining to my plight. While the entire ocean was my source of power, I knew my true form was still a temporary state of being. I'd been suspecting Leia's presence somehow increased the strength of my Kraken, although I'd yet to understand how it was possible.

I need to discuss my various theories with Julius.

My lips pressed together at the conundrum of having a *human* mate. Despite her insistence on accepting our monstrous forms, she no doubt preferred us as humans, not just for logistical reasons, but societal ones. Yes, her kind had been fucking mythical creatures for centuries, but even before we were exiled, there were whispers of this common practice becoming 'taboo.'

Humans are so uptight.

As I neared the boulders, I couldn't shake the feeling of unease churning in my gut. The twelve's shared mission had always been to escape this island, and reverse the curse damning us to a humanoid existence. Now I wasn't so sure I wanted to only inhabit my Kraken form.

Especially if my mate will no longer desire me.

My jumbled thoughts were interrupted as I rounded a boulder to find not Leia, but three unfamiliar women, standing perfectly still, gazing out to sea. They were clearly of Greek heritage, and related—possibly sisters. For some inexplicable reason, they were collectively wrangling a ball of yarn. One held the ball wrapped around a wooden spindle, while the woman beside her absently unspooled the yarn, before handing it to the third. This woman simply fed the strand through her fingertips, the length of it disappearing into the waves in the direction they all were facing.

They had an otherworldly aura, and while I'd never seen them on the island before, they seemed familiar. I took a moment to ponder. Folklore was often shared between cultures, with more similarities than differences between Greek and Norse mythology.

But why are they... weaving?

With a sharp intake of breath, I realized these three were the *Norns*—the demigoddesses of destiny—the *Fates,* as the Greeks called them. To my people they were known as *Urd,* 'The Past,' *Verdandi,* 'What Is Presently Coming into Being,' and *Skuld,* 'What Shall Be.'

Or as the Greeks say—'The Inevitable.'

My cold blood ran colder still as I frantically looked around for my mate. The wind had picked up, heavy storm clouds swirling overhead as punishing waves smashed against the rock formations lining the shore.

"Leia!" I called into the howling wind, desperate to keep her away from these witches, despite knowing any attempts to escape one's fate were futile. *Urd* and *Verdandi* ignored my distress, but *Skuld* impassively met my gaze before lifting her hand and wordlessly pointing out to sea.

No, no, no, no...

I followed the path, horrified to see a small vessel on the distant horizon, rapidly heading for the wall of fog trapping us here. There wasn't time to rouse the others. If I acted quickly, I might catch Leia before she breached the barrier.

Why would she leave us?!

With a roar that echoed off the cliffs, I ran into the foaming surf, instantly taking my true form and propelling myself toward my mate. I didn't understand why she was fleeing, but I was determined to get her back—determined to defy the Fates.

43
LEIA

"Bish! I swear on all that is holy, you need to get your thicc ass on this boat!"

I almost dropped the obol I'd been examining, my mouth gaping as I stared in pure shock. Iola had randomly appeared behind the wheel of a speedboat, bobbing in the waves outside Vann's grotto. Adding to the strangeness was that her normally jet-black hair was now dyed blood-red.

Is Kraken cum... hallucinogenic?

It wasn't weird to see my niece driving a boat—her stepdad's family had a beach house in the Hamptons—but her materializing *here* had rendered me speechless.

Wait.

"Who sent you?" I narrowed my eyes accusingly, tucking the coin into my cleavage for safekeeping before crossing my arms. "Because my *mother* is the last fucking person I want to—"

"*FUCK YO' MAMA!*" she shrieked. "I have put up with Auntie Meanie's bullshit for *months* since you disappeared, and I am D.O.N.E. When we get back to Manhattan, I will personally take you to City Hall and help you get emancipated, or disowned, or whatever adults do to cut ties with toxic family members. But right now, I need you to get your booty on my pirate ship. I'm taking you home!"

Home?

My brain had gone offline, too overwhelmed to function, but my feet moved of their own accord, carrying me across the sand in her direction. It wasn't until the cool ocean water skimmed over my bare toes that the full force of her words washed over me.

"Months?!" I yelped, standing ankle-deep in the surf, twisting my mother's amethyst ring in agitation. "I've only been here for a few days... a week, tops."

Instead of gifting me with another rant, Iola's face fell into unmistakable despair. "You've been gone for almost a *year*, Leia," she croaked. "And it's been weeks and weeks since I saw you at Delphi. Please. Get. In. The. fucking. Boat."

A YEAR?!

"I... I can't leave my..." I vaguely gestured toward the opening of Vann's rave-cave, struggling to process what Iola was saying *and* explain who my men were.

Who they are to me.

Iola rolled her eyes, back to her sassy self. "You've got to be kidding me. You found *dick* on a desert island, hoebaggler? Listen. I'm impressed, not gonna lie, but this is a classic 'forced proximity' trope. Let's be real—would this relationship actually *work* in the real world? Honestly?"

No. It wouldn't.

My shoulders slumped in defeat. I realized I truly had been living in a fantasy—hanging out with actual storybook creatures who could never exist in my world. If I took my monsters home with me, what would they do? Would I expect them to get 9-5 jobs in human form? Or would Ambrose have to camouflage himself among the stone lions guarding the New York Public Library? Would Julius head to the Pine Barrens, so his boar could be mistaken for a sexy Jersey Devil, like in that oddly hot *Carnal Cryptids* book I'd downloaded to read on my cruise? Would Timyn inhabit the Central Park Lake, capsizing gondolas by day and terrorizing muggers by night?

He'd probably love that, actually.

I sniffled dramatically as I waded out to the idling boat, noticing a light drizzle had started. Iola reached down and helped haul me aboard as a sob broke through, and by the time she'd turned the boat around, I was full on ugly-crying.

"Jesus, the sex must have been good," my niece murmured, although she shot me a sympathetic smile. "Leia, I'm so sorry you've been out here—and that your bitch of a mother knew the whole time. I couldn't sit around and listen to her babble about *fate* any longer. Fuck that. *I'm* your ride or die, and that includes full-service jail-breaks. You know that."

I nodded, scrubbing the back of my hand over my eyes to dry my tears. She was right. This was exactly what we did for each other—whether it was staging emergency phone calls to leave work early, or directing the getaway cab to the restaurant's back alleyway to ditch shitty dates. No matter what happened, our motto was always that blood was thicker than water.

And no dick is thicker than that.

My head hung even lower when I realized just how much of myself I'd given up for Dylan, including my other relationships. Iola still hung out with me, even with what limited time I gave her, but I'd ignored her repeated claims I could do better. Like many women nearing their third decade, I'd suddenly decided I needed to check some adulting milestones off my list before I was old and gray. Apparently, that included taking a thankless, low-level job and ditching my BFF for a complete douchebag.

My priorities have been so fucked.

"Uhh... I probably should have asked if Desert Island Dick needed a ride outta here," Iola grimaced, her intense hair whipping in the breeze. "Should we go back and get him?"

My heart soared before shattering once again. I shook my head, murmuring, "No. He... can't leave."

None of them can.

And they're going to wish they'd never met me.

"Hey!" I squinted at my niece. "How did *you* get past the fog?" I pointed toward the wall of white—fast-approaching, thanks to Iola going full-throttle, as if this really *was* a jailbreak. "More importantly, whose boat is this?"

She shrugged. "I'm borrowing it. I randomly met someone who *survived* the same shipwreck as you, and when I told him your story, he offered to help. And get this! It ended up being the same dude who bought your extra cruise ticket—Eury whatever. Weird, huh?"

Oh, hell, no.

"Io, stop!" I shouted above the increasing wind, noticing eerie, greenish clouds had gathered overhead. Drizzle had turned into rain, and the sea was growing choppier by the minute, but luckily, Iola immediately stopped the boat, banking it to the left. The waves tossed us right up against the fog, which was deceptively drifting over the deck, as if it *wasn't* solid. I glared at it, not believing for one second Eurystheus had lent his boat to Iola out of the goodness of his heart.

What is he up to?

"I need you to stick your hand through the fog," I bossed, pulling my niece toward the starboard side, even as I warily eyed the storm brewing above us. She huffed, but obeyed. Her annoyed expression changed to fear when her palm flattened against the wall just as a monstrous roar rang out from back on the beach. I stumbled backward as I spun around, expecting something solid to stop me from falling.

It didn't.

I yelped as I landed hard on the deck. Glancing back, I found my lower half still on the other side of the fog, with Iola. Meanwhile, from the waist up, I was existing in a completely different scene. Calm ocean waters stretched before me, dotted with a multitude of Greek islands and bustling ships, and nothing but a clear blue sky above.

What in the actual fuck?

Terrified of leaving my ride or die behind, I scrambled back through the fog to the chaos of the island side. The clouds over here were now threateningly black, lightning flashing and thunder booming, with waves pouring over the railing of the boat.

"Io!" I screeched above the wind. "Back this shit up, or else you're gonna get tossed overboard if the boat passes through the fog!"

How did she get here in the first place?

Despite her brain probably exploding, Iola sprang into action, yanking down the throttle to throw the boat into reverse before steering us back toward the beach. I helplessly watched her struggle at the wheel against the storm just as I realized there were no life jackets on board.

All part of Eurystheus' plan, no doubt.

I held onto the slippery railing with a death grip as I

desperately scanned the choppy water, stupidly hoping that either Vann or Timyn would appear to save us. For a moment, I thought I spied a tentacle cresting over a wave—which made my pussy inappropriately pulse—but I couldn't be sure.

Why would they save you, Leia?

You.

Left.

Them.

My heart sank at this realization, and my stomach joined it as Iola shouted that we'd now lost power. I closed my eyes, instantly reliving the trauma of the shipwreck that brought me here—the one I'd dreamed about at Auracle.

Like a prophecy.

"This is bullshit!" I shrieked, eyes snapping open so the storm would *know* I was talking about *its* shady ass.

I was tired of being treated like an expendable nobody —by my job, my ex-boyfriend, Eurystheus, this psychotic weather, and even my mother. Although I'd refused to follow in Alcmene's professional footsteps, I'd still never been completely free to make my own decisions. She'd directed from afar, as if she was the heartless author who fed on readers' tears, and I was just a side-character to fuck with.

"I'm the goddamn main character!" I yelled at the water crashing over me, not giving a shit that I'd turned into a person who yells at the ocean. My life was *mine,* regardless of whatever 'fate' anyone thought they were going to trap me with. "I don't care if Zeus *himself* is behind this—I am not going down without a fight and even if I lose, I am taking all you Olympus bitches with me!"

Iola cried out, and I turned, following her terrified gaze past the bow. Writhing snake heads were surfacing from the roiling sea, and I maniacally laughed, making a mental note to give Timyn the best underwater blowie he'd ever had once he got us out of this mess.

My joy was short-lived, as nine heads turned into 20 and then into what looked like 100. As they rose higher into the air—towering over our tiny boat—I saw they were attached to the shoulders of a giant man with enormous black wings and actual *fire* in his eyes.

That is not *my Hydra.*

"Herculeia," the giant boomed, abruptly calming the storm with a flick of his wrist. "Your oath of vengeance against Olympus has been recorded. Now it's time for you to meet your family."

With that, he bent, and gathered our boat into his arms, before pulling us, screaming, beneath the waves.

To be continued...

REVIEWS

If you have enjoyed **The 12 Hunks of Herculeia,** please leave reviews! It helps other readers find my work, which helps me as an indie author. *Thank you!*

Amazon
Goodreads
Bookbub

But don't stop there: Tag me in your reviews, stories, edits, videos, and fan art on social. I love to share these posts with my followers!

HERCULEIA PLAYLIST

Please enjoy this Spotify playlist inspired by Herculeia's Monstrously Mythic duet (and let me know if you have the perfect song to add):

(CENSORED) HERCULEIA
PRINTS AVAILABLE
LINK TO ORDER PRINTS ON THE BOOKS
BY C. PAGE

BOOKS BY C. ROCHELLE

Looking for signed paperbacks, N/SFW art prints, bookplates & other goodies? My store can be found at **C-Rochelle.com/shop** (and **Patreon** members get discounts on art prints and signed books, plus extra swag and personalized inscriptions in their books!)

MONSTROUSLY MYTHIC SERIES (ALSO ON AUDIBLE):

The 12 Hunks of Herculeia (Herculeia Duet, Book 1)

Herculeia the Hero (Herculeia Duet, Book 2) (*sign up for the newsletter for the bonus epilogue: Three Heads Are Better Than One*)

Herculeia: Complete Duet + Bonus Content (*includes Calm Down Monster-Fucker, Three Heads Are Better Than One, & the Thanksgiving Special: Get Stuffed, plus UNcensored art*)

More Monstrously Mythic Tales:

Valhalla is Full of Hunks (Iola's standalone story)

VILLAINOUS THINGS - SUPERHERO/VILLAIN MM ROMANCE (COMING SOON TO AUDIBLE):

Not All Himbos Wear Capes (*sign up for the newsletter to get the Only Good Boys Get to Top Their Xaddys bonus epilogue*)

Gentlemen Prefer Villains (*sign up for the newsletter to get the Yes Sir, Sorry Sir bonus epilogue*)

Putting Out for a Hero (Balty's story)

Villainous Book 4 (the twins)

Villainous Book 5 (reunion book)

THE YAGA'S RIDERS TRILOGY (ALSO ON AUDIBLE):

Rise of the Witch

A Witch Out of Time

Call of the Ride

The Yaga's Riders: Complete Trilogy + Bonus Content *(The Asa Baby Christmas Special & the Too Peopley Valentine's Day Special)*

More Yaga's Riders Tales:

A Song of Saints and Swans *(Anthia spin-off novella, which includes From the Depths & the Halloween Special: It's Just a Bunch of Va Ju-Ju Voodoo)*

WINGS OF DARKNESS + LIGHT TRILOGY:

Shadows Spark

Shadows Smolder

Shadows Scorch

Wings of Darkness + Light: The Complete Trilogy + Bonus Content *(Oversized Cupids V-Day Special, The Second Coming Easter Special, & the Sexy Little Devil Halloween Specials Pt. 1 & Pt. 2)*

More from the Wings Universe:

Death by Vanilla (Gage origin story novella)

CURRENT/UPCOMING ANTHOLOGIES:

Creepy Court: A Monster Mall anthology (featuring my tale - **Vampires Totally Suck**)

And there will be a bonus Monstrous holiday special in the forthcoming **Snow, Lights, & Monster Nights** charity anthology

ABOUT THE AUTHOR

C. Rochelle here! I'm a naughty but sweet, introverted, Aquarius weirdo who believes a sharp sense of humor is the sexiest trait, loves shaking my booty to Prince, and have never met a cheese I didn't like. Oh, and I write spicy paranormal/monster Why Choose + MM, MFF & MMF romance with dark, naughty humor. #loveislove

Want More?

- **Join my Clubhouse of Smut on Patreon**
- **Subscribe to my newsletter at C-Rochelle.com**
- **Join my Little Sinners Facebook group**
- **Stalk me in all the places on Linktree**

ACKNOWLEDGMENTS

There are many people to thank for helping me on this journey, especially as I took the full-time author plunge and brought this latest batch of delicious ridiculousness to life.

My new PA (and loyal smutling) Jessica Schmit - it's incredibly calming to know I finally have someone in my corner who not only gets me and my writing, but always gives 110%. You are a freakin' gem among a pile o' dusty-ass coal. Those other smutlings are pretty special too.

Michelle from Cliterature, for being my very loud cheerleader, and for coaching me through leaving my day job, life in general, and on writing slightly darker shit that still made me squirrelly (even though it will never be dark enough for you).

Thank you to the Monster Dong Aficionados, for welcoming me into your filthy fold - with open... tentacles - as I accidentally stumbled upon writing monster romance. Our group chat is often the brightest spot in my day and I appreciate how hilarious, supportive, and safe that space is.

And a shout-out to my author friends in general, for understanding that I actually am a weird little introvert who often goes radio silent while lost in my own head. Thank you for assuming the best instead of the worst of me.

My longtime alpha reader and author friend, Kailyn (aka Ariel Dawn), who has trained me well in adding just enough descriptions to my writing in exchange for my lessons in sexual tension. We all have our strengths, and I appreciate you always treating me like a brainstorming buddy instead of catty competition.

Thank you to my other alpha readers - Stephanie and Andrea - for being eagle-eyed and honest. I appreciate every hilarious typo and confusing phrase you find (along with the real-time reactions).

A smutty shout-out to my Va Ju-Ju Voodoo Queens on Patreon: Kaylah, Kelly, Kristina, Kyla & Lauren. Thank you for supporting my author journey in this extra spicy way!

A special thank you to my Street Team Hype Squad! There are too many of you to name, but the fact that you care enough about me and my work to spend your time running your mouths warms my little black heart. My ARC Team is also vital to my success, as you are the last line of defense for typos, and the frontline for leaving honest reviews that help my book find its way into the claws of the right readers.

And THANK YOU to my readers - old and new - I still can't seem to "write to market" for the life of me... but I think that's why you're here. Weird-ho's for life!

GLOSSARY

While many people have gone over this book to find typos and other mistakes, we are only human. **If you spot an error, please do NOT report it to Amazon.**

Send me an email:
crochelle.author@gmail.com
or **use the form** (also found in my FB group, pinned under Featured/Announcements)

GLOSSARY NOTE: The men here are speaking Ancient Greek (plus a little Old Norse), which I've mostly written as English, since they "magically" understand each other. You will find a few unfamiliar words, italicized and written phonetically. Please reference the glossary below for definitions. Everything is Greek, unless otherwise noted. **And please note, I'm no historian, simply a history nerd who likes writing filthy retellings, so go easy on me.**

SLANG NOTE: There is also a bit of American slang peppered in, but I didn't bother translating, as much of it is common lexicon at this point. When in doubt, use Google, or contact me using the methods above if you truly believe it's a typo.

The 12 Labors of Heracles: A series of tasks completed as penance by **Heracles*** - the greatest hero of the Greeks, son of Alcmene (a mortal... mostly) and **Zeus**** (possibly her great-grandfather... gross) - in the service of **King Eurystheus**. There were originally 10 Labors, but our hero tried to cheat, so the king tacked on two more:

1. Slay the Nemean lion. (Of **Nemea**, RIP Ambrose's cave home.)
2. Slay the nine-headed Lernaean Hydra. (Of the **lake of Lerna**. This was cheat #1, because Heracles' nephew and original ride or die, **Iolaus** - here a niece and named **Iola** - assisted.)
3. Capture the Ceryneian Hind. (Of **Ceryneia/the Ceryneian valley.**)
4. Capture the Erymanthian Boar. (Of **Mount Erymanthos.**)
5. Clean the Augean stables in a single day. (Heracles achieved this one by rerouting the **Alpheus** and **Peneus** rivers. This Labor was cheat #2, because there was payment involved between Heracles & **King Augeas**, which the king tried to back out of, hence our boy killing him, as one does.)
6. Slay the Stymphalian birds.
7. Capture the Cretan Bull.
8. Steal the Mares of Diomedes.
9. Obtain the girdle of Hippolyta, queen of the Amazon.
10. Obtain the cattle of the three-bodied giant Geryon.
11. Steal three of the golden apples of the Hesperides.
12. Capture and bring back Cerberus.

*A note on Herculeia/Hercules vs. Heracles: I assure you,

I am aware that Hercules is the Roman spelling of the Greek Heracles ("in glory of Hera" - nice try, Zeus). The main reason I based Herculeia off the Roman spelling was because, thanks to Disney, that is the spelling most mortals are familiar with. I do address it in the book, I promise.

A note on the Twelve Olympians: Throughout this series, I make casual mention of many of the major deities of the Greek pantheon, commonly considered to be **Zeus, Hera, Poseidon, Demeter, Athena, Apollo, Artemis, Ares, Hephaestus, Aphrodite, Hermes,** and either **Hestia** or **Dionysus** (special shout-out to our outcasts, **Hades** and his girl **Persephone**). In the interest of saving paper, I'm going to assume my readers have basic knowledge of these gods, thanks to Lore Olympus and Percy Jackson, but feel free to poke around Wikipedia to learn more. I will do my best to explain lesser known gods/demigods, Titans, and other primordial deities.

The Acropolis of Athens, Greece/Acropolis Museum: An ancient citadel on a rocky outcrop above the city of Athens that includes the remains of several ancient buildings, the most famous being the Parthenon. The new Acropolis Museum (est. 2009) is a collection focused on the findings of the archaeological site of the Acropolis.

Aeaea: A mythical island in Greek mythology, where the witch Circe lived and where Odysseus stayed for a year while trying to get back to his homeland, Ithaca. He knocked Circe up while the rest of his men were turned into pigs by our witch.

Aelfmaer *(Norse):* A little mystical nymph.

Amethystos: An amethyst was supposed to possess the magical power to prevent or cure drunkenness in its wearer.

Therefore, the Greeks gave it the name *amethystos,* which comes from the prefix *a-,* meaning "not," and *methyein* "to be drunk."

Amphora: A type of vase container with a pointed bottom used for the transport and storage of both liquid and dry materials, but mostly for wine.

Ancient Greece: A civilization, existing from the Greek Dark Ages of the 12th–9th centuries BC to the end of classical antiquity (c. AD 600).

Athens, Greece: The capital of Greece and the heart of Ancient Greece. Includes the **Plaka District** ("Neighborhood of the Gods" - where The Acropolis is located) and **Piraeus Port** (the chief sea port of Athens, located on the western coasts of the Aegean Sea, the largest port in Greece, and one of the largest in Europe).

"Burden on the earth": An insult meaning waste of space.

Calamari *(Italian):* Squid (and a hilarious nickname for a Kraken).

Charon: The ferryman of Hades who carried souls of the newly deceased across the **river Acheron** (or in some later accounts, across the **river Styx**) that divided the world of the living from the world of the dead. A coin (see **Obol**) was required to pay for passage, and was sometimes placed in or on the mouth of a dead person.

Chiron: The "wisest and justest of all the centaurs" who famously tutored Heracles and Achilles, among others. His death came when he accidentally came in contact with one of Heracles' arrows that had been dipped in the poisonous blood of the Lernaean Hydra. It's a sad story, even if Timyn thinks it's hilarious.

Delphi: Considered by Ancient Greeks to be the center of the world, it served as the seat of the **Pythia**, the priestess/prophetess who was consulted about important decisions throughout the ancient classical world. (See also: **Oracle**)

Eleusinian Mysteries: were initiations held every year for the cult of **Demeter** and **Persephone** based at the **Panhellenic Sanctuary of Eleusis** in Ancient Greece. The rites, ceremonies, and beliefs were kept secret and consistently preserved from antiquity, so while there are many scholarly theories, they are still very much a mystery.

The Fates: Aka, the **Moirai**, a group of three weaving goddesses who assign individual destinies to mortals at birth. Their names are **Clotho** (the Spinner/the Past), **Lachesis** (the Alloter/the Present) and **Atropos** (the Inflexible/the Future/the Inevitable). Their backstory is a little murky *(*cough cough* stay tuned),* but regardless, they had enormous power and even the gods couldn't fight or dispute their decisions. (See also, **The Norns**, below)

Foloi Forest: A native oak forest in Greece, named by Heracles after his centaur friend Pholus (after he accidentally killed him...it was high risk to be friends/family with our boy).

Gorgon: Three sisters who had hair made of venomous snakes and visages that turned men to stone. **Stheno** and **Euryale** were immortal, but **Medusa** was not. She was slain by demigod/hero **Perseus**, who used her severed head to turn the sea monster **Cetus** to stone.

Kamari mou: A term of endearment meaning "little pride."

Kataratos: Curse(d). (In Renaissance France, was considered an obscenity meaning "abominable.")

Kylix: An elaborately painted drinking vessel used in Ancient Greece. The broad, shallow "bowl-cup" with two handles atop a pedestal base permitted the drinker to recline while drinking, as was customary in a **Symposium** (see below).

Kynodesme: A cord, string or leather strip that was worn in Ancient Greece to prevent the exposure of the glans penis in public. It was tied tightly around the part of the foreskin that extends beyond the glans, and could either be attached to a waistband to expose the scrotum, or tied to the base of the penis so that the penis appeared to curl upwards, like a dick dumpling. (I dare you to Google this.)

Ladon, river: A tributary to the river **Alpheus** (see the **Fifth Labor**, above). Rivers cleanse in Greek mythology, and this one serves as that in a few tales, but it's also an Easter Egg for a future harem member…

Leto: A goddess and the mother of **Apollo** and **Artemis** (see **Twelve Olympians**, above). She is the daughter of the **Titans Coeus** and **Phoebe**.

Loukoumades: Pastries made of deep-fried dough soaked in sugar syrup or honey and cinnamon, and sometimes sprinkled with sesame.

Mezze platter: An assortment of small dishes eaten as appetizers or a light meal. Instagram knows them as #grazingboards.

Mount Olympus: The home of the Greek gods and the site of the throne of Zeus (see the note on the **Twelve Olympians**, above).

Mount Taygetus: The highest mountain of the Taygetus range, associated with the nymph **Taygete** (see below) in classic mythology, and dedicated to **Artemis** (see **Twelve Olympians**, above).

Moussaka: Greek beef and eggplant lasagna. Pretty much what Leia and her men are cooking up in bed.

Nereid: A sea nymph—female spirit who symbolized everything that is beautiful and kind about the ocean, particularly the Aegean Sea.

The Norns *(Norse mythology):* **Urðr/Urd** - The Past, **Verðan-**

di/Verdandi (What Is Presently Coming into Being), **Skuld** (What Shall Be). (See also **The Fates**, above)

Obol: A form of ancient Greek currency and weight often used in burial rites to pay for the deceased's passage to the underworld (referred to as "Charon's obol").

Oracle: From the Latin verb *orare*, "to speak" and can refer to the priestess uttering the prediction, the site of the oracle, and to the oracular utterances themselves.

Oread: A nymph inhabiting the mountains or grottos. **Echo** was the famous Oread who loved **Narcissus** (who only loved his own reflection... earning him a seat on the petty couch). She made the bad decision of trying to distract **Hera** from another one of **Zeus'** affairs (see **Twelve Olympians**, above), so the goddess cursed her to only be able to repeat the words of those around her.

Pandora's box (actually a jar): Curiosity led Pandora to open a container left in the care of her husband, thus releasing physical and emotional curses upon mankind.

Peplos: A type of dress worn by women in Greece c.500 BCE. There was no tailoring in Ancient Greece, so this particular type of dress was made of a big sheet of fabric, folded over at the top and wrapped around the body. It was pinned at the shoulders to keep it from falling down and often belted at the waist.

Pholus: a wise centaur and friend of Heracles, who lived in a cave on or near Mount Pelion, and who was part of the hero's Fourth Labor. Like **Chiron** (above), Pholus was civilized, and in art sometimes shared the "human-centaur" form in which Chiron was usually depicted (that is, he was a man from head to toe, but with the center and hindparts of a horse attached to his ass).

Planetes: Our word "planet" comes from this Greek word, meaning "wanderer."

Potnia Theron: "Mistress of the animals," "The Animal Queen," or "Lady/Queen of Animals" is a widespread motif in ancient art from the Mediterranean world and the ancient Near East, with its likely roots in prehistory. The term is first used once by **Homer** as a descriptor of **Artemis** (see **Twelve Olympians**, above), and is often used to describe female divinities associated with animals, regardless of culture of origin.

Rán *(Norse mythology):* A goddess and a personification of the sea, along with her husband, **Aegir**. Together, they have nine daughters who personify different types of waves.

Schvitzing *(Yiddish,* which is practically a second language in New York): Sweating.

Spanakopita: A savory Greek pie with crispy layers of phyllo dough surrounding a filling of spinach and feta cheese.

Strigil: A tool primarily used by men for cleansing the body by scraping off dirt, perspiration, and oil that was applied before bathing in Ancient Greek and Roman cultures. There were actually "sweat collectors" who would gather the leftover concoction (known as **gloios**) to be used for medical purposes (eg. a topical anti-inflammatory), with gloios from famous athletes fetching a higher price.

Symposium: A drinking party or convivial discussion, especially as held in ancient Greece after a banquet (and notable as the title of a work by Plato).

Taygete: was a nymph, one of the **Pleiades** (the seven daughters of the **Titan Atlas**), and a companion of **Artemis** (see **Twelve Olympians**, above), in her archaic role as **Potnia Theron** (see above). Mount Taygetos, dedicated to the goddess, was her haunt.

Thule: The farthest north location mentioned in ancient Greek and Roman literature and cartography. Greek explorer **Pytheas** first wrote about Thule after his travels between 330 and 320 BC, although his work has been lost and the island is still unidentified (although there are theories...possible Easter Egg...or Red Herring).

"To the crows with you": A grave insult. A proper burial was very important to the Greeks, so this is suggesting that your body will be left out for the crows to feast on.

Triptolemus: A figure connected with Demeter (see **Twelve Olympians**, above). During her search for her daughter, Persephone, the goddess taught **Triptolemus** the art of agriculture and, from him, the rest of Greece learned to plant and reap crops. There are many conflicting accounts, but In the archaic Homeric Hymn, he is briefly mentioned as one of the Demeter's original priests, and one of the first men to learn the secret rites and mysteries of **Eleusinian Mysteries** (see above).

Tzatziki: A salted yogurt and cucumber dip that's made of strained yogurt, shredded cucumber, olive oil, garlic, lemon juice, salt, and herbs.